Drilling, Killing, Love, Drugs & Mud

by

B.D. McKay

Published by Precarious Books

© B.D. McKay 2014

The right of B.D. McKay to be identified as the Author of the Work has been asserted by him in accordance with the Copyright, Designs & Patents Act, 1988.

A catalogue record for this title is available from the British library.

ISBN 978-0-9929880-1-2

This book is dedicated to my Mother, to Annabel and to anyone who has ever been there.

Many thanks to Indie Authors Scotland for their help in the publication of this book.

All characters presented in this novel are fictitious. Any resemblance to real persons, living or dead, is purely coincidental.

The Oil Industry in this novel is also fictitious. Any resemblance to any real Oil Industry or any industry masquerading as an Oil Industry is entirely accidental. Honest.

Chapter 1 Dead End

Face down in a dense brown liquid lay the body of John James Webster, fifty-four years on this planet, father of three, husband to none, feared by most, loathed by all. Arms cocked over the blades of the pit agitator, his final, apt embrace was with cold steel. The agitator motor squealed in complaint and sang the only lamentation that would be heard for this Toolpusher, this thief, this liar, this foul and abusive human. His skull was fractured and his lungs were filled with a fluid they called mud. Dead in Active Pit 1 on the Manticore semi-submersible oil rig 110 miles east by north east of Aberdeen, the body circled slowly until a derrickman hit the Off switch in concern for his bearings.

Chapter 2 This Will All End in Fascism

It was at the heliport that Jamie finally left behind the real world. He had entered the rig world. It was an odd world.

He had wobbled from the taxi bearing the unfamiliar weight of two kitbags. He pressed the Disabled button on the doors and lurched inside. The heliport had looked so ordinary from the outside, but as the doors swished ominously shut behind him, Jamie realised that he had entered a parallel universe to the one that everyone else was in. There was definitely something peculiar going on.

For a start, there was a higher proportion of mustaches than in normal society. The place was populated on the whole by men and these men were on some kind of a mission. The atmosphere was muted. No one in this lounge was going on their holidays.

The building wasn't even properly lit. The ceiling was too high. No attempt had been made to hide the massive ventilation ducts. It wasn't clear whether the vents were sucking or blowing. Jamie assumed they were blowing, as there was nothing to suck. The smokers had long since been banished outside. They were gloomily huddled by the door in a makeshift bus shelter surrounded by discarded lighters. The entire place looked like a converted warehouse which could just as quickly be converted back.

To one side there were eight check-in desks, one of them with a small queue of guys in jeans. Behind was a long counter where some other guys in jeans were having their bags rifled through. Everybody was in jeans. To the other side were islands of chairs around small tables. At the back was a shop selling newspapers, teas, coffees and lots and lots of fried food. It even sold apples to the adventurous.

The flight for the Manticore wasn't yet checking in, so Jamie staggered across to an empty island. He was new to the job, new to the rig and he knew no one. He sat down and felt as lonely as he had ever felt in his entire life.

'Cheer up. It could be worse. You could be going to the Manticore.'

'I am going to the Manticore.' Jamie was looking up at a soft-faced, rosy-cheeked guy in his thirties. 'What's so bad about the Manticore?'

The guy sat down beside Jamie. 'It's John Webster's rig.'

'You're not the first person who's said that to me,' said Jamie. 'Does he own the rig?'

'You could say that.' He gave a lopsided grin. 'You must be the new mud engineer on night shift. Reidy's replacement.'

'Yes. I'm Jamie.'

The man's face dropped. 'It was a shame about Reidy. Poor guy.'

'What happened to him?'

'John Webster happened to him. He's off with his nerves. He'll be off a long time.' The man took a sad pause to reflect on this. Then he brightened. 'I take it this is your first trip offshore?'

'Is it that obvious?'

'It couldn't be more obvious if you were ringing a bell and shouting it out to everybody over the tannoy. Webster's going to love you.'

'What can I do to come across as more experienced?' Jamie tried to hide the panic in his voice.

'Don't even try. Don't worry. It's a good crew. We'll look after you.'

'It wasn't much use to poor Reidy.'

'Reidy was a liar. We couldn't help him. He signed his own Death Warrant. You don't fuck around with a man like John Webster.'

'I've heard that he knows every valve and every rivet on the rig,' said Jamie.

'Good. Forewarned is forearmed. But you won't have to worry for the moment. Webster won't be aboard for at least a week. Give you time to get your feet under the table. I'll look after you. I'm Peachy.'

'Thanks Peachy.' Jamie looked at the friendly, mildly red face. "Peachy" couldn't have been a more apt nickname.

Two other men joined them. They were glassy-eyed and reeking of spearmint.

'Scottie. Desperate Dan. This is Jamie, the new Reidy.'

'I don't tell lies,' said Jamie.

'All mud engineers are liars,' said Scottie, the thin, nervous one. 'It's their job.'

'You look as if you're brand new,' said Desperate Dan, pumping Jamie's hand fearsomely.

'I am brand new. No point in lying about that,' said Jamie. Desperate Dan wasn't a man you wanted to bump into down a dark alleyway. He looked desperate, right enough. But desperate for what?

Peachy must have read Jamie's mind. 'Don't go drinking with him,' he whispered.

'Good time off?' Desperate Dan barked at Peachy.

'Very quiet. I just chilled.'

'You fucking needed to. You were in a right state on the last trip.'

'We were all in a right state,' said Scottie. 'It was the well from hell.'

'More like the toolpusher from hell,' said Desperate Dan. 'He's bad enough when he's happy. I've never seen a man get so upset about a supply boat. I mean we unloaded everything we needed. And we backloaded everything we didn't need. Why get so worked up about a boat?'

'They messed him around,' said Scottie. 'He's a control freak. He goes mental.'

'No, it was more than that, Scottie. Something seriously fucked up was going down.'

'Forget it Dan. We've drilled that well. We've moved on. The rig's being towed to the new location. And Webster's not aboard.

Happy days.'

A man arrived. He had the swollen figure of a body-builder. And a twitchy mustache.

'What are you doing here?' said Scottie.

'I'm the driller.'

'Where's Roger?'

'Roger quit.' The body-building driller pulled his face into a fake smile, threw his bag down and marched off to the toilet.

'There's more chance of me being David Beckham than him being driller,' said Desperate Dan.

'There's more chance of you being Victoria Beckham than him being driller,' said Peachy.

'I knew Roger would quit,' said Desperate Dan. 'The shenanigans with the supply boat was the final straw. He's not been right since Fraserburgh.'

Jamie noticed Peachy flinching at the mention of the word "Fraserburgh".

'None of us has been right since Fraserburgh,' said Scottie.

'I warned you all about Fraserburgh,' said a new arrival.

Two men had come: one a well-groomed man in his sixties; the other, who had spoken, a wizened man of dubious age who gave Jamie a dubious look.

'Who the fuck are you?'

'I'm Jamie. The night mud engineer.'

'I'm Ronnie the Roustie. He's Bill the Mechanic.'

'Reidy's quit with his nerves,' said Jamie, helpfully.

'Roger's gone. And Phil McNulty's the new driller,' said Desperate Dan. 'He's in the toilet right now, shitting himself.'

'Phil's a twat,' said Ronnie the Roustie. 'The only way Phil McNulty could last as a driller would be if he had an outstanding assistant driller. 'And we've got...'

'... a Russian assistant driller who isn't an assistant driller at all,' said Desperate Dan desperately.

It was at this point that things started kicking off at one of the check-in desks.

'No way! No fucking way!'

A guy in a mustache and a leather jacket was attempting to check in. The girl at the check-in counter was explaining something patiently to him. Two security men quickly appeared on the scene. Jamie noticed that the check-in staff were dressed exactly the same as the security staff. The check-in staff were security staff. This really wasn't like going on your holidays.

'Drinking?? Of course I've been drinking! You expect me to go out there with those maniacs without a drink in me? What do you think I am? Retarded?'

This was followed by more patient explanations from the girl. Her hair, which was in a neat ponytail, was wagging up and down with each point she was making. She was styled in classic British security staff colours – black and white. Jamie wondered what security and funerals had in common.

'I'm not blowing in to any fucking bag! And I'm not pissing into any cups either! You can fuck right off! You and your two pals. My grandfather did not fight at Anzio so that my bodily fluids could come under the control of three fuckwits in black ties! I'm a freeborn Scotsman. What I stick down my throat, up my nose and up my arse are nobody's business but mine. So long as I check in here clean and sober, it doesn't matter a fuck.'

This was the cue for the security men to grip the yelling drunk by the elbows and escort him to the door.

'Mhe-ee. Mhe-ee.' The yeller made bleating sounds at the onlookers as he passed. 'You're all sheep! Do what you're told! Toe the line! Don't complain! This will end in fascism! FASCISM!!!'

The freedom fighter was catapulted out of the door that Jamie had come in.

'Another satisfied customer,' said Peachy

'That's Gordy Sinclair,' said Ronnie the Roustie. 'Hates the North Sea. Any time his company send him out here, he shows up pissed and gets bumped from the flight.'

'Hasn't his company learned?' said Jamie.

'They're an oil company,' said Ronnie the Roustie. 'They're eternal optimists.'

'Why don't they fire him?' asked Jamie.

'He's the best guy they've got. They're working flat out. He'll be in Russia tomorrow.'

'Drinking in Russia is compulsory,' said Peachy. 'So says our Russian assistant driller who's never been on an oil rig in his life.'

'This might seem like an obvious question,' said Jamie, 'but how does a guy like that get onto an oil rig at all?'

'Welcome to the wonderful world of John Webster,' said Scottie. 'The man spent a year in Russia and came back with all sorts of wonderful new friends.'

'Well this new friend isn't going to be around much longer,' said Ronnie the Roustie.

'What the hell are you doing here anyway?' said Desperate Dan. 'This isn't your crew-change day.'

'I got a call from Webster.'

'So did I,' said Bill the Mechanic. 'Something about wanting reliable people around. He's on the rig.'

The colour left Peachy's face. 'Oh fuck. Webster aboard? Already? This is going to be the trip from hell. New driller, new assistant driller, new night mud engineer – and John Webster in the middle of it all. Christ, get me out of here.'

'Relax. We can work through this,' said Scottie. 'There's nothing we can't sort out.

Phil the Driller came striding towards them. He was a man with a purpose.

'Okay, listen up,' he began, his mustache vibrating. 'There's going to be no problems with Webster on this trip because I'm in charge now. Webster's going to notice the improvement in performance and he'll leave us alone. There will be no hanging about the tea shack. And no lingering. And no sloping off either. I know all the dodges. You'll do what I say. You'll do it one way. Or there will be hell to pay.'

'One way? Or hell to pay? Fuck me,' said Scottie. 'We've got a poet on our hands. You might be an idiot, Phil. But at least your disasters will rhyme.'

Ronnie the Roustie seized the moment.

'My mustache is twitching, my knees are trembly. 'Cos I just lost the Bottom Hole Assembly. My CV will be doing the rounds. 'Cos it was worth three million pounds.'

The others quickly chipped in.

'I've filled my pants, so phone the bosses. The fucking well is taking losses.'

'I am doomed like General Custer. There's no fucking oil, the Well's a duster.'

The canon of world literature may have grown. Civilisation may have expanded. But Phil was not impressed. His first attempt at man-motivation was a disaster. It didn't bode well. He then did what idiotic leaders have done since time immemorial when faced with their own fiascos: he acted like nothing had happened.

'I'm not saying it's going to be easy,' he continued. 'It's not going to be a great big party like it was when we were in the shipyard in Rotterdam.'

'A drillcrew let loose in Holland? I can imagine,' Jamie whispered to Peachy.

'Oh no you can't,' Peachy whispered back.

'But I think things started going wrong in Rotterdam,' Phil went on. 'There's been a funny atmosphere ever since. Even by his own evil standards, Webster's been nastier than normal. So let's not give him any excuse to get heavy with us. I'm as terrified of him as the next man. So let's put Rotterdam behind us. And let us totally forget about Fraserburgh.'

'Is that your attempt at management?' said Scottie. 'What a load of pish.'

'What happened in Fraserburgh?' said Jamie.

But it was too late. Everyone had picked up their bags and gone. Their flight had been called.

Chapter 3 A Desperate Man

As Jamie stood in the queue to check in, he could feel the nerves beginning to take a hold. What on earth was he doing here? He was utterly clueless as to what his job was supposed to be. They might as well have snatched someone off the street to be the night mud engineer. Come to think of it, he had been snatched off the street.

It had all started, as madness frequently does, in a pub. The Lion Rampant had been a good pub. Once. The good times, the good people and the good-looking girls had gone. Jamie remembered when the place was packed with gorgeous Goths in fishnet stockings and Doc Marten boots. At weekends you had to get in early to get a seat. There was good conversation, talk of music, of education, of sex. Sometimes there was even talk of politics. Now the only things in Doc Marten boots were aggressive-looking men. And the only talk was tabloid talk, if there was talk at all. The entire place reeked of defeat. You only went in if you were unemployed, about to be made unemployed, or in a job where you might as well have been unemployed.

Jamie fell heavily into this last category. His career had followed the trajectory of the town itself. Downwards. Every place he worked in eventually closed down. Maybe all the Goths were in Poland. Or China. Jamie had worked hard and worked well, but all to no avail. The tides of global economics were against him. His degree from college had got him lower management, small-sized factory work. One witty machine operator had summed his career up as "Jeans and a Tie" jobs. Jamie had never made it into a suit. His first job had private health care and a pension. Now, hitting 30, there was no health care, no pension and no money in the bank at the end of the month. He was on less money now than when he started. Given the choice between holidays and beer, Jamie had chosen beer.

Jamie's life changed on the day when someone with prospects came into the pub by mistake.

The guy had clocked the surroundings, clocked the people and was about to do a swift turnaround when he clocked Jamie. 'Jamie Chivers!' he cried. 'I'd recognise that acne anywhere! How the hell are you?' He slapped Jamie on the shoulder and pumped his hand vigorously.

'Harold? O'Neil?'

'Bet you didn't expect to see me still alive, eh? You know you were the only person who ever stepped in to stop me getting a kicking?'

It was true. Harold (never Harry) had been one of the odd kids at school that no one ever played with; a serial target of abuse. Something about his personality attracted it. The name, with overtones of Englishness and Catholicism in a fiercely Presbyterian Scottish town, sealed his fate. That he received an education at all was testament to the resilience of the human spirit. Harold was frequently beaten up before lessons even began. Schools didn't have anti-bullying policies in those days. In fact, the school pursued a pseudo-Darwinian pro-bullying policy, if it pursued anything at all. Victims, it was generally assumed, deserved it. Bullies were a gift from God to stop the Scottish population from turning into a bunch of softies. Harold, despite himself, was living proof that the policy worked. Harold wasn't dead. Harold was thriving.

The incident in question involved a second year thug attacking Harold when he and Jamie were both in third year. Jamie's sense of injustice had been pricked. It was bad enough that Harold was being attacked by his own year group. Seeing him being bullied by younger kids was too much for Jamie. No one deserved this. 'Just leave him!' was all that Jamie could think to shout when he stood up as Harold's protector. For some unknown reason the thug had backed down, muttered something, and skulked off. Jamie found himself shaking with fear. Harold had been too gobsmacked to say anything at all.

'So, how are you Jamie?' said the fit and tanned Harold, sixteen years later.

'Things couldn't be better, Harold. I'm fine.'

'You were really kind to me.'

Jamie was reminded of the person he had once been: excitable; optimistic; and caring. 'Yes Harold,' he said. 'I suppose I was kind.'

Harold turned around slowly to get a proper look at the ramshackle establishment, its deflated customers and its dismal décor. 'What went wrong?'

***

Harold offered to buy a meal. Jamie really didn't feel up to it. The whole point of drinking in places like The Lion Rampant was to avoid successful types who reminded you how bad your own life was. But Harold was insistent, so they went to the last restaurant left in the town. It was a serviceable establishment. They drank a serviceable Chianti. Jamie tried valiantly to put a favourable gloss on his life.

'It's a small company, but it has a niche position in the plastic container market. We do the jobs that are too challenging for the big players. So there's a premium that we charge for a boutique service. What's most challenging about working in a Small to Medium Enterprise is the variety of tasks and aspects of the business that you get to taste. And there's a fair bit of international travel involved. I'm really juiced, Harold.'

"Juiced" was a word that Jamie had picked up from a motivational CD that had completely and utterly failed to motivate him. Plasti-Kan was a dump. It was the last port of call for desperate businesses who couldn't get their orders filled by reputable companies. Its owner was a crook. Jamie was his dogsbody. Every day was the same spirit-crushingly dull routine. The international travel had been a trip to Newcastle.

However, after three large glasses of vino, the veritas came out.

'I'm thirty years old and my life is over,' he wailed. 'I haven't had a serious relationship in five years. I haven't had a shag in three. Remember Janice McArthur? Ugly and dull? Dumped me for being duller and uglier. I live alone. I hate my family. I hate my friends. Oh God Harold, I even hate myself. I'm far worse than you ever were. Far worse. You were a wimpy guy that didn't deserve it. I'm a major catastrophe. There's a Black Hole where my personality should be. It sucks in every bit of goodness and light and crushes it into nothing. No fun. No joy. No kinky sex with Goths in fishnet stockings and lipstick. It should be me that gets beaten up every day. You're fantastic. I'm a disgrace.'

Mama Mia's had something that The Lion Rampant notably lacked: mirrors. Here, in mid-wallow, Jamie caught a glimpse of his own reflection. He saw a spotty six footer, angular and undernourished with a doleful face that had been bloated by alcohol. His sorrowful eyes spoke silently and eloquently of his emptiness. His hair topped everything off. It was dark. It was neglected. It had undergone a half-hearted attempt to style it with gel (which had failed). There was no denying it, he was a pathetic character.

'I am pathetic,' he slurred. 'I am completely and utterly fucked. I'm desperate.'

Harold then did something that Jamie would never forget. He smiled. It was a smile of sympathy, mixed with wisdom and spiced with a hint of devilishness. It was an enigmatic smile.

'I think I can get you a job,' Harold purred. 'It's just the thing for a man of your … talents.'

'I'll do absolutely anything.'

'That's the spirit.' The smile hadn't left Harold's face. 'Because you might have to do absolutely anything.'

Jamie waited. Harold, savouring the moment, kept him waiting. Eventually Jamie could bear it no longer.

'Well? What is it?'

'Jamie, you're going to be a mud engineer.'

Chapter 4 The University of Mud

Things moved quickly. This was the 21st century. The oil industry was desperate for people. In Jamie, a desperate industry was about to get a desperate man. Harold's word was enough to secure Jamie an interview with a monumentally hungover Aberdonian.

'All right, sit down. I'm Alan Whiston. Harold recommended you. He's a good guy. I owe him a favour. I've got a slot opening up in maybe a month on the Manticore rig. The night man's only good for one more trip. There's John Webster issues.'

'Who's John Webster?' Jamie asked, keenly.

'John Webster's a long story, son. He'll love you and that's all that counts. Do you know anything about Fabian Mud Systems Ltd?'

'No.'

'Me neither. Do you know anything about drilling fluids?'

'Eh.... no.'

'Knowledge isn't important. Can you tell bare-faced lies and keep a straight face?'

'Yes,' Jamie beamed. He was hitting his stride now.

'So you know all about water-based mud?'

'Yes.'

'And oil-based mud? And emulsion strength? And fluid loss?'

'Yes, yes and yes.'

'Viscosity?'

'I'm an expert on viscosity.'

'What do you know about viscosity?'

'I'll get back to you on that.'

The monumentally hungover Aberdonian scratched his chin. 'So you think you can do this job?'

'I know I can.'

'All right then, you're hired. Now get out of my office, I think I'm going to be sick.'

The next thing Jamie knew, he was doing his offshore survival course. This involved outdoor-types in polo shirts and clipboards trying, and succeeding, to scare their audience half to death at the prospect of working offshore. They gave ominous lectures. They set things on fire. They threw Jamie into a swimming pool and turned him upside down in a pretend helicopter. Jamie listened, asked pertinent questions, put the fires out and tried desperately to avoid drowning. He even breathed a bag of his own air until all the oxygen was gone and his lungs were fit to burst. All of which allowed the government and the oil companies to sleep better, safe in the knowledge that they had Put Safety First. The course also gave the poor, perpetually-bored safety instructors the money to go out and do ridiculously unsafe things up mountains at the weekend. There, bedding down on the summit of some God-forsaken Ben in sub-zero temperatures with a 2,000 ft precipice below, they slept safe in the knowledge that they had Put Safety Last. It was a fair deal all round.

During a break, Jamie had been chatting with one of the instructors. The guy had been a game warden in Africa, but not because of any enduring love of wild animals.

'It allowed me to do what I love most,' he said. 'Fly. Of course I know nothing about flying helicopters. All my experience is fixed-wing.'

These words had caused Jamie a pang of anxiety. Fixed-wing. The wings on an aeroplane were fixed on. The wings on every bird that had ever existed on planet Earth were fixed on. It was the natural way of things. It allowed planes and birds to glide, even if their engines went down. The wings on helicopters were the bits that moved round and round and round at high speed above your head. There was nothing natural about this at all. If anything went wrong with them, the helicopter would drop like a stone.

'Do you know what rig they're sending you to?' the instructor asked.

'I think it's the Manticore,' said Jamie.

'Ah, John Webster's rig,' said the instructor. He gave Jamie an enigmatic smile not unlike Harold's.

'Does he own it?' said Jamie innocently.

The instructor gave Jamie another enigmatic smile not unlike Harold's. 'You could say that,' he said. 'He's definitely stamped his personality on it.'

***

After survival training, it was "Mud School". This sounded fantastic. After all, who doesn't want to have a good play with mud? It conjured up pictures of seaside fun and innocent, carefree days. Jamie's tutor was Bert, a burnt-out mud engineer who didn't want to be a mud engineer any more. He wanted to dedicate more of his time to his interests.

'Make mine a lager and lime,' said Bert.

Lunch with Bert began at eleven o'clock when the pub opened. Lunch with Bert ended when Jamie was unable to drink any more. This was generally at about 8 o'clock at night, when Jamie would stagger back to his B&B. Bert kept going until the small hours and would turn up at the Fab-Mud laboratory in the morning looking perfectly sober, but smelling faintly of whisky. This gave Jamie three hours in the morning with Bert learning about the job. Bert would set Jamie a few tasks and disappear for lunch. Jamie spent the rest of the day running back and forward to the pub asking questions about the chemicals he was mixing. At some point in the day, Jamie gave up and just stayed in the pub. Bert wasn't bothered either way. This went on for two weeks.

'I can't hack it out there any more,' said Bert, taking a sweet sip. 'It's a good job for a drinker, though. A two week bender at home, then two weeks offshore giving your liver a rest. Suited me for twenty years.'

'What went wrong?'

'I got fed up holding onto handrails.'

If you have a pit of 60 barrels of mud weighing 11.5 pounds per gallon, and water weighs 8.33 pounds per gallon, how many barrels of water do you have to add to bring the weight down to 10.7 pounds per gallon? If the mud had a calcium carbonate concentration of 4 pounds per barrel, how many 25 kg sacks would you have to add to maintain concentration?

A triplex pump with a stoke length of 12 inches and 6 inch liners is pumping at 25 strokes per minute. If the efficiency of the pump is 97%, what is the pump flow rate in gallons per minute?

Calculate the annular velocity between 5 inch drillpipe and 9 5/8 inch casing (inside diameter 8.681 inches) if the pump rate is a) 250 gallons per minute   b) 450 gallons per minute

These were the kind of questions that Bert tortured Jamie with if a) Jamie looked as if he was at a loose end in the laboratory or b) if Jamie got on Bert's nerves in the pub. They were what Bert called "fag packet" calculations, the kind of sums you could do on the back of a packet of cigarettes. Jamie did most of them on the back of beer mats. Bert tended to annoy very easily in the pub - until he'd had eight or nine pints. Jamie watched him, his swollen nose and watery eyes, and wondered if that would be him in twenty years. Bert had no money worries, other than what to do with it. His wife had left him. His kids were grown up and working. He seemed to drink from lack of imagination to do anything else. He didn't come across as being an alcoholic. Jamie had seen enough of those in The Lion Rampant to recognise the type.

'The mud engineer's job is to condition the drilling fluid and keep it within the specifications of the fluids programme,' said Bert.

'The mud is sucked from the Active pit by the rig pumps. They pump it up to the standpipe on the drillfloor. It goes through the top drive of the drill string, down the inside of the drillpipe and out through the nozzles of the bit. Whatever the diameter of the drillpipe and drill collars, the diameter of the bit is bigger, so there is an annular gap between the drillpipe and the side of the hole. The fluid carries the cuttings up this annulus, then into the casing and the riser and out into the flowline. Then it passes over massive sieves, also known as shale shakers. These remove the all the large cuttings and most of the fine ones from the mud. The mud then proceeds down another flowline and back into the Active pit where the whole sequence starts again,' said Bert.

'If you report any mud property out of spec on the mud report, you'll get yourself into trouble,' said Bert.

'The most important thing is the mud weight. If you don't

have enough hydrostatic pressure to contain formation gases, you'll take a kick and then you're really really in trouble,' said Bert.

'Watch for the ECD rising,' said Bert.

'What's the ECD?'

'Equivalent Circulating Density. A rising ECD means you're not cleaning the hole,' said Bert.

'The loggers will let you know,' said Bert. 'Unless they're useless.'

'All loggers are useless,' said Bert.

'Do you know what rig they're sending you to?' said Bert.

'The Manticore.'

'Ah, John Webster's rig.' Bert didn't smile enigmatically. He smiled gleefully.

'There's not a rivet on the Manticore that John Webster doesn't know about,' said Bert.

'There's not a valve open on that rig that John Webster doesn't know about,' said Bert.

'John Webster is the best toolpusher in the North Sea,' said Bert.

'John Webster is a lovely fellow. You'll get on like a house on fire,' said Bert.

Well, one thing was for sure. Bert was a lying old bastard.

Chapter 5 Checking Out the Check-in

Jamie now found himself at the front of the queue for checking-in. The ponytailed girl who had explained everything patiently to the drunken, ranting, anti-sheep freedom fighter, nodded expectantly.

'Passport?'

'I was confused about that,' said Jamie. 'I've got an offshore ID card. A Vintage card.'

'Vantage card,' she corrected him. 'I'm glad you've got a Vantage card, but I need to see your passport.'

'Why? Am I going abroad?'

'You might get evacuated to Norway.'

'Oh, is there a problem on the rig?'

'No, but there will be once you arrive. Hand it over.'

After some rummaging in his bag, Jamie did so. 'Do you get a lot of people trying to check in as somebody else?'

'We get a lot of everything. Can you place your bags on the scales? Yes, there. You know, those things that look like scales? That's it.' Her voice had assumed the tone of a playgroup teacher talking to a particularly slow three year-old. 'Do you mind not leaning on my counter?' Jamie's hands shot back instinctively, as if he'd done something very naughty. The girl blinked slowly. 'I need to get an accurate measurement of your weight. You're actually standing on scales yourself.'

'Sorry.'

'Do you have a mobile phone?'

'Yes,' said Jamie emphatically.

The woman made a note on her clipboard. 'Where is it?'

'Ayrshire.'

'Are you taking the piss?'

Jamie lowered his voice. 'It's my first trip offshore. I don't know anything.'

The girl lowered her voice. 'There's no point in trying to keep it secret. They'll spot you a mile away, believe me. Do you have any medication? That you're actually carrying today? Not something that you've left with some auntie in Tobermory?'

Jamie lowered his voice again. 'Well I do have some. Pills. For acne. Does that count?'

The girl turned and yelled at the top of her voice. 'BILLY? DO ACNE PILLS COUNT AS MEDICATION?'

'ACNE? ARE THEY PRESCRIPTION?'

'ARE YOUR ACNE PILLS PRESCRIPTION?'

'Yes.'

'THEY'RE PRESCRIPTION ACNE PILLS!'

'ANYTHING PRESCRIPTION NEEDS TO BE REGISTERED, EVEN ACNE!'

Ronnie the Roustie smiled sympathetically. 'Could have been worse, son. Could have been haemorrhoids or gonorrhea.'

'Or haemorrhoids with gonorrhea,' said the girl.

Jamie stepped forward to the bag search counter where his medication was sealed in a plastic bag and taken note of on another clipboard.

'You'll get your acne pills back from the rig medic. He needs to know what everybody is on,' said the Security Guy in tones of deep seriousness.

Jamie put his bags on the counter. Everybody had their bags searched. It was part of the deal. Nobody knew what they were trying to prevent. Everything required to destroy a rig was already aboard. It must have been a drugs / alcohol thing.

'Do you have a lighter or any matches?' asked the Security Guy.

'You can't light up in here,' said Jamie, 'it's non-smoking.'

'Who said anything about smoking?'

'You asked for a light.'

'No I didn't.'

'I don't smoke.'

'Neither do I.'

'So what are you asking for a light for?'

'I'm not asking for a light,' said the Security Guy testily. 'I'm asking if you have any sources of ignition on your person or in your luggage. They're banned.'

'Explosions?' Jamie ventured.

The Security Guy nodded.

'Are the rigs no-smoking?'

'There are designated areas for smoking provided with safety matches. Any knives?'

'Do I need one?'

'No. Knives are banned'

'Are knife fights a problem offshore?'

'No.'

'Knife crime then?'

'No!' The Security Guy was getting annoyed.

'What's the knife ban for then?'

'To stop people hurting themselves.'

'They're self-harming? Offshore? I knew it was bad, but I never thought they'd resort to cutting themselves. I mean it's the kind of thing you associate with teenagers who don't get out enough. That wear dark clothes. Maybe into Marilyn Manson a bit too much. But rig workers? Mutilating themselves? It's worse than I thought.'

'Is this your first trip offshore?' said the Security Guy.

'Is it obvious?'

'Yes.'

Jamie leaned toward the Security Man confidentially. 'Is there any advice you could give me?'

The Security Guy looked around and leaned toward Jamie confidentially. 'The best piece of advice I can give you is to run through those doors. And keep running. Until you get home.'

With this endorsement ringing in his ears, Jamie turned to go.

'Wait a minute,' said the Security Guy. 'Three layer policy.'

'What?'

The Security Guy rummaged in Jamie's bag and threw him a sweatshirt. 'You need to wear three layers of clothing under your survival suit and fleece. To keep heat in when you hit the water.'

'Oh,' said Jamie, who was wearing a t-shirt and jumper. 'That's the top half covered. Do I need to put something over my jeans and pants?'

'It's only to protect your major organs,' said the security guy.

'You mean my cock isn't a major organ?'

'Hey guys!' shouted Ronnie the Roustie, 'Jamie's cock's not a major organ.'

Ronnie the Roustie laughed. The security guy laughed. All of Jamie's new crew-mates laughed.

'Don't worry Jamie,' said Peachy, sympathetically. 'They wouldn't laugh if they didn't like you.'

Having been relieved of their bags, the crew sat back down and settled into a morose silence. 'This is the worst part of the trip,' said Peachy. 'Everything's ahead of you. Once we get out there and get a couple of shifts under our belt, you'll see us brighten up.'

'Either that, or John Webster will heap misery on us like a ton of shit,' said Ronnie the Roustie. 'Then you'll see us really come in to our own. I mean look at us. We've got to be the most miserable crew in the North Sea.'

He was right. The people at other tables appeared to be much happier. The spectre of John Webster hung heavily on them. This was a haunted crew. John Webster was a living ghost.

'Look on the bright side,' said Peachy. 'Antonio Banderas is aboard.'

'Is he really?' said Scottie. 'That's one good-looking logger.'

'Aye, he's a braw lad,' said Bill the Mechanic.

'What's a logger?' Jamie whispered.

'They're geologists and they provide the rig with all the data about bit depth and hook height and stuff,' Peachy murmured.

'I'm not ashamed to say that if I was to go gay, Antonio Banderas would be the man for me,' said Scottie.

'Hear hear,' said Ronnie the Roustie. 'It proves that sexuality has truly moved on in the oilfield.'

'As you boys know, things like that hadn't even been invented when I was a lad. But if anything was ever to happen to Theresa, I'd happily take up with Antonio Banderas. The grandchildren would soon come round,' said Bill the Mechanic.

'This Antonio Banderas sounds like some guy,' said Jamie, dubiously.

'He's a big boy,' said Ronnie the Roustie with a wink. 'He'll love you.'

Chapter 6 Suiting Survival

Having sat grimly for twenty minutes, being pitied by their fellow travellers, the passengers for the Manticore were called through to departures. After going through a body scan, Jamie was confronted by yet another person with a clipboard. The industry seemed to breed them.

'Suit size?' said the man with the clipboard.

'I've no idea,' said Jamie. 'I don't own a suit.'

'I'm talking about your survival suit. What size would you like?'

'What size do they come in?'

'Small, medium, large, extra large, extra extra large and extra extra extra large. Small tall, medium tall, large tall, extra large tall, extra extra large tall and extra extra extra large tall,' said the man with the clipboard, drawing from his reservoir of infinite patience.

'What do you think?' said Jamie.

'I think you've been sent by Satan as a test of my faith. Medium tall. Room four.'

'Room for what?'

'Not "room for", I said "Room four".' The man with the clipboard's voice rose. His reservoir of infinite patience obviously wasn't an infinite reservoir of infinite patience. He pointed his propelling pencil. 'See that room with the big "4" above it? That's departure lounge four.'

'Where's the suit?' said Jamie.

'I have to go and get it from the stores! It will be brought to you once you've all watched the safety video.'

The safety video didn't make Jamie feel very safe at all. It was an ominous little film. It was all about bracing yourself for impact and launching the life rafts. It gave the impression that some kind of catastrophe was highly likely. But it tried to pretend that the chopper wouldn't drop out of the sky like a stone, smack into the sea and smash them all to pieces.

After the checking-in debacle, the putting-on-the-survival-suit fiasco was even worse. There's an art to putting on an offshore survival suit. It was an art that was utterly beyond Jamie.

The secret was to take your shoes off, tuck your trousers into your socks, step into the suit and pull it up to your waist. The really secret bit was putting your shoes back on while you could still bend over i.e. before pulling the suit up over your torso. Jamie put the entire thing on, sealed himself up and zipped himself in. He was feeling pleased with himself that he'd noticed the tucking-your-trousers-into-your-socks bit. Then he tried to put his shoes back on. He couldn't.

There were two problems. The air trapped in the foot bit of the survival suit had ballooned up so that his feet didn't fit into his shoes any more. And the suit was so stiff that Jamie couldn't even reach his feet. He grabbed a shoe and made a wild lunge for his toes. The toes made it into the shoe but the rest of his foot was having none of it. Then his leg jerked forward and catapulted the shoe across the room, smacking it into some bottles of water. The room was a heaving sea of 32 arms and 32 legs. Jamie bobbed and weaved and ducked. He retrieved the shoe. On his way back, he narrowly missed an elbow to the head, but took a right to the stomach.

A little winded, he took a seat and took stock of the situation. Guys were squatting like Sumo wrestlers, holding their neck-seals open to expel excess air from the suits. Jamie did the same. This solved the elephant foot problem. It was time for one last desperate go at the shoes. He loosened the laces as far as they would go.

Jamie grabbed a shoe and made several lunges for his toes. He fell off his chair. His head was beginning to swell. The neck seal on the suit was too tight. Sweat was pouring out of him. He got onto his hands and knees and crawled back to his chair. He stared at the conundrum that his shoes had become. His audience (for that's what it now was) watched him with a morbid fascination. They were probably thinking about what John Webster was going to make of this man. Jamie was convinced that he could hear some tittering.

Peachy motioned to Scottie and the two of them set about Jamie like a Formula 1 Crew changing tyres. They knelt and rammed Jamie's feet into his trainers. They tied the laces and stood Jamie up. Jamie thought he could put his own lifejacket on. He couldn't. He soon found his head being poked through a hole and a clip being tightened at the side. A hand appeared up between his legs and fastened a crotch strap. Scottie patted Jamie on the head and sat him down.

Another man with a clipboard arrived. 'Is there anyone who hasn't been to the installation before?'

Fifteen fingers pointed at Jamie. He looked around to see if anyone else was in the same boat as him. They weren't. He stuck his hand up. The man with the clipboard ceremoniously placed a green armband on it. It was the final humiliation.

'Don't sit in the two seats nearest the door,' the guy advised.

'Why not?' said Jamie.

'Because the men in those seats are first out of the chopper. And you don't have a clue what you're doing.' The man with the clipboard turned to the others. 'Please make sure he gets to heli reception without a major catastrophe.' He turned back to Jamie. 'Make sure you hold onto the handrail.'

'What handrail?' said Jamie.

'Any handrail.'

Suited and booted, they sat, sweltering in silence. Each man drifted off into his own particular reverie. Jamie wondered what was waiting for him offshore. What would the rig be like? His room? Would he have to share a bed? What would the food be like? What other characters would he meet? What challenges would he face? What mistakes would he make? He felt his stomach lurch. There were bound to be a few clangers. He'd be alone and humiliated. This guy Webster sounded like a complete nutter. Failure was certain. The consequences were too awful to contemplate. Jamie pictured himself being bent over a table and shagged remorselessly by a deranged sodomite who wasn't even gay, but was just doing it to be bad. Someone like the ominous-sounding Antonio Banderas.

To cheer himself up, Jamie thought about the money he'd

earn. He'd spend three weeks in a world exclusively of men and return with money to the world which had women in it. Women liked money, so he'd heard. And he'd be able to buy things once again. Not just beer. He was re-joining the world of the living – if he could survive the world of the rigs. And what kind of world was that? The world of the dead?

A sound made everyone in the room stir. The sound grew in strength, becoming a roar. The pitch was lower than a chainsaw, but much more powerful. There was a serious piece of mechanical equipment outside. Their helicopter had arrived.

They rammed foam plugs into their ears and followed the other man with the clipboard out onto the tarmac. A weak sun illuminated the scene. Jamie was grateful for the chill of the air around him. Aberdeen airport lay beyond. Jamie longed to be with the people there, leading normal lives, headed for normal destinations. Another chopper was disgorging lucky workers returning home. Jamie wondered how changed he would be when he returned.

The pilot was a reassuring, roger-tango, we'll-take-it-on-the-chin-when-we-plunge-into-the-sea type of a guy. 'Just relax and we'll give you a shout five minutes before landing,' he said airily. He made it sound like they were all going to Torremolinos.

They spent fifteen minutes waiting on a take-off slot. Jamie suspected that the real reason he hadn't been allowed to sit by the door was to prevent him making a last-minute escape bid. Or leaping to a desperate death in mid-flight. There was a pause when they got on the main runway. Then the noise levels rose as the engines powered up. Then the craft lifted ten, twenty feet. Then, disconcertingly, it dropped. Then the nose dropped even more. And then they began to move forward. And upward. They banked immediately. It was a textbook take-off. The trees and the fields were ruddy and green. Jamie looked at them for what felt like the last time. Aberdeen was silver and distant. They were on their way.

The North Sea was a dark, depressing, steel grey colour. Intermittent wisps of foam made it look like a massive spittoon. It made Jamie feel sick – and faint. The survival suit made Jamie feel even sicker and fainter. Between the rubber seals that bound Jamie's wrists and neck and the Three Layer Policy, there wasn't a lot of his body heat escaping from the suit. The crotch strap on the lifejacket had been pulled too tight, so that his neck was being pulled down. And he was overtaken by a desperate need to pee, which was surprising given the amount of sweat he was generating. He was gasping for a drink. But he was too frightened to place any more strain on his bladder. There was no toilet on board the helicopter. There were no stewardesses. There was no tea, no coffee and no complementary biscuits. They weren't passengers. They were freight.

Chapter 7 Meet & Greet

Jamie had imagined the rig to be large and impressive. It was neither. It looked small and lonely. It seemed to have four legs along each side which reached down to pontoons at the water's surface. The exterior was in desperate need of a good lick of paint. Jamie felt deflated. This rusting little hellhole was to be home for the next three weeks.

The helideck crew were all dressed as firemen. One was standing sentry by a fire hose, waiting for an explosion. Preventing fires was clearly an obsession.

For some reason they opened the door slightly while their luggage was placed in a neat line on the helideck. After a few minutes the doors were completely opened, the crew unbuckled their four-point seat harnesses and disembarked. Jamie followed the line, struggling to find his footing on the rope mesh which covered the helideck. He picked up both his bags, making sure to sling one over his shoulder so that he had one hand free to hold onto the handrail. He didn't want to get into trouble before he'd begun.

They filed down some stairs. This part of the rig felt more like a boat than a rig. A large sign above a storm-proof door read: Heli-Reception. Inside was a linoleum-floored room with a large television and chairs around the walls. The departing crew, ready in their survival suits, were waiting for them.

The crews met up like old friends, shaking hands and exchanging life-jackets. Each crew member met up with his "back-to-back" – the person who did the same job while the other was at home. The arriving crew listened to whatever verbal handover could be given in the few minutes they had together while the chopper was refuelled and loaded with luggage. The departing crew were clearly delighted to be the departing crew.

Jamie had no one to receive a handover from. His job was being up-manned, whatever that meant. One of the heli-crew took his lifejacket. There were fewer people going home.

'All right, let's go gentlemen!' shouted the helideck guy.

The departing crew needed no second invitation. They had completed their hitch. They were in one piece. The money was in the bank. Now they were going to go back to "the Beach" to spend it. But first, they were going to get very very drunk.

A very tired and defeated-looking guy came up to Jamie. 'Wait behind. You'll need to be inducted. When this is over.'

'When what is over?' said Jamie.

The rest of the crew were already out of their survival suits. They sat patiently in their chairs. The sense of foreboding was building.

'This is the worst part of the hitch,' said Peachy glumly. 'Look at us. Sitting here like condemned men waiting on that psychopath.'

'Shut up,' said Ronnie the Roustie. 'He might come in. Then you'll be in trouble.'

'It's too late for that,' Peachy snorted. 'All our problems would be sorted by one man's death.'

'We could toss him over the side,' said Phil the Driller.

'Not painful enough. We need to organise an industrial accident. Chew the fucker up in a lathe,' said Bill the Mechanic.

'No,' said Ronnie the Roustie. 'If it's done well, it's better it's done quickly. Sneak up on the bastard. Bish. Bash. Bosh.'

'Steady,' said Scottie. 'We'll be in our beds soon enough. And then we'll get the first shift under our belts.'

Whenever a chopper landed, it was traditional to have a Meet and Greet with everyone who had just arrived. It provided the opportunity to update them on rig activity and any pressing safety issues. It provided John Webster with the opportunity to impose himself on the new faces. He never missed a Meet and Greet.

The door opened and the man himself came in. Jamie had been expecting someone enormous and six foot five. What he got was five foot nine of utter menace.

Webster clocked every face in the room and then locked his gaze on Jamie. 'Who the fuck are you?'

'J-Jamie. The new night mud engineer.'

'What happened to Reidy?'

'He's had a nervous breakdown,' said Jamie, who was about to have one of his own.

There was a small movement at the edges of Webster's mouth. It should have been a smile, but it was obvious that his face didn't like it and wasn't used to it, so the effect was undermined. That a smile was brought on by someone else's misfortune was typical of Webster. This was already apparent to Jamie, after thirty seconds with the man.

Webster's concentrated his entire speech on Jamie. But it was meant for everyone.

'I am John Webster. And this is my rig. You will do things my way or you will be fucked. I'm well-known in the North Sea. I believe in speed and efficiency. I believe in destroying anything that stands in the way of the goal. I believe the goal is to drill a highly directional well to a Total Depth of ten thousand three hundred and sixty seven feet. Do not stand in the way of that goal. I believe in having an impeccable safety record. There will be no reported accidents while I am aboard. Accidents are a symptom of a man with his mind elsewhere. While you are here your mind will be focused where I want it.'

Webster's eyes were already dead. The rest of him was soon to catch up. He had hooded eyelids which, instead of blinking, closed slowly like a shark's. The face was sculpted by cynicism and contempt. There was an explosion of small veins on each cheek. The hair was thick and wavy and almost long. There was no grey. Grey hairs were for him to give to others. The large hands with calloused, swollen fingers were not designed for intricacies. Webster's was a brutal body. The words were spat from a bitter mouth.

'I believe that this is a working rig, not a leisure rig,' he continued. 'When you are outside you will focus like a laser on work. When you are inside you will maintain impeccable standards of cleanliness. If you do not tidy up after yourself and assist our stewards in every way, you will suffer. I believe that personal slovenliness carries over into the workplace. If the stewards inform me that your room is in a mess, every aspect of your work will be gone through with a fine toothcomb down to the last nut and bolt. If there is a single thing out of place, not only will you be run off the rig, you will have me as a personal enemy. Does everybody appreciate the seriousness of the situation out here?'

No one dared to raise their voice.

'As I say to my three daughters, there's no point in doing anything unless you do it one hundred percent. So is everyone committed to me?'

'Yes,' said the crew.

As a parting shot, Webster made one last threat. 'Enjoy your time on the Manticore,' he said.

Webster walked over and rammed his face into Jamie's. 'You. I want to see you in my office. Now.'

Jamie's walk to Webster's office was an agonising and feeble affair. Convicted killers have strode more confidently to the gallows. Webster motioned him to take a seat. Jamie was relieved to make it without his legs giving way. The environment of an oil rig is a very strange one. The first encounter with it is a heady experience. The combination of this and Webster's aggressive strangeness was almost too much for Jamie. He could see that Webster was sensing this.

'Why is your company fucking with me?' was Webster's opening question, delivered in a flat and unchallenging tone.

'I don't know,' said Jamie, trying not to whimper.

'They know I hate green hands. And they've sent you.'

'I'm sorry they sent me.'

'You will be.' Webster fell silent as if he was calculating a suitable punishment for the wretch standing in front of him. Jamie felt himself diminish under Webster's gaze. He wondered if he was already wearing the haunted look that was the hallmark of the Manticore's crew.

'Who sent you?' said Webster.

'Alan Whiston.'

'I don't like him already. Sounds like a wanker.'

'He is a wanker,' said Jamie. He had made the logical decision not to defend someone he didn't know and who was over a hundred miles away while he was confronted with Webster, whom he did know, who was terrifying and who was three feet away.

'Maybe it's time your company felt some pain,' Webster mused. The eyes remained locked onto Jamie, who squirmed under their relentless and horrible penetration. At that point he'd have taken anything to go home. Ten years of permanent unemployment. Fifteen years of abject poverty. Starvation. Anything. But he was going nowhere. The chopper was gone. He was as doomed as anyone else on the Manticore. He was being stared at by a deeply unimaginative man who was intent on causing his company some serious harm. Webster would probably revert to doing something that he had done before. Something that worked. Something that hurt.

If Webster made some kind of decision, his eyes didn't show it. Nor did his face. He changed subjects. 'There's nothing for you to do for the next couple of days,' he said. 'Other than try to calm down. Then you'll be mixing spud mud. Not even you can fuck that up. In the meantime, the only thing that I will allow you to touch are door-handles. Do you understand?'

'Yes,' said Jamie.

'Everything that you lay your fingers on will turn to rat-shit. I can tell just by looking at you,' said Webster.

'Can I work with our lab equipment?' asked Jamie.

'No,' said Webster.

'I have to test the mud.'

'You'll test the spud mud by sticking a broom handle in it. If the broom handle stands up and then slides away, it's thick enough to make kill mud. If the broom handle stands up and stays up, it's thick enough for spud mud. You can use your computer. I suppose you've got a report to send.'

'Yes.'

'The only person you can embarrass with your report is yourself. Nobody reads the Mud Report anyway,' Webster mused, running a finger across his chin like a knife. 'Unless they want a scapegoat.'

Being a scapegoat: something else for Jamie to look forward to. Just when Jamie felt that he had hit rock bottom, a new low was found. Webster had a talent for things like that.

There was a small commotion outside. Webster's head snapped round. Two men came in. The second of them approached sheepishly, as Jamie and Webster would have expected. The first, the cause of the commotion, had breezed in fearlessly. He addressed Webster confidently. 'Boss, he said, 'here's Stevie. You going to show him the ropes?'

Jamie could only imagine that the ropes were nooses. The man's accent was Russian. His English was flawless though. He had managed to communicate the word "boss" with heavy irony. Webster was not his boss. Both Jamie and Stevie could sense Webster's unease. Stevie sneaked occasional glances. Jamie, now out of Webster's eyeline, took it all in.

'Thanks Alex,' said Webster, loading the words with his own bitter irony. 'You can go now.'

'I'm leaving,' said Alexei.

'I know,' said Webster. 'That's why I brought Stevie onto the rig. That's why I'm showing him the ropes. You're not going to show him fuck all, are you?'

The speed with which Webster reasserted his superiority was frightening. Jamie was impressed. And frightened.

Alexei managed to smile. 'I'm leaving tomorrow,' he said.

'There's no chopper tomorrow,' said Webster forcefully.

A grimace came across Webster's face. His head dropped slightly. He stared at the Russian as if in anger. Jamie wondered what on earth was going on until he realised: Webster was thinking.

No light came on, but the head rose slightly. The Russian, for all his bluster, remained silent. 'There will be a chopper tomorrow,' Webster announced. 'And you will be on it.'

Can I be on it too? Jamie wanted to yell. Please!!! But no words came out.

'I might be back,' said Alexei.

'Not on this rig you won't.'

'Did you think about what we discussed?'

'No I didn't,' said Webster emphatically.

Jamie sat, thinking that this was a conversation that Webster didn't want to have in front of the children, so to speak. The Russian was either very brave, very stupid, or he had some very big friends.

'But you will think about what we discussed,' said Alexei. 'I promise you. And I tell you this: you are now very likely to be killed.'

He walked out. Webster took the threat well. No reaction. Jamie and Stevie studied the floor. They were both painfully aware that they were now likely to be on the receiving end.

'Look on the bright side Stevie,' said Webster darkly, 'you can't be a worse AD than that twat. And he's only been here two trips. Useless bastard. Talking of which,' Webster turned to Jamie. 'Do you need to be told to fuck off?'

Jamie rose. He tried to smile but the muscles in his face were having none of it. He had been drawn inexorably into Webster's desolate universe.

'Door-handles,' warned Webster.

As he left the office, Jamie saw Stevie being given his first lesson in management, Webster-style. It was the only lesson that the man was capable of passing on.

'Come outside,' Webster said, 'and I'll show you how to treat the boys like shite.'

Chapter 8 Great Expectations

Outside Webster's office, Jamie bumped into the depressed man with the clipboard from heli-reception. They went back to heli-reception.

The man with the clipboard was Ritchie the Medic, perhaps the most profoundly depressed man on the planet. There was a reason for this. Actually there were several reasons for this. But the main reason was that Ritchie was about to embark on the one thousand eight hundred and seventy sixth induction of his sorry career.

'Welcome aboard the Manticore,' Ritchie droned, his voice in perfect harmony with the dismal surroundings. 'What I am about to tell you is crucial to your safety on the rig,' he whined, 'so pay close attention.'

'Yes I will,' said Jamie. 'But I have a major safety issue to raise. Someone's just threatened to kill the toolpusher.'

'You might want to write that down on a safety card,' said Ritchie. 'I'll explain about those in a minute.'

Ritchie droned straight into his usual script. It wasn't his fault. He had taken the job in order to save lives in dramatic circumstances without the bother of going through medical school. The Manticore had double-crossed him by being depressingly safe. What minor incidents there were tended to happen when he was at home and his back-to-back was aboard. He'd remained grimly enthusiastic for over ten years. He liked the money. He liked the time at home. His wife liked the money. His wife liked the time he was away. Ritchie contented himself with dishing out headache pills, haemorrhoid cream and advice about Viagra. Then, six years ago, his enthusiasm fell off a cliff. He began to loathe the job. But he was unable to find anything else that paid so well. Ritchie wasn't willing to take a drop in his standard of living, so he was stuck on the Manticore, counting down to retirement. Ritchie was forty eight. It was a long count.

On and on Ritchie droned. One thousand eight hundred and seventy six down, two thousand more to go. What a life. Through his haze Jamie heard snatches about lifejackets and escape routes and Station Bills cunningly placed on the back of bedroom doors. Nothing about psychopathic toolpushers and pretend Russian assistant drillers.

'And if we fail to work together as a team,' Ritchie continued, 'it will have serious ramifications.'

Ritchie was proud of "ramifications". He had introduced it into his act nine years ago. It really rammed the fications of teamwork. It was a big word with big ramifications. He felt that it made an impact on his audience.

Ritchie looked at his audience: Jamie. He didn't look particularly inspired. Paul McCartney got his audiences in tens of thousands and he inspired them with songs. Ritchie got his audiences in ones and twos and threes and failed to inspire them about things that might save their lives. It was no wonder that he was depressed. His career audience might total four thousand souls. More people would see him if he was in a Christmas pantomime for a week. It would be funnier too.

'Any questions?' Ritchie asked, hopelessly, once everything was over.

'The assistant driller's just threatened to kill the toolpusher. And the rest of the crew all want to kill him as well. There's going to be some serious violence out here.'

'Write that in the "Potential Hazards" part of the safety card. Put it in one of the boxes around the rig. And then the safety committee will get together, review the issue and close it out.'

Ritchie smiled. 'Now I'll take you to see the OIM.'

'OIM?'

'The Offshore Installation Manager. He's in overall charge of the rig.'

'Above Webster?'

Ritchie took a long look at Jamie. 'Technically, yes.'

They ambled along a corridor and then discovered a door, which led to some stairs. At the top of the stairs, they went past the service office and ambled down another corridor, parallel to the first one on the level below. It wasn't a difficult rig to get around, but Jamie was permanently and hopelessly lost. Finally, they came upon the largest office on the rig. There, sat behind the biggest desk on the rig, sitting in the biggest chair on the rig, was the OIM. Meeting him was part of the induction. The Offshore Installation Manager was the man in overall charge of the rig's safety. He could overrule the client, the toolpusher, everyone. What he said went. It was his rig. Technically.

The OIM was a jolly-faced, whisky-nosed man. He was an optimistic and antagonistic fellow. Thirty-seven years offshore hadn't dampened his conviction that things generally turned out for the best, but only if you fought for them. Originally from Newcastle, he had become a landowner in Perthshire. His name was Walter.

'Now then,' Walter began, 'they tell me this is your first trip offshore.'

'That's right,' said Jamie.

'God help you. God help me. And God help the rig. What the hell did John Webster say to you?'

'I'm only allowed to touch door-handles.'

'Is that all? You must have caught him on a good day. John Webster gaily skipping through a day on the Manticore. Who'd have believed it?'

'But he was terrifying,' said Jamie.

'Son, I've had people in here who were unable to speak. Babbling wrecks. Terrifying is as good as Webster gets. He's obviously taken a shine to you.'

'Oh shit.'

Walter laughed. 'Don't worry son, John Webster won't be around for much longer. Not if I have anything to do with it.'

'Do you want to kill him too?' said Jamie.

'Who said anything about killing Webster?'

'The assistant driller more or less promised to have him killed. And the entire crew wants him dead.'

'That's just knockabout stuff you get on all rigs. If I had a fiver for every time someone wanted to murder the toolpusher, I'd be sitting in a mansion in Beverly Hills.'

'They seemed deadly serious.'

'They always seem deadly serious. It's all bullshit.'

'Wanting to murder the toolpusher is normal on rigs?'

'It's standard throughout the industry.'

Walter waved an arm airily and changed the subject. 'Now, my primary concern out here is that everybody goes home safely. And on the Manticore we've been very successful at that. It's been four hundred and fifteen days since our last LTA. Do you know what LTA stands for?'

'Lawn Tennis Association?'

Walter sighed. 'Idiots. They're sending me idiots. LTA stands for Lost Time Accident. That's an accident that causes the injured party to lose time at their work. We're very proud of our LTA record and we don't want you ruining it. So we want you to go home...?'

'Safely.'

'Correct. With ten fingers and ten toes. And all your major organs intact.'

'And my cock too,' said Jamie.

A cloud of incomprehension passed briefly over Walter's face. Then he smiled. 'Especially your cock. And remember if you want to keep all your fingers, don't put them anywhere you wouldn't be happy to put your cock.'

A cloud of concern passed briefly over Jamie's face. 'Oh, I've put my fingers in all kinds of places I wouldn't put my cock.'

'Let's not go into detail. You get the idea.'

'I do.'

'So we'll start with door-handles. Then we'll go on to handrails and work our way up.'

'Whatever you say, Walter.'

Walter beamed. He liked people agreeing with him. Even idiots. 'Now this meeting is all about expectations. You expect to be going home in one piece, with ten fingers, ten toes ...'

'One cock and two balls.'

'And we expect you to help us to go home in one piece. That's not unreasonable, is it?'

'No,' said Jamie, thinking that Walter's question-and-answer-method was the same one pioneered by Socrates in 500 BC. He also thought how far humankind had come in the intervening 2,500 years. Or maybe it hadn't come far at all.

'The law,' Walter continued, 'expects us to provide a safe environment and safe working systems. And it expects you participate fully in our safety culture. By law you must adhere to the safe working practices and procedures that we lay down. By law. Do you understand?'

'Yes.'

'Good. I expect. England expects. Scotland expects. Jamie expects. Expectations.'

'I understand and comply,' said Jamie. Comply? 'I mean I'll join in as much as I can. I'll be safe for the entire rig.'

'We have other expectations which aren't legal. You'll know all about John Webster's expectations. Meet them and you won't go far wrong. But don't think that once he's gone the expectations are any less.'

'It's just the stress that's less.' Jamie smiled affably.

Walter returned the smile. 'John Webster's days on here are numbered. Now, do you have any questions Jamie? Feel free to ask me anything.'

'Anything?'

'Don't be shy. It's very important that you're not afraid to make a fool of yourself. I'd rather you looked stupid and lived, than saved face and got hurt.'

'Why have you only got nine fingers?'

Walter threw his head back and laughed. 'I was a good roughneck who had a bad few seconds on the chain tongs. That was in the bad old days when the attitude to safety was: "This guy's broken; get rid of him; get a new guy out and we'll see how long he lasts." You'll hear people complaining about safety bullshit. Don't listen to them. There were no good old days out here. It was brutal.' Walter held up the stump of his left forefinger. 'I've got a daily reminder of just how brutal it was. Today we drill faster, more accurately and with less damage to the environment. There's also less damage to people. We're far far safer. I'm proud of that. Make sure you look after the boys. And they'll look after you. Is that a deal?'

'It's a deal.'

Expectations. Expectations. Leaving Walter's office, it dawned on Jamie that his best bet might be to lower everyone's expectations of him as much as possible. It wouldn't be difficult. Five minutes in his company would be enough for most people. But of all the expectations that were held on the rig, there was one expectation that almost no one expected. No one expected the Senior Toolpusher to be bludgeoned and tossed into a mud pit.

Chapter 9 Gray Outlook

Alan Whiston had briefed Jamie about the mud engineer that he would be working with on the Manticore, the so-called "lead engineer" on days. He told him that he was one of their most experienced men, a go-getter who loved nothing more than mentoring new recruits. He was a man of integrity. A man of energy. A man with an obsessive attention to detail. A man dedicated to running outstanding mud systems. A man called John Gray.

But here, in the service office, Jamie was confronted with a fat man with no energy, no integrity and an obsessive hatred of new recruits. The only thing he was dedicated to was putting as much money in the bank in return for the least amount of effort.

'Whiston told me you had two years' experience,' Gray wailed. 'Have you even been to Mud School?'

'Two weeks in the pub with Bert.'

'Oh fuck,' said Gray. 'Fuck. Fuck. Fuck. Fuck. Fuck.'

Stevie the Assistant Driller, surfing the net in the corner, smiled ruefully at Jamie.

'In my day we did two months in Houston,' said Gray.

'I think they're desperate,' said Jamie helpfully.

'Look at you. You're useless. I knew I should never have called Whiston a "wanker" in that conference call. You've been sent out here to punish me.'

Gray was fifty-two, overweight and seething. He had a full head of grey hair, neatly parted in the centre. He had a mustache which was slightly overgrown, the kind of mustache that Jamie associated with laid-back types. Gray wasn't a laid back type.

'Sending an untrained clown onto the most pressurised rig in North Sea. With John Webster aboard. It's beyond belief.' Gray buried his face in his hands.

'Oh, that reminds me. Maybe this isn't the best time to bring it up, but Webster said something about punishing our company. For daring to send me out.'

'What???!!!' Gray shrieked. 'Punish us! John Webster's going to punish us? Oh God, it's horrible, horrible.' Gray eyed Jamie with something approaching hatred. 'Gee thanks Jamie.'

'I'm sorry,' Jamie offered.

'I'm going to have to do everything!' said Gray, ignoring Jamie completely. He took a couple of deep breaths and calmed a little. 'First things first. We have a problem.'

'Just the one?'

Gray allowed himself a brief smile. 'There's a pit full of oil-based mud left over from the last well. It should have been backloaded. Webster went mental when he heard about it. There might be a boat if we get onto location tonight.'

'What does "onto location" mean?'

Gray looked at Jamie as if he was an idiot. 'The rig's being towed. Didn't you see the boats when you landed?'

'No. I was trying not to fall over. I seem to remember someone saying something at the heliport.'

'Can't you feel us moving?'

'I thought that was the way rigs felt all the time.'

Gray rubbed his forehead wearily. 'When we get on location they might let us pump the mud onto a boat. First, you need to flashpoint test it. Have you seen a flashpoint tester?'

'No.'

'There's instructions in the mud lab. It's yet another piece of health and safety bullshit sent to make our lives more difficult. It basically involves heating two millilitres up to sixty five degrees centigrade and then trying to set it on fire.'

'I'm not trying to set anything on fire,' said Jamie nervously. 'Webster said door-handles only.'

'Webster won't know anything about it,' said Gray. 'He'll be in his bed.'

'Talking about door-handles,' said Stevie, 'that useless welder still hasn't fixed the door to the cement unit. And if the welder needs a Hot Work Permit for welding, Jamie will need a Hot Work Permit for the flashpoint testing. Trust me, Webster will know all about it.'

'Okay,' sighed Gray. 'I'll have to do that myself too. If they do take mud off during the night, your job is to stand by the side of the rig and check for spills.'

'And what if there is a spill?'

'Get a Samurai sword and commit Hari-Kiri because Webster will blame you and you'll wish you were dead,' Gray replied, in tones of complete seriousness. Jamie didn't doubt him. Gray lowered his voice. 'If somebody took a Samurai sword to Webster all our problems would be solved. And I'm just the man to do it.'

'No,' whispered Stevie, 'you want to do it slowly. Make the bastard suffer. Have him tied up. Attack him with a blunt instrument.'

'Can you imagine the kind of abuse he'd be screaming at you?' said Gray. 'Webster would be saying things that would turn your hair white. No, with a man like that you want to be quick. He knows every dirty trick in the book. One swift blow. His head bouncing across the deck and over the side. Plop. Causing a Lost Time Accident and an environmental spill at one and the same time. Ruining the man's impeccable record. Death and disgrace.' Gray spoke with relish.

'Pity about the knife ban,' said Jamie.

'They're not daft,' said Gray. 'Webster wouldn't be the only one getting it.'

'Tell you what Jamie,' said Stevie, 'we'll take you down to the mechanic's workshop and get you tooled up with some serious weapons. You can ambush Webster in the mud lab.'

'If I get any more stressed, I might just take you up on it,' said Jamie.

'Stress?' said Gray. 'Wait until something goes wrong. Then you'll know about stress on the Manticore. Tonight there's nothing for you to worry about. Get a few jugs of oil-based mud and practise mud checks. I'll print out the instructions. When you get bored with that, you can input the new well details on MudMap.'

'What's MudMap?'

'Our reporting system. It generates the Daily Mud Report. Are you telling me you've never seen it?'

'I've never even heard of it.'

This led to another outburst of "fucks" from Gray; more groaning; and a wail as he put his head in his hands again.

'Don't worry, John Webster says that no one reads the Daily Mud Report anyway,' said Jamie, trying to cheer Gray up.

It didn't work.

'So why have I been filling one out every day for the last twenty five years?' Gray yelled. 'Why do you think we're out here?'

'To run a mud system?'

'Don't be stupid. The mud runs itself. We're here to take the blame for everyone else's incompetence. And they're all incompetent! The Mud Report has to be perfect. Because the day it isn't will be the day the well collapses. And they all pore over it so they pin the blame on us. Do you understand?'

'I'll learn the reporting system....'

But Gray was on an unstoppable rant. 'A pump packs in. They don't blame the derrickmen, they blame the mud. A cement job goes wrong. They don't blame the cementer, they blame the mud. The top drive breaks. They don't blame the driller. They don't blame the mechanic. They blame the mud. John Webster has an attack of flatulence. He doesn't blame the chef. He doesn't blame the Brussels sprouts. He blames the fucking mud!'

Gray collapsed into his chair, whimpering. He turned to Stevie. 'I just want an easy life.'

'This might not be the best time to mention it,' said Jamie, 'but Webster said I couldn't do mud checks.'

'Which just goes to prove that he might be a psychopath, but he isn't daft. He goes out on the prowl at nine o'clock. After ten, you'll be safe. I better go and see him. Find out what brand of punishment he's lining up for us. Pray for me.' Gray left the office.

'Don't mind Gray,' said Stevie. 'His bark is worse than his bite.'

'It's Webster I'm frightened of,' said Jamie.

Stevie smiled. 'I see the great man has made first impressions count. Don't worry. You're well below his radar. Take my advice and stay there.'

'You obviously haven't stayed under his radar. It sounded to me as if Webster has requested that you come to the rig. What have you done to deserve that?'

'I've been frighteningly competent,' said Stevie, whose appearance was frighteningly neat. 'I was Webster's old derrickman on here. I was good, so he didn't bother me. But I was smart enough to manufacture an exit to another rig. Then Webster double-crossed me by going to Russia. By the time he came back here, I had two years' assistant driller experience under my belt. So when he needed an AD in a hurry, guess who got the call?'

'What's in it for you?'

'Money. Webster's got the clout with the oil company to organise it, so I asked him to organise it.'

'You're a brave man.'

'Away with you. Webster was asking me for a favour. Even he can't just yank me off another rig. With me aboard, there's a lot less for John Webster to worry about. Out here, you only need to lose, say, a driller and then you have a series of promotions on your hands. The assistant becomes the driller, the derrickman becomes the AD, a roughneck becomes derrickman, a roustabout becomes a roughneck and you get a brand new roustie out the box. All of a sudden your experienced crew doesn't look so experienced any more. You've got five hands that are brand new in the job. The industry's flat out at the minute. There's a lot of people learning on the job. And when that happens, people get hurt.'

'I'm learning on the job,' said Jamie gloomily.

'Any problems, you wake Gray up,' said Stevie. 'Besides, grab it while you can. You've only been hired because oil's $100 a barrel and they're desperate.'

'Thanks for the ego boost,' said Jamie.

'You want to see it out here when oil is $20 a barrel and you've got a dozen rigs stacked in Invergordon,' said Stevie. 'Then it works in reverse. You get toolpushers working as drillers, and drillers working as roughnecks. The ADs and derrickmen are all rousties.

'What are the rousties doing?' said Jamie.

'Sitting at home. Unemployed.'

'They say the oil price will never come down.'

'I've been listening to that bullshit for the last twenty years. Although this time maybe they're right, what with China and all. Personally, I wouldn't take the chance. It's a cyclical industry, so take my advice and save your money.'

'So how come you're out here looking for money?'

Stevie smiled. 'You don't miss much. The wife wants to send the boys to private schools. So I get to work with Webster. And the wife isn't just my wife. She's Gray's sister. It's a small world out here, so watch what you're saying to people. They're either all related or they were at school together. Aberdeen's just a glorified fishing village. I'm a Geordie. I had no idea what I was marrying into.'

'I'm a West Coaster,' said Jamie. 'I had no idea about Aberdeen. It's like a different culture.'

'They're all weirdos,' said Stevie. 'Talking of which…'

Gray returned. 'Do you want the good news or the bad news?' he gasped.

'The good news,' said Jamie.

'If Webster has anything to do with it, this will be your one and only trip on the Manticore.'

Jamie let out a whoop of delight.

'Shh! The bad news is: he intends to make this trip a complete and utter nightmare.'

'Oh crap. What's the punishment for the company?'

'The mud's going to take the blame for everything that goes wrong out here.'

'The mud always gets the blame for everything that goes wrong out here,' said Stevie. 'I blame the mud for everything that goes wrong out here.'

'That's because you're a bastard,' said Gray.

'And I hate you,' said Stevie.

'There's some weird shit going on with Webster,' said Gray. 'Just now, while he was ripping me a new arsehole, he wasn't relishing it at all. His mind's distracted. I don't like it.'

'The Russian assistant driller threatened to kill Webster,' said Jamie. 'And he meant it.'

The two men stared at Jamie.

'The Russian's never even been on a rig. I'd stake my life on it,' said Gray. 'He's as clueless and useless as you are. The only difference is: he's not a nervous wreck.'

'How does a Russian pretending to be an assistant driller get out here?' said Jamie.

'He's been sent by the drilling company,' said Gray. 'Webster's drilling company.'

'Webster owns the drilling company?' said Jamie.

'No,' laughed Stevie, 'it just seems like it. But now the Russian AD has been sent out behind Webster's back.'

'Webster's losing control over his own rig,' said Gray.

'No wonder he's spooked,' said Stevie.

A silence fell and they all thought dark thoughts which had dark implications. Jamie was glad of the company. He was even gladder to feel some empathy with these men on what was his most vulnerable day ever.

'You'll have to excuse me gentlemen,' said Stevie. 'I have to go and see Peachy about joining his film club.' He went out.

Gray spoke up. 'The best thing that could happen to you would be to get run off today. My fear is that Webster will want you on board as an excuse. For everything.'

'Is there any need for me to go out tonight at all?' said Jamie hopefully.

Gray smiled. 'You're safer outside. Webster will be mainly inside. He worked in Russia for a year. Got involved in all sorts of shit. Some say drugs. Some say prostitutes. Some say drugs and prostitutes.' Gray mused for a moment. 'Watch you don't get caught up in the crossfire. Before this well is drilled, there's gonna be some weird shit going down.'

Chapter 10 The Best of Nights, The Worst of Nights

It was the first night that Jamie Chivers would ever spend on an oil rig. It was the last night that John Webster would ever spend on earth. It was a cloudless night, a chilly night. It was a starry night, a moonlit night. It was a night of unbearable emotion. It was a night of unbearable tears. It was the most surreal night of Jamie's life thus far. It was the night he fell in love.

Jamie had managed a couple of hours sleep. He then went to the mess and forced down some cereal for breakfast at 4:30 pm. He sat alone, amidst the smell of beef stew being prepared for the evening meal. It made him feel sick. He met Gray at 5pm.

Gray looked wearily at Jamie, 'You've got your rig tour to do. Then meet Scottie the Derrickman in the pit room at seven,' he said. 'I'm away to my bed. Do not wake me up under any circumstances.' He left. That was Jamie's first handover.

Jamie was given a whistle-stop tour of the rig by Ritchie the Medic. He was shown the luminous orange lifeboats fore and aft, 2 at either end, capable of holding over fifty men each; the inflatable life-rafts for launch in a hurry; the escape ladders to the sea for times of complete desperation; he was shown the pipe deck; the V-door; the drillfloor; the heavy tool store; the doghouse; the catwalk; the logging shack; the mud lab; the riser deck; the shale shakers; the Moon Pool. He was even shown the mud pits, which would become the centre of his universe - and the end of John Webster's. It all looked very industrial, functional, oily and rusty. The predominating colour was battleship grey. That was traditional. There were walkways outlined in yellow paint and a small blue logging shack. There were skips for wood and metal and general waste. There were wheelie bins for glass and paper and plastic and oil filters. There were even some that contained small absorbent pads for small oil spills. There were massive bins with massive absorbent pads for big oil spills. There was a liberal sprinkling of fire hoses. Nothing had been overlooked. There had been a lot of catastrophes over the years.

Inside, he was shown the offices of the toolpusher, the company man, the maintenance department, the OIM and the occasional office of the geologist. He was even re-familiarised with the office for the service hands – directional drillers, cementers, wellhead specialists, casing hands, wireliners, control system experts, mud engineers and the like. They walked around corridors on two levels, passing rooms which were opened and closed. They saw the laundry and the TV lounge and the smoking TV lounge and the galley and the locker room and the tea shack and the smoking tea shack and the radio room. The entire rig was coordinated via the control room, which was the ship's bridge when the rig was on tow and from where the rig was ballasted when it wasn't. It had large white panels displaying numbers that Jamie would need. There was a small telephone room which was timed to allow you five minutes of communication with a loved one. There was a small shop under the stairs which could have sold duty free cigarettes but wasn't allowed to. The boys could have brought fishing rods and fished over the side, but that wasn't allowed either. It was allowed in Norway, but the Manticore wasn't allowed in Norway. It had been condemned in Norway as unfit for purpose.

The tour ended when Ritchie the Medic made a presentation to Jamie: he presented him with the key to a very badly positioned locker. Jamie didn't know it, but this was a good omen. He'd made a favourable impression. The worst lockers on the rig were reserved for those who were hated. This was as good as it got for a new hand from one of the service companies. The best lockers were taken by the drilling crew. So were the best rooms, although Jamie didn't yet know what constituted a good room. He was soon to find out.

PING PONG! The tannoy sounded. It was Scottie: 'Ritchie the Medic call the pit room.'

Ritchie's face lit up. It could be a broken leg, a mangled hand or severe trauma. The gruesome possibilities were limitless.

'Nothing important,' Scottie added. 'I need to sort out next week's lottery bonus ball.'

Ritchie's face deflated as the optimism left it. 'Scottie's an experienced hand. If you ever tannoy me, always say whether it's urgent or not. If Scottie hadn't added the bit at the end, everybody would assume there was an injury in the pit room. Webster would have been there like a shot. Tannoys for the medic to go to the drillfloor always mean trouble.' Ritchie sighed.

'Cheer up,' said Jamie. 'I'm sure there will be something horrific for you soon enough.'

These words would come back to haunt Jamie.

Ritchie dialled the pit room. 'All right, I'll be there in a minute,' he said. He turned to Jamie. 'That's us finished.' And he left.

And that was it. Jamie was now allowed to venture outside all on his own. He wondered if the oil company knew what it was letting itself in for. To identify him as a brand new hire and to make him feel utterly ridiculous, they made him wear a luminous green hat.

Jamie stood in his brand new ill-fitting coveralls and his brand new ill-fitting boots. He put on his stupid green hat, his safety glasses and his leather gloves. He wrestled with the water-tight door and stepped over the large ledge to the strange and peculiar world outside. Bert had told Jamie that the first thing experienced hands did outside was to look up. He looked up.

'What are you looking up for?' said an unknown passer-by in a Liverpudlian accent.

'To see if the cranes are working,' said Jamie. Bert had told him this too.

'Don't be stupid,' said the passer-by, 'we're still on tow. When you're on tow, you can't work the cranes.'

'Why not?' said Jamie.

'Because the rig is high out the water. It's not ballasted. If you swung the cranes about you could capsize.'

'I suppose that makes sense. And what do you do on the rig?'

'I'm the fucking crane operator.'

Jamie meant to ask him for directions to the pit room, but the guy was gone. Jamie was five feet outside and he was already totally lost. The light was failing, and so was he. The rig was in semi-darkness and didn't look willing to yield any of its secrets. Jamie clumped forward and took some steps up to a higher level. The derrick, over 100 ft high, was in the centre of the rig. Jamie took in its sheer immensity. The pontoons were visible at the water's level. Normally submersed and out of sight, they were huge. The water flowed past them with a reassuring whisper. Jamie could see the two tugs half a mile away, thick wires stretching back to the rig's metal superstructure. Jamie was impressed by the incredible amount of steel in the rig. Just building the thing had been a feat of engineering. It looked robust enough to withstand a serious storm, if not a hurricane. Its sheer scale was soothing. Not even an incompetent like Jamie could make much of a dent in the Manticore. He could only break little, insignificant bits of it.

Presently a door appeared, marked "Pump Room". Jamie went in, suspecting that the pit room couldn't be too far away. When he had been doing his sums with Bert about pumps, Jamie had somehow imagined pumps the size of bedroom drawers. The pump looming in front of him would have struggled to be contained in a four bedroomed detached house. It was bigger than a combine harvester. There were three of them. This was how you pumped a fluid three miles down a hole and back again. Numbers, which until now Jamie had toyed with in classrooms and offices (and pubs) were assuming a physical shape in front of his very eyes.

A door on the other side opened. Ritchie came in. And when he saw Jamie, he glared.

'You didn't take long to figure out the short-cuts.'

'I was checking out the pumps. Bet these can generate a bit of welly. Two, three tons? Per square inch?'

'I don't know anything about pumps,' Ritchie barked.

'You wouldn't want to be around if one of these boys blows.'

'There's lots of things out here you don't want to be around when they blow.'

Ritchie left.

Jamie went to the door that Ritchie had come through. It was marked "Pit Room". On the other side were Scottie and Peachy.

'You shouldn't be in there,' said Scottie. 'Things explode.'

'Did you see anyone?' said Peachy.

'Ritchie the Medic.'

'If anyone asks, you didn't see Ritchie. Okay?' There was an edge to Scottie's voice.

Jamie nodded. The atmosphere was ice cold. Something had happened.

Phil the Driller burst in. 'What happened?' he shrieked.

Mark Z, Desperate Dan and Stevie the Assistant Driller were trailing in his wake.

Scottie interposed himself between Phil and Peachy. His eyes were inches from Phil's. His voice was calm. 'Until you're calm enough to contribute something positive, we're going to ignore you.'

'You will listen to me! I'm the driller!'

'We'll see.' Scottie moved slowly away, guiding Peachy with him.

'I could have lost a hand,' said Mark Z.

'And I could have been mangled in the derrick,' said Desperate Dan.

'And it had to happen right in front of Webster. On my first shift,' said Phil.

'Shut up,' said Scottie.

'I'm sorry,' said Peachy. 'I don't know what came over me.'

'You could have killed two people!' said Mark Z. 'What a crew. I'm the only professional on it.'

'Don't start that crap again,' said Desperate Dan, squaring up to him.

'What sort of state are you in, Peachy?' said Mark Z, looking over Desperate Dan's sizeable shoulder. 'You're worse than last trip. How are we going to get through three weeks with Webster - and you in permanent meltdown?'

'I'm so sorry,' said Peachy desolately.

'He'll be fine,' said Scottie. 'I'll see him through the trip. We'll be drilling most of the time. He'll be safe down here with me.'

'Scottie, that's not good enough,' said Desperate Dan.

Mark Z pointed a finger at Peachy. 'You need to take a chill pill.'

'Everybody needs to take a chill pill,' said Stevie the Assistant Driller.

There was a silence. Stevie, at least, was respected.

It was at this point that Phil the Driller became aware of Jamie's presence. 'What are you doing here?' he snapped.

All eyes turned to Jamie. He didn't know what to say. He realised how easily and how quickly you became utterly isolated on a crowded rig.

Amazingly, it was Peachy who spoke up. 'He's got every right to be here.'

No one said anything, but the focus moved away. Jamie had moved from loneliness to acceptance in a split second. He couldn't have been happier. It might have been a disintegrating crew, but he was now part of it.

Stevie now asserted himself. 'We all need to focus. Before Webster performs his Highland Fling. Mark Z – you nearly lost your hand because it was in the wrong place. None of you were communicating properly with each other. Phil, you should have cleared the drillfloor. Or at least coordinated what was happening with the tugger.'

'I'm not listening to you!' Phil's mustache was on the move again. 'I'm the driller!'

'It's your first trip as a driller. You need to proceed with some humility. You can listen to us and succeed. Or you can fail all on your own.'

Phil reverted to his default setting: sullen silence.

Stevie continued, 'Peachy, we need to know exactly what you did...'

Bill the Mechanic came in. 'Peachy did exactly nothing. The tugger's broken, mechanically and electrically.'

'It's the other bloody crew,' said Mark Z. 'We're the only professional crew on this rig.'

'Webster thought he'd sort it out,' Bill continued. 'The tugger had other ideas. Started itself. Went forwards. Went backwards. Nearly electrocuted him.'

'If only,' said Peachy wistfully.

'You've dodged a bullet. Webster's on the warpath with the day shift. Let's all go get a cup of tea.'

Scottie turned to Peachy. 'Show Jamie the set-up.' He whispered to Jamie on the way out. 'Keep an eye on him.'

After everyone had gone, Peachy showed Jamie around his and Scottie's empire. It consisted of the pump room and the pit room and the sack-store. The pit room was a maze of pipes and valves and handles. They were colour co-ordinated. There was a red mixing line, a blue mixing line, seawater pipes were painted green and drillwater pipes blue. Drillwater was like fresh water, only you couldn't drink it. Brown pipes took mud to the boat. A black line led to the cement unit. Peachy patiently explained it all. Jamie instantly forgot it all. A whiteboard contained a plan of the pits: four large reserve pits; two medium-sized Active pits; two smaller reserve pits; and something called a slug pit. There were sand traps too. Why anybody wanted to trap sand was beyond Jamie. The shaker house wasn't in the empire, but Peachy showed it to Jamie anyway. The shale shakers were sieves the size of two double beds. The sack-store was a little warehouse, where Jamie and the cementer could store their chemicals. There were some pallets of chemicals there already: soda ash; sodium bicarbonate; lime; guar gum. Jamie had no idea what any of them were for. Two mixing hoppers and a couple of mix pumps rounded the empire off.

'What's that?' said Jamie, pointing at a small, corrugated shed in the corner.

'The caustic store.'

'Looks like the wee shed from The Bridge Over the River Kwai. The one they locked Alex Guinness in.'

'Don't say that in front of John Webster. You'll give him ideas. We have an early warning system on here. Someone watches Webster's door all the time. If he comes out, they ring the tea shack, so the boys have a couple of minutes to square things off.'

'Webster's door is watched all day?'

'Welcome to the Manticore.' Peachy cast his eyes around the

sack-store as if he was looking for something he'd lost. Jamie also looked around. It was an odd space. It didn't look like the rest of the rig. It could have been a warehouse anywhere. It even had a forklift truck.

'What's in the hoppers?'

'Oh just the usual stuff. Barite. Bentonite.'

Jamie looked blankly at Peachy.

'Er, barite is barium sulphite, a powdered solid 4.2 times heavier than water. We use it to add weight to our fluids. Bentonite is a form of clay. It mixes in water for thickness. It'll support the barite and remove cuttings from the well.' Peachy took a long look at Jamie. 'Jamie, I think you're supposed to know this stuff. It's the basis of your job.'

'I learn quickly,' said Jamie lamely.

'Don't worry. If push comes to shove, we can always get Gray out of his bed.'

'What's that shiny hopper at the back? It looks new.'

'That's not been brought online yet. It'll give us more options. The rig's in transition.' Peachy paused for a moment, his face serious and troubled. Then it lit up. 'Do you like porn?' he asked eagerly.

Jamie felt as if everything that had been said by Peachy was merely a preamble to this question. Peachy's face had been transformed. Jamie had never seen someone who looked so animated. It was as if this one word had opened Peachy's mind to the limitless possibilities of life itself.

'I love porn,' Jamie lied. He didn't want to disappoint Peachy.

'I can get you anything. Anything. There's some great stuff coming out of Asia. I'm amazed it's taken them so long. Bangkok's been the centre of Asian sex for decades. I'd love to go to Bangkok, but the wife won't have it. Just once before...' Peachy's voice trailed off. His eyes dimmed momentarily, then brightened. 'Have you been to Bangkok, Jamie?'

'No.'

'Are you married?'

'No.'

'Girlfriend?'

'No.'

Peachy's face dropped again. 'Why haven't you been?'

Jamie wanted to explain, but it was obvious that Peachy lived in a universe where any sane single man blew every last penny he had on Thai prostitutes. 'I've just come out of a long term relationship,' he said. 'And I'm saving up.' It wasn't that Jamie wanted to be one of the lads. It was that he felt compelled to keep Peachy's spirits in orbit.

'I've got all sorts on my hard drive,' said Peachy, his eyes dancing. Then a pause. 'No kids, mind.'

'No,' said Jamie emphatically.

'I'm the Porn King on the Manticore.' Peachy's eyes shone. His cheeks glowed. His smile was beautiful and sincere.

I wonder what Webster thinks about that, Jamie wondered. Does he get a cut? What does he like to watch?

'How long have you been out here Peachy?'

'Fifteen years.' Peachy rearranged his features into their normal, amiable state. He was wearing a white rag around his neck; like a cravat. He was the rig dandy too.

Mark Z returned. 'Figured it all out yet?'

'No, said Jamie.

'Don't worry. It's the oil industry. Everybody's useless. That's why we don't build rockets out here. Because there's no fucking rocket scientists.'

Bill the Mechanic approached.

'But there are one or two outstanding people,' Mark Z continued quietly, 'and Bill the Mechanic is one of them. Just don't get stuck alone with him in the tea shack.'

'Greetings,' said Bill grandly.

'You should be in your bed, Bill. Your shift's long since finished.'

'What's the point? Vlad the Impaler's throwing a hairy about that new hopper.'

'Tell him to poke it,' said Peachy, 'you're about the only person out here that's not frightened of him.'

'Because you're the only bugger he's terrified of losing,' said Mark Z. 'This rig's got less downtime than anything in the fleet.'

'Don't count your chickens. He won't let me touch the pumps. They'll cause us serious down-time on this well. The clown's obsessed with that new hopper. He'll meet a sticky end. Believe me. His goose is cooked.'

'What's this, a conspiracy?' They had been joined by the Alexei, the pretend Russian assistant driller.

'The mutiny begins at nine. We're demanding that the rig gets towed to the Caribbean. And Webster walks the plank.'

'Sounds good. But I leave tomorrow. We deal with John tonight. I get rope. You do plank. We make him scream. For fun.'

No one smiled. Alexei appeared to be perfectly serious.

Alexei turned to Bill. 'I need to talk to you.'

'What about?'

'About the work that was done in the yard. In Rotterdam. On the new hopper.'

Bill rolled his eyes. 'I thought you were leaving?'

'I need this information before I go. I come back soon.'

'Shift's over. Come and see me tomorrow morning.'

'My flight is early.'

'There's nothing I can tell you that you can't find out in the Aberdeen office. It's all documented.'

'Do not tell me that everything John Webster does is documented.' Alexei's tone was threatening.

A sliver of sweat trickled down Bill's cheek. 'Everything I do is documented,' he said.

Alexei watched Bill intently. He looked at Jamie and Mark Z. Neither moved.

'Why don't you ask Webster?' said Jamie. 'I'm sure he'll be glad to help.'

'His memory's not so good any more.' He jabbed a finger at Bill. 'You and I need to talk.' Alexei retreated a couple of steps, staring at Bill all the while. He turned slowly and walked away.

'Honestly,' said Mark Z, 'this company's really gone downhill. The people they let onto oil rigs these days...'

'Are you all right Bill?' said Jamie. He handed Bill a clean tissue.

Bill took off his hard hat, threw his safety glasses in and mopped his brow. It was a small thing, but it felt enormous to Jamie. He had done something useful for one of his colleagues. His first night was a success.

'I'm fine Jamie. Thank-you.' Bill rearranged himself. 'There were some strange goings-on in Rotterdam. I stayed well away.'

'We all stayed well away,' said Mark Z.

'Remember what I said about Webster's goose?' Bill slipped his hard hat onto his head. 'That Russian came here to tell Webster that the cooking stove has been lit.'

Chapter 11 Antonio Banderas is One Hot Guy

Armed with a jug of oil-based mud, Jamie decided to do his first ever proper mud check. His first ever proper mud check was a fiasco. The spinning-whatsit spun mud all over the wall – and all over his face. The pressure-thingummy sprayed hot mud all over the worktop – and all over his hand. The heaty-up water/oil/solids measurer performed perfectly, but Jamie forgot to put the measuring cylinder under the spout, so it dripped oily water all over the inside of his fume cupboard.

Jamie was burned, muddied and beaten. There was only one place to go. Countless thousands of defeated oil workers over countless years had wended their weary way to the same place in the same circumstances. Jamie went to the tea shack.

The tea shack was an Aladdin's cave of coffee, tea, sugar and

UHT milk. It was a container like the ones you see on the backs of trucks on the motorway, but with a door in one side and some kind of ventilation system poking out of the top. It was plumbed in. It had a linoleum floor, plastic chairs and a couple of formica tables. There was a large bin. At one end there was a high-tech tea urn which provided an endless supply of boiling water without ever having to be filled. It sat next to the sink, on a counter where the ceremonies of hot drink creation could be performed. The walls were covered in safety posters which no one saw any more.

There was only one other person in the shack. Ronnie the Roustie was sitting alone, rolling a cigarette. He was deep in thought.

Jamie made some tea. The milky water in the polystyrene cup struggled to take on much colour from the teabag. Jamie added another teabag and stirred frantically. He finally attained a light beige colour. He was pleased with himself. He felt like an alchemist. He sat down and took a sip. 'Whooooragghhh.'

'Shite, eh?' said Ronnie the Roustie.

'It's the worst tea I've ever tasted.'

'It's the teabags. They're the same all over the rig. All over the fleet. Not even management gets better teabags. Everyone drinking the same piss. It's a socialist nightmare created by an ultra-capitalist enterprise.'

Jamie must have looked surprised.

'Surprised?' said Ronnie.

'Well, I don't know. You don't sound like a roustabout.'

'What's a roustabout supposed to sound like?'

'I don't know.'

'Rough?'

'Well..'

'Like a moron?'

'No. I'm sorry. It's just unexpected. Capitalism. Socialism. Out here. You know? I'm sorry. I didn't mean to offend you. I'm not very smart myself.'

'That's obvious. I bet Gray's really glad to have you out here.'

'Gray's cock-a-hoop. Compared to Webster.'

A smile.

'He says this will be my one and only trip out here.' Jamie found himself smirking at the prospect of losing his job. He had come an awfully long way in twelve hours.

Ronnie the Roustie looked at Jamie derisively. 'He says that to everybody. Getting run off here is a badge of pride on other rigs. A must-have on any CV. If you really want run off, make a stand. Pick a fight with Webster. Your feet won't touch the ground. You'll be on a nice rig before you know it, instead of this God-forsaken shit-hole. It's full of defeated people. Losers. Every one of them. Maybe it is time for a revolution. It only takes one person with some backbone.'

Jamie checked around to see that no one was about. He lowered his voice. 'Ronnie, tell me, what exactly does a roustabout do?'

Mocking Jamie, Ronnie lowered his voice. 'Exactly? Exactly any shite job that's going. We work for the crane op. Loading, unloading boats. Moving stuff about the rig: containers; skips full of cuttings. We swab decks. Might even mix some of your chemicals. Painting. Needle-gunning. Mainly crane work.'

'Doesn't sound too taxing for a man of your intelligence.'

'Ambition is over-rated. Look at Webster.'

'Is that why you haven't been run off?'

A smile spread slowly across Ronnie's weather-beaten face. 'Who knows? I could be a coward too. Maybe the biggest coward on the rig. Do anything for an easy life. But all that is about to change. Just watch.'

Ronnie ground his cigarette to death. He got up and threw his cup dismissively into the bin. He threw a sharp glance at Jamie as he left. It left Jamie wondering whether he'd made his second enemy on the rig.

Phil the Driller was scarcely in the door and he had a cigarette lit. A coffee was quickly improvised and the guy planked himself directly opposite Jamie and stared at him through his protruding eyes. 'We need to talk,' he snapped.

'About what?'

'Mud. I don't want any fuck-ups.'

'Me neither.'

Phil didn't see the joke. He twitched. 'I don't want us running out of spud mud. And don't go giving me seawater and telling me it's spud mud. I'm not daft. I was seven years derrickman on here. I know all the dodges.'

'I don't know any dodges,' said Jamie. 'I've just started.'

'And don't listen to Gray. He's an arse. I want to see written plans for everything. None of that "wing it" nonsense that Gray goes in for. He's a clown.'

'Thanks for the warning.'

'You taking the piss?' Phil stroked an over-developed bicep.

Jamie sat in silence. Phil's mustache was twitching at both ends. Jamie couldn't take his eyes off it. 'Gray seemed a bit grumpy,' he said, finally. 'Maybe he's not having a good day.'

'Maybe he's not having a good life. He's always grumpy. The only time that twat smiles is the day he's going home.'

'This doesn't strike me as being a happy rig,' said Jamie.

The hairy caterpillar under Phil's nose performed a couple of sit-ups. 'Happy? Happy!!??' Phil shrieked. 'The Manticore? We're not here to be happy. We're here to make hole, strike oil, log it, case it and fuck off home with money in our pockets. End of story. And remember. No fuck ups. And don't you so much as fart without giving me a written work instruction first.'

Phil downed the last of his coffee and stubbed out his cigarette aggressively. These boys were certainly enthusiasts for extinguishing fires, however small. Fires on rigs were no joke. But smoking seemed to be keeping most of the guys going. Nicotine was certainly the drug of choice. This was an industry that clearly ran on its nerves. Coffee. Cigarettes. Work. Fret. Jamie was beginning to understand why rig workers went nuts when they hit the land of alcohol.

Phil was gone, muttering away to himself. Jamie thought about staying in the tea shack for the entire shift. It was the best way to meet the crew. But he didn't seem to be making any friends, so he decided to go outside again. This was also his best hope of avoiding Webster, who was sure to pay the tea shack a visit.

Outside, it was getting colder.

'By Christ, you're lucky,' said the Crane Op. He was coiling rope. 'Webster caught Phil the Drill coming out the tea shack. Gave him a hell of a roasting. I had to hide behind a container to hear the whole thing. Brutal it was. Brutal.'

'I'm getting run off,' said Jamie.

'Bollocks,' said the Crane Op. 'You'd be on a chopper already. Webster's got you marked down for special entertainment.'

'What the hell is that?'

The Crane Op lowered his voice to a murmur. 'He likes to amuse himself by making someone suffer. His present victim is almost burnt out. You're fresh meat. And you'll believe anything he tells you.'

'But I won't believe anything you tell me. I can spot a wind-up when I see one.'

The Crane Op laughed. 'I had you going for a minute, though.'

Walter had told Jamie never to put his hands anywhere he wasn't happy to put his cock, so Jamie went around the rig looking for places to put his cock. Since most of the options involved cold metal, the search wasn't a very fruitful one. He declined to put his cock in the shale shakers or the mud pumps, although he would have been happy to dangle it over the mud pits. The pipe deck was out of the question, as was the drillfloor. He wasn't for putting it up the derrick either. The various containers looked as if they could do without its attentions too. No, it was definitely staying where it was – and his hands wouldn't be venturing out much either.

There was a warm light coming from a container just outside the mud lab. It was the logging unit. Jamie thought about going in to introduce himself and maybe fall out with some more people. He had decided against it when he thought he saw the ominous shape of John Webster heading his way. He opened a heavy metal door and went in. He then found himself in a dark little vestibule. It was about four feet square. What an odd decorative feature,

Jamie thought. He could hear music coming from the other side of a second door.

'Close the door!' chorused the loggers.

Jamie heaved the door shut. He opened the second door and entered the logging shack, closing the second door quickly behind him.

'The container is pressurised,' said a husky Spanish voice. 'If you leave the door open, the unit shuts down and we have to reboot everything.'

There, standing in front of Jamie, was a girl. But this wasn't just any girl.

'Hola,' she said, 'I'm Antonio Banderas.'

She had perfect teeth, high, Iberian cheekbones and a classical nose. Her gorgeous brown eyes sat below two stylish eyebrows and her voluminous dark hair was swept into a casual ponytail. Michelangelo couldn't have sculpted better, or more nibble-able ears. They were adorned with subtle silver earrings. Antonio had removed the top half of her coveralls and tied the sleeves stylishly together below her waist. It was a touch of flair that only the continentals seem to manage. The trouser legs were neatly, yet haphazardly folded so that her pristine, steel-toecapped boots looked like something more likely to be seen on Kate Moss on a Paris catwalk than on a sweaty roustie on the Manticore's catwalk. She was wearing a figure-hugging blue cotton top whose top two buttons she had absent-mindedly left undone. Her thirty-four inch hips curved sleekly inward to what looked like a twenty-six inch waist. Her breasts were understated and petite. They hinted at passion and athleticism. Her nipples were sticking out.

Jamie drank this vision in. Finally, he thought, somewhere that I'd be happy to put my cock.

'Why are you blushing?' said Antonio Banderas.

'I'm not blushing,' said Jamie. 'It's an acne attack.'

Antonio's eyes sparkled. Her full, yet tender and sensitive lips arranged themselves first into a half smile before broadening into a full beam. Then the lips parted to give a grand finale of gleaming, glistening white-toothed glory.

An acne attack? Acne attack? Where did I think that up from? Are they to be the first words to the love of my life? Love? Did I say "love"?' thought Jamie. Oh my God, it's love. And I've only looked at her. No, it is. I feel faint. It must be love. I need to sit down. I'm in pain already. It's awful. No, it's not. How do I get out of this mess? Do I want to? Help!

'You are funny,' said Antonio.

She thought the acne attack was a gag. Her loveliness simply grew in Jamie's mind. How perfect could a girl be?

'It's my first night offshore. I wasn't expecting to meet... a Spaniard.'

Antonio Banderas giggled. She had a wonderful giggle.

'I bet you weren't expecting to meet an Indian either,' said Antonio's Indian colleague.

He was short and had a mustache.

'Who are you?' said Jamie crossly.

'Lat.'

'Haven't you got things to log? Outside?'

'Jamie,' said Antonio Banderas. She made it sound like "Jaime". It was so erotic. Being "Jaime" opened a world of possibilities for Jamie. "Jaimes" got invited to all the right parties. "Jaimes" had great sex with great girls like... well, with great girls like Antonio Banderas. She had read his name from his coveralls. She had initiative too. 'Why don't you sit down? You are still under attack. Would you like a cup of tea?'

Jamie didn't want tea. Jamie was awash with tea. 'Yes please,' he breathed.

Antonio sat back down in her chair. 'You make it. Everything you need is in the corner,' she said. She was passionately independent as well.

As Jamie staggered to the corner, he saw how nicely things were set up in the logging unit. It was clean, bright and well ventilated. They had classical music. Lat was playing a computer game and Antonio was reading. The many monitors blinked in pleasing tones of blue. They even had de-ionised water for the tea.

As Jamie fiddled with bags and boiling water, he realised that he wasn't just going to make a fool of himself in his job; he was going to make a fool of himself in love too. He didn't care. His life had been utterly transformed in five minutes. Cocking up the job wasn't important anymore. Pursuing Antonio Banderas was all that mattered now. But in order to woo her, Jamie needed to keep his job and remain aboard.

The awful truth was that John Webster now held the key to Jamie's heart in his hands.

It was vitally important for Jamie to somehow get on the right side of John Webster. It was equally vitally important that Jamie keep his true feelings for Antonio Banderas hidden from everyone else aboard. Jamie looked at Lat. Lat looked back at Jamie, gave him a dirty grin and winked. Oh fuck, Jamie thought, the cat's well and truly out of the bag. He turned to the matter in hand.

'I suspect you're not really called Antonio Banderas.'

'My real name is Antonia Ruiz Velasquez de Sabartes Casagemas.'

'Antonio Banderas it is then.'

'My full name is Lat….,' began Lat.

'Lat'll do fine,' Jamie interrupted.

Antonio Banderas giggled deliciously. 'You're hilarious,' she said.

She thinks I'm hilarious, thought Jamie. She's amazing. It really is love. He stood, taking in her Iberian wonderfulness. 'How well do you know John Webster?' he said.

'Well enough to want to see him dead.'

'You too?'

'I'd laugh to see that son of a bitch in hell.'

'I wondered if he might behave differently toward women.'

'I'd quite happily administer the poison myself. Something slow acting. A horrible, lingering, death of agony. Or the garrotte. It is the Spanish method. Slow strangulation.'

I wouldn't take a busted pay packet home to her, Jamie thought.

Antonio smiled. 'See what a bad man does? Such thoughts. The world will be a happier place without him for sure.'

'Have you any idea what I can do to get in his good books?'

The loggers roared with laughter.

'He is not having any good books,' said Lat. 'With John Webster, it is all bad books in his library.'

'Why do want him to like you Jaime?' Antonio searched Jamie's eyes deeply.

Jamie tried not to blush too much. 'I don't want to get run off. I'd like to stay here, for a while at least.' He watched carefully for Antonio Banderas's response.

Antonio Banderas smiled gently. Behind her back, Lat winked lewdly.

Antonio stroked her neck absent-mindedly. 'My advice is to agree with everything Webster says. If you fuck up, tell him at once. Or he will crucify you. It is a strange time. Unusual things are happening. Apart from that, enjoy yourself.' She shrugged erotically. 'As much as you can.'

'You're doing that Spanish lisping thing,' he said. 'It's so sexy. Or maybe I should say "tho thexthy".'

Antonio Banderas smiled and turned a little red. She ran her hand lightly through her hair. Her eyes shone fiercely. Jamie felt that he had a real chance with her. Jamie also felt so nervous that he was ready to vomit. It was time to quit while he was ahead. He gulped his tea down and rose. 'Nice to see you Lat. We'll need to talk again soon,' he lied.

Jamie turned to Antonio for his grand exit. 'Lovely meeting you. I'll thee you thoon.' Jamie tried to wink at her, but scrunched both of his eyes up instead. He left the unit to the sound of her cruel peninsular laughter. His heart sank into blackness. His body went outside into the dark.

Jamie hastened to the mud lab to deal with the storm of emotions that was battering him. She was beautiful, she was scary. She was lovely, she was strange. She was strangely lovely. How could he feel so much so quickly? It didn't make sense. If there was one thing Jamie prided himself on, it was a grim logic about himself that guided him through life. Okay, it was a shite life, but now wasn't the time to get picky. What really was he in love with? A smile, a couple of perky nipples, a few lispy words? Was this all it took? Judging by his throbbing heart, his throbbing head and, it had to be admitted, his throbbing cock, the answer was "yes". Whatever else, Antonio Banderas was a puzzle that Jamie / Jaime had to work out for himself. Jamie's grim logic made him feel better - but only for a moment. A girl? A puzzle? Worked out? What was he thinking? More importantly, what was he feeling? The grim logic, Jamie realised, could be saved for the job. The rig was grim. The mud was logic. Antonio Banderas was something else altogether. She was a gorgeous woman. Not grim. And definitely not logical. She was a puzzle that first and foremost he would love.

A shout broke through Jamie's concentration. It came from the sack-store. Jamie crept over to the escape hatch and eased it open. Below him were Peachy and Phil the Driller.

'You had better pull your socks up or I'll kick your arse so hard I'll knock you into next week.'

'Phil, I'm sorry. I'm trying.'

'You're trying my patience. If there's anybody going down on this rig, it's not going to be me. And I'm taking you fucking with me.'

'Don't worry Phil, I'll cover your arse.'

'I want to know everything that goes on down here. I want to hear every single thing that Scottie says. I don't trust that scheming bastard. And keep an eye on that new mud muppet. He looks like a complete loser. And remember: if you think that Webster can give you a hard time, wait till you see what happens when you cross me. Now fuck off you useless piece of shit.'

Phil immediately contradicted himself by fucking off himself. Peachy, who hadn't looked too bothered by Phil's words, made a "wanker" gesture behind his back. Jamie thought this an odd thing for the rig Porn King to do. However, honour had been satisfied on both sides. Phil felt superior as bully and manager. Peachy felt superior, having stood up to a pathetic tirade from a jumped-up, idiotic, brown-nosing clown who couldn't even manage an erection.

Such was the way the world worked. Jamie closed the hatch.

He had only just begun to study the mud splattered on the walls and muse upon the nature of love when there was a huge explosion outside. It was the watertight door being slammed.

'You wait. You!' Alexei's unmistakable Russian tones.

The noise moved around the lab, from the short corridor outside into the pit room. Alexei was chasing someone. Boom! The watertight door to the sack-store slammed.

'You think you fuck with us and live?'

One set of feet on the steps down to the sack-store. Followed by another. Jamie moved back to the hatch. He cracked it open. Someone walking quickly, almost running. Alexei close behind.

'You don't ignore me. You!'

A pause. Only Alexei was visible. His prey was obscured by a pallet of guar gum.

'You can't run away. You can't fuck with us. We find you anywhere on the world. Do you think we are stupid? You know how easy it is to have you killed?'

Mumbling from the other person. Inaudible.

Alexei lowered his voice. 'It is here somewhere.' He looked up. He saw Jamie. 'I promise you death very soon.' Jamie closed the hatch. More words, all inaudible.

Jamie now had a decision: stay or flee? The viciousness of the exchange had left him feeling physically sick. The decision was made for him. There were footsteps on the stairs. The wheel on the hatch turned. The hatch opened. Alexei, smiling, pressed a finger to his lips. Shhh.

Jamie nodded.

Alexei nodded. We understand one another. 'Where is derrickman?'

Jamie shook his head.

'Tell him I want to see him. In private.' Alexei's voice was as cold as a Siberian winter.

Jamie closed the hatch. He went to the sink. He vomited. He rinsed his mouth out. The tap water tasted disgusting. It was brown. There was a five gallon drum marked "Distilled Water". Jamie doused himself with it. He sat with his head in his hands. He took breaths in large gulps.

A minute passed. Fifteen minutes passed. Jamie calmed. The next thing he knew, he could hear someone sobbing. At first he thought it was himself. He lifted his wet head up. It was a quiet grief, coming from the other side of the lab wall. Someone was hiding in a corner of the pit room. Jamie dried himself with blue paper towels. There were small pools of water on the worktops and on the floor, as if someone had been crying here too. As the sound grew louder and more anguished it became unbearable to listen to. Jamie mopped up the water as best he could with the rags available. He had to stop. There was a real human being on the other side of the bulkhead. That person was suffering. They were inches away. Jamie touched the filthy bulkhead gently. He wanted to help. He could sense so much pain in the cries. He didn't want to intrude on private grief. The rig was a very public place. Would Jamie have wanted to be found if the roles were reversed? But the cries seemed to plead for comfort.

Jamie found these sounds of pain unbearable to listen to. Ultimately, he realised that he couldn't live with himself if he didn't offer some kind of consolation to someone in such distress. Whatever problems he had were nothing by comparison. What a day. Jamie took a deep breath and went to help. The door to the mud lab opened noisily. By the time that Jamie went through the water-tight door to the pit room, the other person was fleeing.

'It's okay! I won't tell anyone! I can help! Please!'

Jamie's words had no effect. To pursue the chase would have been to humiliate the man he was trying to help. The person who was crying, whoever it was, wanted to be left alone in their suffering.

All Jamie had seen had been a leg as it disappeared, clad in the orange coveralls of Manticore Drilling. He also caught a glimpse of a sock – a red sock.

Chapter 12 Webster's Dead

The tiredness hit Jamie at around 3 am. The rest of the shift was just about survival.

He was glad not to have any major decisions to have to make and he understood implicitly why so many catastrophes occurred in the early hours. Sleep deprivation was a very real issue for rig workers. Phil the Driller decided not to give the boys an easy first shift. He had them doing all sorts of heavy maintenance on the drillfloor. This lost him what little respect he had. It would come back to haunt him.

As it was, most guys quit and spent the last two hours of the shift in and around the tea shack. Jamie joined them, enjoying some tall tales of what they had got up to on their time off. He himself had no stories to tell.

At around 5:30 the company broke up. John Webster was out of his bed for the final time. Jamie saw him, with Bill the Mechanic, up in the gantry around the new hopper that wasn't working. Jamie went into the mud lab to clear up the mess. Once he had restored everything to its original state, he opened the escape hatch that looked out into the sack-store.

There was a lot of coming and going. The sack-store was a crossroads of short-cuts around the rig. Scottie and Peachy went up to the drillfloor. Antonio Banderas went into the pit room. Phil the Driller went by, glared at Jamie, and went through the cement unit. Bill the Mechanic came and went, taking measurements and gathering materials. He saw Lat the Logger, Desperate Dan, Mark Z, Stevie the real AD and Sergei the pretend AD. Ronnie the Roustie was the last person he saw going into the pit room. Except one.

Jamie gasped with fright. John Webster's face loomed large in the hatch opening. He had climbed the small escape ladder to take Jamie by surprise.

'I don't like you looking out on my business,' said Webster. 'This is an escape hatch. It's not a ventilation hatch. You're lucky I don't weld it shut. Then you'll never escape. Or ventilate.'

Webster closed the hatch. He turned the wheel which slid the bolts home with finality. Jamie never saw the man alive again.

***

The handover was a bad-tempered affair. Jamie hadn't slept in over 30 hours. Gray was just out of his bed and wasn't a morning person. He wasn't an afternoon person or a night person either.

'I suppose I should say "Good Morning",' said Gray irritably, and fifteen minutes late.

'You can say what you like,' replied Jamie peevishly.

'Get the report sent?' said Gray grouchily.

'After three hours messing around with the templates that you never explained,' said Jamie crossly.

'Sorry. And I could have wiped your arse while I was at it,' said Gray churlishly.

'You'd probably have fucked that up as well,' said Jamie cantankerously.

'No boat for the mud?' said Gray brusquely.

'What do you think?' snapped Jamie.

'Just as well. You'd have put most of it over the side,' said Gray crabbily.

'Only to spite you,' said Jamie petulantly.

'Webster won't be happy,' whined Gray.

'He'll be happier than you,' said Jamie testily.

'Everybody's happier than me,' said Gray sullenly.

Jamie's spirits plunged when he returned to his bedroom. Room 14 was as bleak a place as he had ever seen. Fifteen feet by seven feet of compressed misery. This was supposed to be home for the next three weeks. What was most depressing was how nakedly functional everything was. There wasn't a hint of softness nor a suggestion of comfort anywhere to be found.

It was a hard room designed for hard men.

The overwhelmingly dominant colour was brown, an old, depressing brown long before the brown-is-the-new-black brown. Floor tiles: brown. Walls: beige with a strong undercurrent of brown. Porthole curtains: brown. Bed Curtains: brown. Wood-effect plastic table: brown. Telly: brown. DVD: brown. The two lockers were light brown. This, presumably, was to cheer the place up.

Even the air was brown.

At least the bed linen was light blue, the angle poised lamp red and the sink cream. Jamie had to be grateful for small mercies.

Jamie stuffed his survival suit and fleece into the empty, bright yellow emergency grab-bag. Did he need to put the fleece in first, or the survival suit? Jamie assumed that he'd be needing the fleece first when the rig blew. There was a smoke hood at the bottom. In a pocket to one side were some flameproof gloves, a torch and a light stick. You snapped the stick apparently, and light issued forth. Jamie could picture himself in his survival suit and smoke hood, crawling along the floor with his gloves, feeling his way through the murk to safety outside. They'd thought of everything. For when the rig blew.

The survival bags were the brightest things in the room.

At the foot of the bunk beds was the shower and toilet cubicle. There was a small ledge dividing the toilet area from the shower, and barely enough room to squeeze in between the two. There were about half a dozen abandoned bottles of shampoo and shower gel. The shower curtain was hooked up behind the soap dish to help it dry out. The air here was really stale. Damp and stale. As the rig heaved to one side, dirty water bubbled up through the drain in the shower. It reminded Jamie of the legendary character who had been sitting on the toilet when a rig had pitched violently to one side. He had been given a massive sewage enema.

Jamie sat on the toilet and put his head in his hands. He let out a long, low groan. When he opened his eyes, he saw something that cheered him up. Beside the toilet, attached to the wall and unused for many moons, was a remnant from a bygone age. It was from the days of heroic smoking on the toilet. It was an ashtray.

Teeth brushed and undressed, Jamie considered his bunk. It looked uninviting. The cover had outgrown the mattress. It sat limply on top. The pillows had died several years before, but had been refused a decent burial. The duvet was in its death-throes. The mattress had simply given up the ghost. It refused to give Jamie any meaningful support. Everything was swathed in sagging nylon, which drooped like geriatric lettuce.

Sprucing up rig rooms was clearly no good for profits. Jamie would sleep like a pauper so that some people in Texas and London and New York could sleep like kings. But sleep, for the moment, was out of the question. Outside, someone was grinding, making a sound like hair-clippers on acid. Then it stopped. Then it started again. It wasn't even a continuous sound that Jamie's brain could get used to and allow him to nod off.

As his mind wasn't drifting off to sleep, it drifted instead back to the tour of the rig's accommodation. He thought of the bedrooms that he had seen. Some of the doors had been opened, some of them closed, their occupants asleep, or trying to sleep. The opened doors afforded glimpses into others' lives. There was something about the rooms that disturbed him. They were all depressingly similar. Only small attempts had been made to humanise them. This mainly involved female breasts, revealed on posters or calendars. Some rooms had no girls at all, just pictures of machines – cars or motorbikes. These rooms all exhibited the same kind of dull lack of imagination. Perhaps humanising your room was one of the many things forbidden offshore. Or perhaps not. There was one perfectly human and homely room that Jamie saw. It belonged to the stewardesses. It was a shocking indictment of Jamie's sex.

Mercifully, the grinding stopped. Jamie allowed himself a deep sigh. He could feel himself drifting off into blissful oblivion. He would get some rest after all.

BOOM! BOOM! BOOM! BOOM! BOOM! BOOM! BOOM!

The entire rig was vibrating violently.

BOOM! BOOM! BOOM! BOOM! BOOM! BOOM! BOOM!

It sounded like someone was pounding on the gates of hell.

Jamie leapt up out of his bed.

He cracked his head off the ceiling.

"Oyah!"

He ricocheted off the side of the bed. He fell from the top bunk onto the hard floor below.

"Ooooof!" The wind was knocked out of him.

BOOM! BOOM! BOOM! BOOM! BOOM! BOOM! BOOM!

Jamie writhed in pain on the floor. Fortunately his arm had wrapped itself around the ladders up to his bed, breaking his fall — and damn near breaking his arm.

"Fuck! Bastard fucking fuck fuck!"

BOOM! BOOM! BOOM! BOOM! BOOM! BOOM! BOOM!

The sound was like enormous anchor chains being dragged. It was enormous anchor chains being dragged.

Jamie's head hurt. His right arm hurt. He felt nauseous. He was mildly concussed. He was incompetent at his job. He was terrified of the psychopathic toolpusher and he was in love with a girl he barely knew. He was exhausted and unsure whether he would ever sleep again.

There was only one logical thing to do: Jamie rolled across the floor and laughed.

***

Jamie was awoken by a fuzzy-sounding Gray. He could barely hear him because of the foam earplugs that had solved the anchor chain problem. Utter exhaustion had taken care of the sleep problem.

'Walter wants to see us,' said Gray. 'There's some kind of blockage in the oil-based mud.'

Jamie joined a motley crew in Walter's office to ascertain who had thrown what into the pit of mud. There was Jamie, Gray, Scottie, Peachy, Billy the Fish the derrickman on days and Wayne, his assistant.

'Everyone directly responsible for the pits and fluids is here,' said Walter.

'What about Webster?' said Gray.

'We suspect that he might be the thing in the pit causing the problem. No one can find him.'

'You mean someone has really murdered him?' Jamie shrieked.

'Let's not get ahead of ourselves,' said Walter. 'It could be a suicide.'

'The only way that bastard would kill himself would be to blow the entire rig up and take us all with him,' said Peachy earnestly.

Everyone agreed about this. Everyone was also innocence itself when asked about dumping anything, particularly bodies, into the mud.

Gray brought up a salient point: 'If the mud's been contaminated with a body, I don't think our boys in Aberdeen will take it back for credit. You better tell the client. That's three grand down the drain.'

'I'm not paying for it,' said Walter.

'It's your toolpusher,' said Gray.

Walter rolled his eyes. He let out a deep sigh. He had a feeling that there would be a lot of eye rolling and sighing in the days to come.

There was then some minor fisticuffs when it became apparent that Billy the Fish had turned the agitator off without bothering to investigate the squealing and John Webster had probably languished in mud for another eight hours. Scottie was indignant. He took this as a sure sign of the day shift passing yet more work onto the night shift. Just like the broken tugger winch the night before, which had almost claimed Mark Z's hand and Peachy's reputation. Peachy then became indignant.

Walter calmed everything down and explained that he wanted to use Scottie and Peachy because of their experience and the severity of the situation. Billy the Fish and Wayne became indignant and then did what countless thousands of indignant oil workers had done in the past; they stormed off to the tea shack in a huff.

Filling out the permits and doing the Risk Assessment for the task seemed to be taking an age. There was no sense of urgency whatsoever. And Webster could potentially still be alive. Jamie pointed this out.

'Let's concentrate on getting the paperwork correct,' Walter replied. 'We don't want to get into trouble.'

'Rig toolpusher killed by safety bullshit. The irony is too good to be true,' said Peachy gleefully.

Since John Webster was unable to authorise the Cold Permit to Work for the recovery of his own body, the night toolpusher was woken and made to sign. But he wasn't told anything. 'He's an idiot,' Walter sighed.

*****

The recovery of John Webster's body was not without incident.

The oil-based mud had to be pumped out of the pit into a reserve pit. Scottie wasn't pleased about getting another pit dirtied, but the task was performed with relative ease: the suction valve on the Blue mixing line was opened; the discharge valve from the blue mixing line to the pit receiving the liquid was opened; the blue mix pump was turned on. The fluid cascaded into the pit with a small, thunderous burst and then a reassuring whoosh.

Scottie and Peachy worked together smoothly. They had flashlights which allowed them to look into the dark pits from the small hatches above.

'We can suck the pit almost dry,' Scottie explained to Jamie. 'Maybe an inch or two left on the bottom. The mix pumps are well below the pits, so you can always get good suction, just by gravity. With the huge pumps, what we call the rig pumps, we always want at least four feet of fluid in the pits to guarantee suction. Because if they run dry, they jack off and smash themselves to pieces and then the rig's shut down and Webster throws a hairy.' Scottie paused. 'THREW a hairy.'

Jamie, Gray, Walter, Scottie and Peachy had been joined by Ritchie the Medic and, for some reason, by Bill the Mechanic. When the pit was empty, a hoist was set up above the hatch to the pit. Scottie and Peachy put harnesses on, so that they could be rescued by the hoist, if required. They were wearing steel-toecapped wellington boots and water-proof slicker suits over their coveralls.

Peachy stuck his head into the hatch. 'There's something down there, right enough. It doesn't look pretty.'

A gas detector was lowered into the pit on a piece of string.

'Give it a couple of minutes,' said Walter.

'Cigarette?' said Scottie. Peachy nodded. They left.

As they waited, listening to the echoing bleep of the gas detector, Jamie realised that these were the most surreal moments of his entire life. Ritchie was standing by gamely in his wellies, with his portable defibrillator set at the ready. 'I've waited years for something as good as this,' he said.

Jamie had never imagined that Ritchie could be so happy.

Scottie and Peachy took an age to come back, explaining that the entire rig was buzzing with rumours and conjecture, but that the phones were down, so no one could phone home to spread the gossip. Walter rolled his eyes.

'You all right to do this?' said Scottie, slinging a leg over the hatch.

'Oh I'm ready for anything,' said Peachy, going down the ladder after him.

A fluorescent light was lowered and Ritchie the Medic went down after it. Everyone else gathered around the hatch. There was a bit of grunting.

'It's definitely him.'

'He's stone cold... and pretty stiff.'

There was more grunting, some confusion - and quite a bit of swearing. They were having trouble unhooking the body from the agitator blade. The next request was totally unexpected.

'Can we have a fire hose?'

'What the fuck do you want a fire hose for?' said Walter.

'He's a bit gloopy.'

'I bet John Webster never thought that it would end like this,' said Walter.

A hose was duly passed down. There was a familiar hissing sound as it was turned on and then some shouting and more swearing as the splashes ricocheted everywhere. There were some grunting and wrestling sounds.

A cheery shout: 'We've got him! .... It really is him ..... He looks a bit shocked.'

Then, 'What are you doing?'

'I'm going to defibrillate him,' said Ritchie.

'You can't defibrillate a corpse with rigor mortis.'

'Just watch me.'

As the shocking sounds of the defibrillator came up, Bill whispered, 'Is that an explosion risk?'

Walter shook his head.

'He's definitely dead,' said Ritchie. 'Never mind, I've covered all the bases.'

'Guys!! Just get a harness on him and get him out.'

'Could you pass us down an iron bar?'

'What the fuck do you want an iron bar for?'

'His arms are sticking out. You won't get him through the hatch.'

'You are not breaking his arms,' said Ritchie sharply. 'We'll need to wait for the rigor mortis to subside. This is a crime scene. We can't go smacking the corpse about.'

There was an ominous sound of unzipping and rustling. The next event was truly shocking – and not in an electrical sense.

'What are you taking that out for?' Scottie shouted.

'I need to pee,' shouted Peachy. 'Stand back.'

'Not there!!!'

As the pitter-patter sounds came up, Scottie retreated to the hatch. He looked up. 'Peachy's pissing on Webster's corpse,' he said.

Walter let out his biggest sigh yet. 'Peachy! Get your arse up here!'

When Peachy emerged, his face was all determination. 'I've been waiting for years to do that.'

'It's easy for you to piss all over the toolpusher's corpse,' said Walter. 'I've got to phone Aberdeen and explain it!'

'S'all right Walter,' Scottie shouted up, 'I'll give him a good dousing. No one need ever know. What happens on the rig stays on the rig.'

Walter rolled his eyes. 'If only that were true.' He shook his head sadly at Peachy, I've a good mind to make sure you get charged.'

'Charged with what?'

'Soiling the dead!'

'It was John Webster! He was soiled already!'

The men were inches apart. Jamie thought he might have to intervene to stop a fist fight from breaking out.

'Go on Walter,' said Peachy. 'Charge me. Just try it. I'll go on the sofa. On Breakfast TV. And I'll tell them exactly what goes on out here.'

Even Jamie, with one shift under his belt, could tell that having assistant derrickmen going on sofas and spilling the beans on what went on offshore wasn't a good idea.

Calmly, Peachy went over to the telephone and put out a tannoy: PING PONG – 'Anybody who wants to piss on the toolpusher's corpse come down to the pit room now.'

Most of the rig showed up. Things got a bit heated and Walter almost had a riot on his hands. Had the corpse not been down a pit that required a Confined Space Permit to enter, Jamie shuddered to think what could have happened to it.

As it was, Walter could only get them to disperse by promising to let them all have a good look at the bashed body once it had been recovered. John Webster was to lie in state.

'They'll take photos and send them all round the world,' said Bill the Mechanic. 'You'll lose your job.'

'It won't be happening,' said Walter. 'I'll get them all to calm down.'

But they didn't calm down. They threw a party.

Chapter 13 It's My Party and I'll Cry if I Want To

It was a curious bash. There was no alcohol. There were no drugs. There were hardly any women. It didn't matter. Their nemesis was gone. The man, who had terrorised every person on the rig, was no more. And what's more, one of their number had brutally terminated his life and then cruelly dumped his deformed carcass into a foul liquid. The crew couldn't have been happier.

Night shift nor day shift, no one slept. No one could have. The music was cranked up to eleven and the entire accommodation block throbbed to its beat. Jamie didn't know whether it was garage music or house music. It may as well have been garden shed music. It was music to take drugs to and this made things even more surreal. The Camp Boss was acting as the dealer. He had opened the bond and was doing a roaring trade in sweets, fizzy drinks and tobacco.

The place was a seething mass of bodies. Desperate Dan was doing a deranged dance, holding a knife in front of him and eviscerating a phantom Webster. It gave Jamie the creeps. Everyone else cheered Dan on.

Phil the Driller was freaking out. His eyes were wild. He poured Coca-Cola all over his head. 'Freeedom!! He can't fire me now! I'm the driller! I'm the driller. I'm gonna drill a hole. I'm gonna drill a hole! I'm the man! It's me!'

Phil banged his chest like an ape.

Jamie found himself being kissed on the cheek by Ronnie the Roustie. Bill the Mechanic ruffled his hair, Peachy rammed a fruit gum into his mouth and Scottie emptied a packet of crisps over his head. Their faces were a sea of smiles.

Shredded paper was being thrown around like confetti. It was a beautiful bedlam. The burden which had been lifted off the crew was enormous. They were elated, as high as kites.

Jamie couldn't help but grin. At the end of the corridor, he saw Antonio Banderas. She was so gorgeous. He was so in love.

She gave him a smile and waved. Jamie's heart soared. Ronnie the Roustie approached her. He whispered something into her ear. She looked deeply into his eyes. Their faces drew closer. They kissed. They kept kissing. Then they weren't kissing. They were snogging furiously.

Jamie felt physically sick. His life was over as surely as John Webster's life was over. He was dizzy. He reeled through the revellers. The music was now just a din, the party merely an eruption of bile.

Phil the Driller rammed his face into Jamie's. 'Enjoying your first trip offshore? Bit of a coincidence? You arrive one day. Webster dies the next? Don't worry, we won't hold it against you. In fact, there's a couple of derrickmen I want you to take care of.' Phil laughed manically and unpleasantly.

Ronnie the Roustie and Antonio Banderas were still playing at tonsil tennis. Jamie took a deep breath to try and control himself. He'd have given anything not to have witnessed that kiss. He was now in genuine grief, the sole mourner at this bizarre funeral party.

Antonio Banderas ran her hand tenderly through Ronnie the Roustie's hair. She looked at Jamie and smiled.

Then Jamie's heart almost stopped. A shrill, intermittent tone rang out.

'Attention all personnel. This is the OIM. This is not a drill. All personnel are to assemble at their Muster Stations. Repeat: this is not a drill.'

The speaker was pelted with hard-boiled sweets. The hard-boiled personnel gave a two word response: 'Fuck Off!' The dancing intensified.

It took about half an hour to finally calm everyone down and get them to their Muster Stations. There were about fifty of them mustered in the television lounge. The others were in the mess hall, with a handful coordinating things from the control room. Jamie sat morosely, trying not to catch Antonio Banderas's eye. Or Ronnie the Roustie's.

'Cheer up,' said Gray. 'At least we won't have to backload that oil-based mud. It will be syphoned into tote-tanks by the police for evidence. We won't have to test it and we won't have to fill out any paperwork.'

Jamie was coming to believe that Gray was the laziest person in the entire world.

'Rigor mortis. Bloody brilliant,' beamed Ritchie the Medic, resplendent in his luminous green Muster Checker's bib.

'The alarm will now be silenced to aid communication,' tannoyed Walter. 'Remain at your Muster Stations. This has been the worst muster ever. We were one short. Some muppet forgot to count the toolpusher. Please remain at your Muster Stations until further notice. We may be some time.'

Having got the fact of Webster's death out of their system, the crew turned its attention to speculation about the murder itself. There were all kinds of conspiracy theories flying around. Jamie was even implicated in some of them. He wasn't much bothered. Every time he caught sight of Antonio Banderas, she looked even more achingly beautiful – and even more heartbreakingly unavailable. He concentrated his stare firmly on the carpet tiles.

The most popular theory involved a crazed loner finally snapping after years of dog's abuse. This didn't really narrow it down much. Some had Webster expertly lassoed, or blundering into a Viet-Cong style mantrap. Sergei the phony assistant driller featured prominently in most scenarios. Jamie was mooted as an international hit man who had shot Webster with a silenced gun smuggled aboard on a pallet of Sodium Bicarbonate. Everybody laughed at this, especially Antonia and Ronnie the Roustie.

The one thing that everyone was agreed on was that the police stood no chance of finding the killer. Unless the crazed loner cracked, there was no chance of a conviction.

'I wonder how many cops they'll send?' wondered Ronnie the Roustie.

'I wonder how long they'll keep us out here?' wondered Bill the Mechanic.

Their ruminations were brought to a swift end. Walter the OIM was about to deliver the most extraordinary tannoy announcement of his forty year career.

'Attention all personnel,' he began. 'It is my sad duty to confirm that John Webster, our Senior Toolpusher, was pronounced dead at two twenty six this afternoon. Foul play is suspected. Looks like he had his head bashed in. Now, no one disliked John Webster more than me, but I think somebody's over-stepped the mark a wee bit. If anybody wants to confess to murder, please make yourself known to your Muster Checker.'

Ritchie stood, pen poised, clipboard at the ready. No one came forward.

Walter continued. 'If anybody knows who committed the deadly deed, please make yourself known to the Muster Checker.'

Nothing.

'Given the popularity of the deceased, I'm not hopeful of much cooperation. We have ninety-six people on board, well ninety five. And ninety five suspects - all with a good motive, because let's face it everybody hated the bastard. May he rest in peace. Not that he deserves to. Although there is a killer amongst us, I'm pretty sure that this will be a one-off, so don't worry. But don't hang about isolated bits of the rig on your own either.'

Around the room, the sound of Walter's voice was having a calming effect.

'The cops are on their way,' he sighed. 'Bastards. But don't worry folks, Uncle Walter has made sure that a son-of-a-bitch lawyer is coming too. You don't have to say a word without a lawyer present. We'll all be interviewed. It's the usual story out here. Don't take any shit off no man. I'll be telling them fuck all. What you do is up to you.'

There was a small cheer. 'Good old Walter,' said Ronnie the Roustie. 'Always looks after his boys.'

'How I'm going to explain this to Head Office in Houston is something else,' Walter continued. 'Over the years I've had a few cock-ups to confess to, but this takes the biscuit. Let me make one thing perfectly clear: in no way is this a Lost Time Accident. Having John Webster bludgeoned to death and tossed into a mud pit was no accident. It might be an incident, I'll give you that. But it's no accident. I'll be fighting every inch of the way to keep our safety bonus. That could be a thousand pounds a man.'

There was another cheer.

Walter slurped some water. 'Now, the brutal murder of the Senior Toolpusher is going to knock us back a few points in the rig of the year competition. Which is a pity, 'cos we were in third place. But if the Phoenix 919 can be in first place with a leaky leg and a four degree list, anything's possible. Rest assured, I'll be battling on your behalf once this has all blown over.'

'Fuck me,' said Peachy, 'Walter's talking about this as if it's a minor oil spill.'

'For safety reasons, we're all going to have to remain at our Muster Stations until the Old Bill gets here. They'll have a quick word with everybody to see if anyone is willing to spill the beans. Failing that, we'll be formally interviewed. The night shift are going to have to stay up for a few hours, so there will be no normal rig activities tonight. It's no big deal because they're having problems setting anchors. Hopefully the rig will return to normal activity on day shift tomorrow.'

'Walter's an old bastard,' said Ronnie the Roustie. 'Always profit before people.'

'Communications to the outside world are suspended. I'll try and get them up as soon as possible. The office in Aberdeen will phone through any urgent messages to loved ones. The official line will be that the Manticore is suffering technical problems with the satellite dish. If you ask me, it's totally pointless. News of this will spread round the North Sea like a dose of the clap. But who am I to question the balloons running the business? One last thing: the oil-based mud will be pumped into tote tanks and sent to the Beach for forensic analysis. There's a forensic team coming out with the cops and it looks like they'll do the pit cleaning for us, which is a wee bonus. In the meantime, the stewards can return to the galley to prepare a special evening meal. Then you'll be allowed to go and eat in supervised groups. A good, hot supper will do us all good. If we can get through the next day, it'll be plain sailing. Don't take any shit from the cops. Webster's dead, long live the Manticore.'

The room burst into a spontaneous round of applause. They could also hear applause coming from the other Muster Stations. Whether the applause was for Walter or for the killer was unknown.

'I see a rosy future ahead for all of us,' said Bill the Mechanic.

'God Bless us, everyone,' said Ronnie the Roustie.

'I think I might confess,' said Peachy.

Chapter 14 Speak Nothing But Good of the Dead

The police decided to split the 95 suspects into two groups. Those with a criminal record were to be interviewed first. The other seven people were to be interviewed after.

Being naïve, Jamie refused the services of Walter's son-of-a-bitch solicitor. Having led a blamelessly dull, unarrested life, Jamie was also one of the last in. This was unfortunate. Having spent hours getting nowhere with a cynical, uncooperative and smug crew intent on protecting the murderer, the cops were in no mood to be messed about.

'Have you had any coaching regarding this interview?' said Detective Inspector Findon, the surly senior cop.

'No,' said Jamie.

This was a lie. Scottie had come up to Jamie and told him not to mention anything anyone had said, or anything he had heard, no matter how banal. And he was definitely not to mention anything about Russians. Or Fraserburgh.

Then Peachy came to have a word. And so did Desperate Dan, Mark Z, Phil the Driller, Bill the Mechanic, Lat the Indian Logger and, finally, Walter himself. 'Cooperate with the police and I'll make sure you never work in this business again,' he said. 'Where do you think the oil industry would be if we just cooperated with the authorities willy-nilly?'

This was an excellent question. But it didn't help Jamie in his present situation. He didn't have to pretend to be clueless. He really was clueless.

'And what does the mud engineer's job involve?' said Detective Constable Brody, playing the part of the Good Cop.

'I've no idea,' said Jamie honestly.

Detective Inspector Findon grabbed Jamie by the lapels. 'I've had about as much of this as I can take from you smart asses.'

'Leave him Bobby!' said DC Brody, pulling Findon away. 'Don't let them get to you.'

'It's bad enough dealing with you scumbags on the Beach.' Findon was becoming tearful. 'Now you think you can run rings round me out here too! Let guarantee this: someone is going down for this murder. It might as well be you.'

DI Findon paraded around, like he'd seen them do on the telly. 'Have you noticed anything unusual since you came on the rig?'

'Yes,' said Jamie earnestly. 'Everything.'

'Why you little shit...' Findon grabbed Jamie again.

DC Brody prised him off and took over. 'Let us turn our attention to other matters,' he began. Brody was a fan of courtroom dramas. 'What would you do if I told you that the recently murdered toolpusher John Webster was having a passionate affair with Antonio Banderas?'

Jamie threw up on the floor.

'Let it be noted,' said DC Brody to the recording device, 'that the suspect has just vomited on the floor – clear proof that he is in love with Antonio Banderas.'

'Oh shit,' said Jamie. 'Is it so obvious?'

'It's the talk of the rig,' said Findon.

'Who told you?'

'Scottie, Peachy, Phil the Driller, Desperate Dan, Lat the Logger, Stevie the Assistant Driller, Walter the OIM. No one's said anything about the murder. All they want to talk about is how you've made a complete tit of yourself since you came aboard! I put it to you that in a fit of jealous rage, you lured John Webster to your pit room smacked him about on the head and pitched his body into your mud to drown.'

'Was she really having an affair with Webster?' said Jamie.

'She was his plaything,' said Brody. 'He used her cruelly. But then she started to enjoy it and kept coming back for more. You know what these Spanish birds are like.'

Watching Brody do his LA Law / Ally McBeal / Sex and the City act made Jamie realise that the whole Webster affair thing was a load of nonsense.

'You've got two choices,' said Findon, jabbing a rude finger in Jamie's face and standing in the vomit. 'You can tell us everything about everyone. Or we'll fit you up for this murder.'

'Oh, I'll tell you everything,' Jamie grinned.

If they were going to lie to him...

***

The police, convinced that the crew were a bunch of deranged assassins, had taken to going around the rig in pairs. The evening's events didn't improve their perception of rig workers.

The Camp Boss pulled out all the stops for the John Webster Memorial Meal.

He wanted to give the boys a feast to remember on a day they'd never forget. There was "Blood Pit Soup", a minestrone-style concoction full of floating objects. There was a magnificent seafood platter "Drowned in a Marie Rose Sauce". The "Murderer's Mince Pie" came with "Bludgeoned Potatoes" whilst the "Webster Bully Beef Wellington" had been "Tenderised and Marinaded to Suit All Tastes". As a finale, the "Toolpusher's Pavlova" was a work of art. It had strawberries haemorrhaging out of a brain-shaped meringue.

'Do you think this is funny?' said Detective Inspector Findon.

'I think it's hilarious,' said Walter.

'You condone this?' said Findon, brandishing one of the souvenir menus.

'Condone it?' said Walter. 'I provided the laminated paper for it.'

'You can tell the Camp Boss that I'm putting him to the top of my suspect list.'

'You can't do that.'

'Why not?'

'You'll make the other lads jealous.'

Findon erected his rude finger and jabbed it in Walter's direction. 'You are unfit to run this rig.'

Walter erected his own rude finger and jabbed back. 'I don't give a shit. I retire in six months. And I'm fucking loaded.'

'I don't think you realise the seriousness of this situation.'

'And I don't think you realise the pressure-cooker atmosphere that John Webster created out here. I intend to defuse things in a controlled manner. If we don't allow the boys to let off steam, I won't be responsible for what happens next.'

What happened next was the Dead Toolpusher Celebration Olympics.

Jamie was determined to perform well in several events, impressing Antonio Banderas with his manhood and hopefully humiliating Ronnie the Roustie in the process. Ronnie, after all, was a chain smoker of legend. He'd even developed Repetitive Strain Injury on his finger - from pressing the button on the electric cigarette lighter in the smoking shack.

Despite his spent lungs, Ronnie put up a decent performance on the 5 minute static bike challenge. He was a useless runner, but so was Jamie. Neither of them could bench press. They both got sand kicked in their faces by the regular gym users.

In the electronic games, Jamie died in the ruins of Stalingrad at Bill the Mechanic's hand. He had a commendably high body count of innocent bystanders in Grand Theft Auto, but Ronnie proved more ruthless. His Formula 1 aspirations came to an inglorious end at Maggots, wherever that was. However, Ronnie's lap was so slow that he came out looking even worse.

In the Karaoke, Jamie belted out "You Give Love a Bad Name" by Bon Jovi. He tried not to look at Antonia, but everybody knew what was going on and stared at her throughout. Her face turned bright red. Ronnie's heartfelt "Coward of the County" caught the mood perfectly. It didn't take a genius to work out that Webster was represented by the evil Gatlin boys who took turns with the lovely but vulnerable Becky (the rig crew) and that the murderer was Tommy, the erstwhile coward. Ronnie received a standing ovation. Antonia wiped away a tear. Jamie felt sick.

The prizes were gift vouchers put up by Walter. These were normally used to reward safety suggestions. That they were rewarding winners in games played to celebrate the brutal murder of the Senior Toolpusher didn't bother Walter in the least. The rig, to his mind, was a safer place with the games being played. Walter walked around the accommodation wearing a large smile. He couldn't have been prouder.

Jamie and Ronnie the Roustie came head-to-head in the final of the cribbage. Jamie hoped that his superior intelligence would shine through. There was just one problem: Jamie didn't have superior intelligence. He held his own in the hands, but Ronnie's superior strategic thinking saw Jamie trounced in the boxes.

'And one for His Nob,' said Ronnie. 'And that's the game.'

'One for whose knob?' snapped Jamie.

'We cut the Eight of Hearts. That's the Jack of Hearts. You play the Jack of the same suit, you get one for His Nob.'

'Everybody knows that,' said Bill the Mechanic.

'It's not like it's close,' said Antonio Banderas. 'You are not even at the turn.'

'We thought you were an expert on knobs,' said Ronnie the Roustie.

They laughed at Jamie, particularly Antonio Banderas, who gave her gorgeous, toothy, jiggly laugh.

Jamie stood up. 'Great! Fine! Fine! Super! Wonderful! Have it your way. It's just a stupid game anyway.' And off he flounced.

He sought refuge in the filthy haven that was the tea shack. The crew, fuelled by fizzy drinks, chocolate and nicotine, were pinballing around the rig like hyperactive children. The excitement surrounding Webster's death hadn't worn off either. Walter was right. There was a head of pressure which had to be worked off in a controlled manner. Still, the entire crew had participated in the games, which said something about rig unity.

The only person who hadn't joined in was Peachy. He had stayed in his room watching porn.

Jamie was steering well away from sugary drinks and chocolate. His mind was hyperactive enough as it was. He felt no need to add petrol to that particular fire. He was also drinking lots of water to counteract the effects of the rig's vicious air conditioning. The lips were the first things to suffer. His neck was also cracking. Sometimes he swore he could feel his eyes drying out. He had noticed a few of the boys using the anti-chap sticks. There was hand cream in the toilets.

It wasn't exactly what Jamie had envisaged for tough North Sea tigers battling the elements: "We're hard. We drill. We moisturise. It's a constant battle between our sensitive skin and everything the ventilation system can throw at us."

One person aboard certainly didn't have sensitive skin, or perhaps their skin was too sensitive. Jamie took a moment to himself to mull over the ramifications of John Webster's sudden and violent demise. The murder felt like a one-off event. Webster had stretched someone beyond breaking point and they had snapped. What was interesting was the cool and calculating way in which the killing had been executed. There was no obviously bloodied perpetrator for the police to round up. No, perhaps the killer hadn't snapped. Webster had crossed a line. The killer had decided that things had gone far enough. He instigated a plan. He lured Webster to the pit room and calmly and efficiently ended his life. Was it Alexei? Was he simply the catalyst? Was he nothing to do with it? Had the police even arrested him?

Detective Findon came in. Sometimes it was really difficult to find peace and quiet on a rig.

Jamie took a good look at Findon. His hair was slightly too long. It was untidy rather than unkempt. His clothes were slightly shabby. His body was bloated. He didn't inspire confidence.

In noting all of these things, Jamie made a realisation: If I'm criticising people for untidiness, I must be getting older.

'I hear you made a right twat of yourself in the cribbage. Had a hissy fit. Stormed out.' Findon busied himself making a cup of tea.

'Either bad news travels fast or you really are a Detective.'

'I'm a Detective all right. I know all about you and Antonio Banderas. Love at first sight was it? There's just a slight hitch, Jamie. She doesn't love you. You've made yourself the laughing stock of the rig. And only on board a day and a half. Quite an achievement.'

Jamie tried desperately not to look desperate. 'She's very attractive. I would love to go out with her. As most men would. But I don't even know her. What's to fall in love with?'

'You're not much of a liar, Jamie.' Findon stirred his tea thoughtfully. 'Did you kill John Webster?'

'Yes I did.'

'You're not convincing as a killer. You're even less convincing as a boyfriend for Antonio Banderas.'

'You're not even convincing as a Detective.'

Findon raised his rude finger. It was becoming a habit. 'Listen. If there's anyone going to be sniffing about Antonio Banderas, it'll be me. She's really really pretty. With gorgeous nipples. And she's much more likely to go out with a man who catches murderers for a living than some spotty mud boy.'

'The only thing you'll catch out here will be pneumonia.' Jamie couldn't believe what he was hearing, even as the words tumbled out of his own mouth. 'I've got more chance of catching the killer than you. I bet you haven't even found the Russian yet.'

Findon choked on his tea. His cheeks were purple. 'What Russian?'

'The one who left on a special chopper this morning.'

'The boys in town are taking care of that.'

'Now who's an unconvincing liar?'

'Nobody mentioned a Russian to me.'

'You were too busy checking out Antonio Banderas's nipples.'

It was at this point that Antonio Banderas came in. Her nipples were indeed prominent. She gave Jamie a thunderous look, turned on her heel and went straight out.

'You've blown it now. You've no chance!' Findon laughed.

'I knew that. She was snogging Ronnie the Roustie earlier.'

'Him? He's a nobody. I was at school with his brother. The whole family's a joke.'

This revelation cheered Jamie up. A relaxed silence broke out. Then there was the sound of a helicopter.

Findon rose. 'My taxi.'

He left, tea in hand. But he hadn't put the lid on it, like you were supposed to. It confirmed all of Jamie's prejudices. Findon was careless; careless with his hair; careless with his talk; careless with other peoples' safety. Good grief, Jamie thought, I really am getting older.

Webster was dead. Findon was useless. Antonio Banderas was out of reach. If ever Jamie needed someone to explain to him how the world worked, it was now. He didn't have long to wait.

Chapter 15 Golfing With The Wrong People

The man who came in was a porky-faced guy. Jamie had last seen him head-butting the wall at Webster's wake.

'You the night mud engineer? I heard you made a twat of yourself at the cribbage. I'm Dave Martin, the night pusher. I shouldn't really be talking to you.'

'Why not?'

'It's Golfing With The Wrong People.'

'It's what?'

This was a question that Jamie would regret asking. Dave Martin wasn't just porky and portly, he was ambitious too. He had had a moment of clarity that had changed his life.

Dave's own road-to-Damascus incident occurred on the fourth hole at Westhill Golf Club on the Manticore Drilling golf day. He'd had his heart set on partnering Steve Phelps the Western Division General Manager, Jim McMenaman the Rig Superintendent and Candy Gillies from HR. Two bigwigs and a babe. Instead, he found himself with Peachy, Mark Z and Ronnie. Two roughnecks and a roustie.

Dave was ten over par and in a poisonous mood when he stepped onto the fourth tee.

'Shit. Shit. Shit,' he thought. 'I'm golfing with the wrong people.'

It was then that the heavens opened and the beam of light illuminated Dave. A choir of angels sang. The universe revealed an eternal truth. Dave's world was forever changed.

Every single action that he took in his life from that moment on would divide into two categories. The next morning, in the teeth of a massive hangover, Dave drew up two lists.

Golfing With The Right People

Shagging (Fit Birds)
Impressing The Beach
Bullshitting with the Client
Blaming Others
Getting the Credit
Hanging out with Top Management

Golfing With The Wrong People

Shagging (Ugly Birds)
Wanking (?)
Eating Crap Food
Talking to roughnecks and rousties
Getting called things behind my back
Drinking Bacardi Breezers
Making a tit of myself
Impressing People That Don't Count
Getting the Blame

Dave's life transformed itself instantly. He even got his six year-old daughter Golfing With The Right People when he saw her at weekends. She was riding horses with posh little girls, swimming with posh little girls and skating with posh little girls. He was going to pay for her to go to school with posh little girls once he'd persuaded her bitch mother. If only he'd known about Golfing With The Wrong People, the marriage to that lying, scheming, credit card abusing, fat-arsed, bad-taste-in-clothes slapper need never had happened. Their ten year union had been an endless round of bunkers and bad lies. Still, he'd only been a roughneck at the time. Now, on the verge of senior management, what Dave needed was a wife who could Golf With The Right People, look good, wear stylish gear and not embarrass him by getting pissed and abusive in public. Or throw up at the Christmas dance. No, Dave's new belle would be quality. She'd be fun, open-minded and into top-notch porn.

Spending time in the tea shack was definitely Golfing With The Wrong People, but Dave was willing to make the sacrifice once a trip. He needed some kind of relationship with the lads, otherwise they'd go out their way to make him look bad. And he hoped that word would get back to town that he had the common touch. Senior managers in the oil industry prided themselves on it.

By the time Dave had explained all this, Jamie was convinced that he was in the presence of a madman. It was the description of the lists that had pushed Jamie over the edge. As time passed, Dave grew sullen, unwilling to hide his disappointment at Jamie's company. Drinking tea alone with the brand new night mud engineer was definitely GWTWP. The chopper was still on the helideck, its sound vying with that of the generators and the air con.

'They leaving any police behind?' Jamie wondered.

'They're all going home. But eight have come out for the night shift.'

'To keep us from attacking each other?'

'Murdering the toolpusher and tossing him in a mud pit is Golfing With The Wrong People.'

'Unless it's Webster.'

Dave turned sharply on Jamie. 'You've only been here for one day. What have you got against him?'

'You don't need a day, Dave. Five minutes with Webster was enough.'

'I suppose.'

Dave grew sullen again. He was being possessive. They'd hated Webster longer. Much longer.

'When are they going to let us go home?' said Jamie.

'We're all to stay aboard until further notice,' said a bespectacled, gormless man who had just arrived.

He looked like a Nigel.

'I'm Nigel,' said Nigel.

'So we're being held prisoner?' said Jamie.

'Welcome to the oil business,' said Dave.

'You can understand their thinking,' said Nigel, who was an understanding person. 'There will be formal interviews tomorrow. Then we should be able to go home.'

'Or go to prison,' said Jamie.

Nigel smiled.

Dave looked a little peeved that Jamie's joke had been well received by Nigel, who was the client rep, aka the night company man. He sat in silence for a moment, but Jamie could practically hear the gears clunking in his head. Eventually, out it came. 'What are we going to do with Jamie?' he asked in mock innocence.

'What do you mean?' replied Nigel, in genuine innocence.

'He's useless. He shouldn't be out here.' Dave turned to Jamie. 'No offence.'

'Hm, well I don't know,' said Nigel. 'We all have to start somewhere.'

'Why can't he start somewhere else? With everything that's going on, he's a complete liability.'

'Well ooh.' Nigel became flustered.

Jamie knew exactly what was going on. Dave had decided that humiliating him in front of the night company man was Golfing With The Right People.

'I've got five years' experience in the lab,' said Jamie. 'There's nothing about mud that I don't know. If I've got a problem, you'll be the first to know, Dave.'

'Oh, well that seems to be all right,' said Nigel. 'I think there's been enough unpleasantness on the rig this trip.'

Jamie reckoned that it was high time for a lot more unpleasantness. 'How long have you been night toolpusher, Dave?'

'Four years.'

'You must be in line for promotion.'

'What do you mean?'

'I believe there's a vacancy for the Senior Toolpusher's job.'

'I didn't kill him! I'm not that ambitious.'

'I would never accuse you of ambition,' said Jamie. 'Have the office been in touch? To tell you to move onto days?'

'Webster's still aboard. It's only decent to wait.'

'Walter mention anything?'

Dave's eyes moved evasively. 'I'm staying on nights as a familiar face to help the boys through this difficult time.'

'Are they, by any chance, sending somebody else out to replace Webster? Keeping you on nights? Not promoting you? It's not exactly a ringing endorsement, is it Dave?'

It was Dave's turn to become flustered. How quickly Golfing With The Right People turned into Golfing With The Wrong People. Blushing was GWTWP too. Another one for the list.

'They're sending one of the pushers from the Griffin rig. It's in the yard.'

'But they won't be able to help the boys through this difficult time. How much easier would it have been just to move you onto days? Unless they thought that you were completely and utterly fucking useless, not up to the job, and not to be promoted under any circumstance.'

Dave stood up. He searched for a devastating response. 'I, I, I didn't want the job!' His mind was blank and having a blank mind when you needed a devastating response was GWTWP. He'd add that to the list as well. Trouble was, his mind was blank most of the time. There was nothing else for it. He would have to prepare for conversations and have his devastating responses ready. He'd set up conversations and ambush people in front of senior management. Jamie would be his first victim.

For now, Dave Martin had nothing else to say. The quickest way for him to resume GWTRP was to leave immediately, go back to his office and nurse his grievances. This is exactly what he did.

Jamie and Nigel were left together, alone and bemused.

'Did I go too far?' said Jamie.

'Just a bit,' said Nigel. 'You've made an enemy, albeit a useless one. The trouble is, in trying to make you look bad, Dave will end up making everybody look bad. That's how stupid he is. I don't know what it is about Manticore Drilling, but anyone above assistant driller behaves like a complete twat. It's their corporate style.'

'No wonder the crews are revolting.'

'Given what happened to Webster, you'd think he'd be a little more sensitive. Dave Martin's always been an ignoramus. Wouldn't surprise me if he'd murdered Webster in a mad bid for promotion.'

'He's certainly not going to get there by brainpower.'

'We informed Manticore that if Dave Martin got anywhere near the Senior Toolpusher's job, we'd be hiring another rig.'

'I'm amazed he's got as high as he has.'

'His promotion was a blessed relief. You should have been on here when Dave Martin was driller and John Webster was night toolpusher. "Horrible" doesn't begin to describe it.' Nigel shuddered. 'Dave's far less dangerous in an office. Much better pottering about on nights. By the time he's mastered the paperwork and Excel, it'll be time to retire.'

'Can't imagine his big fingers are very deft on the keyboard,' said Jamie.

'What Dave needs is a computer with massive keys that he can hit with mallets. It's a nightmare all over the industry. Guys that are good at drilling a hole in the ground are an absolute disaster in the office, a disaster on computers and a disaster at organisation. I used to laugh at the geeks in the office who had no experience. Now I'm bloody glad they're keeping things ticking over.'

'Why did I ever think the oil industry was well run?'

'Because of the huge profits it makes,' said Nigel. 'The truth is, the money comes too easily. If it costs eighteen dollars a barrel to extract oil from an existing well and the price goes up from twenty dollars a barrel to twenty-two dollars a barrel, your profits have just doubled and you've done absolutely nothing to deserve it.'

'My God,' said Jamie, 'and if the price goes up to a hundred dollars a barrel..'

'Multiply profits times fifty and crack open the Champagne.'

'Nice work.'

'Give or take potential climate catastrophe and the end of human life on the planet, I agree. You see how a business like that can lead to lazy management.'

'Surely somebody must know what they're doing?'

'That's what ten dollars a barrel is for. Sorts out the decent workers from the clowns. And then the price goes back up and the clowns get hired again. The way China and India are, I don't think we'll see the back of the clowns ever again.'

Nigel paused and thought for a moment. He smiled. 'Actually Jamie, I take all that back. When oil is ten dollars a barrel, they fire all the decent guys and keep the clowns. It's amazing that anything gets to the petrol pumps at all.'

'A lot of the stuff out here looks pretty impressive,' said Jamie. 'Somebody got something right.'

'I'll give you that. There are some very smart people working in Research and Development. Steerable rotary bits. Measurement While Drilling. Logging. Some of the geologists and reservoir engineers are pretty clever. I suppose that drilling a well the shape of a piece of spaghetti and then hitting a target the size of your front door five miles down is slightly better than mediocre. I suppose we are quite good.' Nigel appeared stunned by the revelation. 'You get so used to all of the cock-ups along the way that you forget. There are some pretty bizarre characters, some of 'em completely useless, but we do generally get there in the end.'

Jamie sat, thinking that if the industry could carry him, it could handle just about anything.

'Goodness me Jamie,' said Nigel. 'We're actually good.' Nigel began to laugh. The laughter quickly turned hysterical. 'We're good! We're good!' Nigel wailed.

It took half a cup of ionised tea before Nigel was able to calm himself. He kept breaking down into uncontrollable sobs. 'We're good. We're good. We're good.'

Finally, when he had got his breath back, Nigel put on his most serious voice. 'One thing before I go Jamie,' he said. 'Please don't bullshit me. I know I come across as a bit wet, but I've been out here nine years and I'm not stupid. If I know about a problem, I can do something about it. Town only needs to hear about it in the last resort. You do know what you're doing, don't you?'

'Haven't a clue.'

'You're not the only one. Believe me.' Nigel sighed. 'Gray will keep you right, but you'll need to kick his arse. His mind wanders.'

'Thanks Nigel. I really do appreciate it. You're the first person out here who's made me feel less alone.'

'Did you hear about Webster's room?' said Nigel. 'It's been ransacked.'

The noise of the chopper intensified above their heads. As they had talked, the body had been loaded onto the helicopter. There had been no ceremony about it. The chopper's engines roared the way the man himself had roared. It then took flight. John Webster was making his final journey back to the Beach.

Chapter 16 Watching the Detectives

Jamie's second night offshore was even stranger than the first. No one was venturing outside. They didn't expect anyone else to be murdered, but they didn't want to chance it either. The only place that Jamie could have gone to was the mud lab and that was too close to the murder scene for comfort. Inside, he could go to the mess, the locker room, the TV lounge or the service office. With all of the drillcrew inside, things were pretty claustrophobic. It was difficult to avoid Antonio Banderas or, for that matter, Ronnie the Roustie. Jamie decamped to the service office and picked up the only novel abandoned there which wasn't a murder mystery. It was a weird and compelling tale of a preacher in the American midwest. Jamie wondered who would bring such a book to an oil rig.

Jamie also had a minor problem with the midnight Mud Report. It contained a box headed: "Rig Activities".

Jamie wrote: "Blockage found in oil-based mud in Active Pit. Transferred fluid to Reserve Pit and investigated same. Bludgeoned body of (unpopular) Senior Toolpusher unable to be revived. Wait on Rigor Mortis to recover to surface. Called cops and shut down communications. Everyone interviewed, no arrest yet. Partied, had fabulous meal and played games. Celebrations ongoing. Continue setting anchors."

Gray was not himself the next morning. He was quite cheerful. But he still couldn't be bothered to give Jamie any help or advice. Jamie kept asking questions about how to mix the fluid they required. Gray kept rambling on about his family, his holiday home or anything that was nothing to do with rig operations.

Jamie's sleep was troubled. They would be drilling that night. He'd have to mix mud. Things were likely to go badly and he would get shouted at. Things had already gone badly with Antonio Banderas. He was in love with her. She was in love with another man. Because of the nipple incident, it was likely that he would get shouted at. His heart ached. Rigs were no place to be thwarted in love. It wasn't just Lat who was winking at him now. The entire crew were winking at him.

Jamie dreamt of a dull thudding sound, coming as Webster banged the side of the pit looking for help that would never come. Findon was banging, shouting for the killer who would never come. Then he was shouting for Antonio Banderas. She would never come. Then it seemed like the entire rig was banging. They were alone, in the middle of the sea. No one was coming.

Jamie woke up. The dull thudding was the sound of the anchor chains being tensioned. His ear plugs has fallen out.

***

Night shift was confusing. The next day was the same day and things were getting serious with the police. In Jamie's second interview, it was all Bad Cop and no Good Cop. DI Findon did all the talking. Someone had turned the heat up on him.

John Webster had died at around 6 am. This placed his murder firmly in the hands of the night shift. The blow to his head hadn't been fatal. His lungs were full of mud. He had died by drowning.

'We've got a suspects' list and an innocent list,' said Findon. 'We had to start a new list for you: the gormless list. Why should Antonio Banderas be interested in your acnied attentions? You're a joke.'

Jamie sat and took it. He had no choice.

'You're not even worthy of contempt. The day shift pretend to know nothing. The night shift pretend to know nothing. You're the only idiot that really knows nothing.'

Jamie evidently knew a great deal more than Findon. He knew about Sergei, the pretend assistant driller, who had been allowed to disappear into Russia's vastness. He knew about Fraserburgh. And he knew that Webster had some kind of special interest in the night shift. But the main thing he knew was that Detective Inspector Bobby Findon would never solve this murder.

Findon raised his voice. 'You can go. Send the next man in. I'm done with you.'

The next man in was Antonio Banderas. Jamie couldn't look her in the eye.

***

There was something unusual about the service office when Jamie returned: Gray was still in it.

'Shouldn't you be in bed?' said Jamie, 'Or have you suddenly taken an interest in helping me?'

'Thank God you're here,' said Gray. 'I think I'm a suspect.'

'You are a suspect.'

'I didn't do it!!! What makes people think I did?'

'You were telling me that you thought that Webster's goose was cooked. That he wasn't long for this rig.'

'And you told the police?!!'

'Of course I didn't. Calm down. Keep your voice down. There were lots of people saying the same thing. Bill the Mechanic. Walter.'

'Yes.' Gray's features softened. 'The three of us were in Walter's office, having a bit of a bullshit together. Then Webster came in. He was behaving really strangely. He was nice. That's when we knew things were seriously wrong.'

Jamie listened. Listening, he felt, was the best way to help Gray. Perhaps, in return, Gray would help him.

'He said he was leaving,' Gray continued. 'He had one more thing to do out here. He was moving onto greater things. Misery on a bigger scale, no doubt. He said that the Russians had taught him a great deal. And then he said he wasn't frightened.'

Jamie nodded understandingly.

'Of course, he really was frightened. And that was frightening to see. I was relieved that he was going, but worried about what he'd do before he left. He wasn't a man to leave quietly.'

'He hasn't left quietly.'

Jamie got his reward. Gray gave him a quick run-down on how to mix spud mud – the thick mud they used to sweep the hole clean when they were drilling with seawater. The kill mud was thin spud mud with barite powder added for weight. This heavier fluid would be pumped into the well at the end of the section, or if shallow gas started to come up and the well needed to be "killed".

'Here's mixing instructions with recipes on them. Keep on top of things. You need to get Scottie and Peachy down from the drillfloor in plenty of time to mix. In fact,' Gray looked at his watch, 'you better go and get them now.'

Jamie went to the locker room. As he was putting on his coveralls, he could hear Findon, nearby, talking to someone. Jamie kept out of sight and listened.

'I was on secondment. Spent six months with the Metropolitan Police in London. Some anti-terrorist work, some murder, some with the Vice Squad.'

Findon was using his man-of-the-world voice. Jamie knew immediately who Findon was talking to.

'People have no idea what's really going on. It's a constant battle against organised crime and organised terror gangs. If it wasn't for our vigilance, the whole thing would fall apart. As for Vice, well, the amount of money that changes hands is phenomenal. A good-looking girl with an open mind and a bit of practice can make a fortune. Not, I mean, not that I'm suggesting that you'd want to do that. But we're worldly people. We know what's going on. All sorts was put on the table. Don't get me wrong, I was flattered. Not all cops get offered for free what others pay thousands for. I was sorely tempted. I'm a professional. I politely refused. You could see that some of the girls were disappointed.'

Findon paused to slurp some tea.

'That mud engineer that's chasing after you, he's just a boy really. He'll never see what I've seen, know what I've known. No one will ever entrust him with catching a killer.'

'You're here to catch the killer?' said Antonio Banderas incredulously. 'I thought they'd sent you just to get you out of the office.'

Jamie's heart soared. Did Antonio Banderas just stand up for him? Or was it simply her hatred of Findon's bullshit?

Findon chuckled. 'I like your sense of humour. I like a feisty girl. I like the Spanish. Their weather. Their wine. Their leather goods. Bullfighting.'

'I hate bullfighting,' said Antonio Banderas bluntly.

'I love the Spanish passion,' Findon continued. 'You are a passionate people. Just like the Scots. Well, like the worldly Scots from the north-east, not the spotty ones from the west coast. Jamie's a pathetic soul really. He's out of his depth. He's in a joke job. He's ugly. He hasn't seen any of the world. He's awkward with women. I mean it doesn't get much worse, does it?' Findon laughed cruelly.

Jamie felt his blood rise. He wanted to burst in and smack the guy. Hit a policeman? Not a good idea. No, he had a cooler head than that. He'd avenge himself in other ways. HE'd solve the murder. Yes, he'd get to the bottom of it. He already knew more than Findon would ever find out. He'd humiliate Findon with proof of his own incompetence. He'd do his own job brilliantly and show Antonio Banderas that he wasn't useless. That, at least, would be a start. He might not win her, but he wouldn't be a joke either. Jamie had never been more determined about anything in his life. He clenched his fists and pressed his head against the cooling metal of the lockers.

Jamie wished that Antonio Banderas might have said something in his defence, but she was silent. Jamie hoped that she was rolling her eyes, or simply letting Findon's guff wash over her. He edged closer to take a peek. It was better than he could possibly have hoped for. Antonia's face was one of utter contempt. Findon's was riven with panic.

Findon pressed on. 'I feel I know you Antonia. I know what you need. A real woman like you needs a real man. You could go out with Jamie. But come on, Antonia, would you want to settle for second best?'

'Second best?' she laughed. 'Men ARE second best. And you are a sad apology for a man, so you are ninety billionth best. You will never find the killer. Never. You know why?'

'Er, no,' said Findon.

'Because we despise you.'

This was the moment when Findon realised that he would never, ever get Antonio Banderas's knickers off. How Jamie enjoyed witnessing it. Findon's mouth was slightly open and his eyes were wide and unblinking. It made him look even more stupid than normal. But what was even better was the panic and astonishment that were also all over his face. He'd really thought he was in with a chance. Failure hadn't been a consideration, let alone an option. And now it was a reality; a juicy, delicious reality.

Antonio Banderas put her hard hat on with a disdainful flourish and stormed out. Jamie could barely contain his laughter. The more he learned about this girl, the more he loved her. He sighed. Coming onto the rigs had been the best thing he had ever done. Rigs were fabulous.

There was no one in the pit room. He went up to the drillfloor to ask Phil the Driller if he could have Scottie and Peachy come down to mix mud. He had no sooner come into the driller's lair, the doghouse, than Phil turned to him.

'Fuck off,' said Phil. 'I'll send them down when I'm good and ready and not before.'

Jamie went down to the rear deck to think things over. There was nothing he could do. His fate was in Phil's hands. If it wasn't for Antonio Banderas, he'd be quite happy to get run off the rig. He could only do his best. There was no accounting for the Phils of this world.

With a feeling of calmness settling upon him, Jamie looked at the horizon. There was a beautiful sunset, tinting the clouds in gorgeous shades of red. Even the rigs in the distance were silver in this light. It was comforting to see them. It made this odd world feel less isolated.

Jamie felt more than ever that the rig existed in a parallel universe. Who else would see oil rigs shimmering in sunset? Platforms lighting the night sky as they flared gas? The standby boat nodding softly in the calm sea? Who else would work under such bizarre circumstances?

"The Beach" was less than an hour's flight away. It may as well have been on a different planet.

These thoughts brought Jamie to a decision. There was nothing else for it. The lance had to be boiled. His mind was in flux. There were never good circumstances in which to make such an apology. You could only take a deep breath, go right into the logging shack and confront the beast.

When Jamie got to the logging shack he wasn't confronted by a beast. He was confronted by Antonio Banderas. She was heartbreakingly gorgeous. What was worse she was standing up. It already felt confrontational. Jamie had imagined being able to look down on her soft face as he eloquently smoothed things out between them. Now she was there, arms folded and her hip stuck out in the way that only a woman can manage. She had a steely look on her face – albeit made from high-grade and beautifully polished steel. She was silent, but communicating quite effectively.

'I'd like to apologise to your nipples,' said Jamie.

Antonio Banderas batted her eyelids derisively. The steel grew steelier.

'Oh God no,' Jamie yammered. He could feel his stomach trying to climb up his throat. His mouth had double-crossed him and was drying up. 'What I mean is, I'm sorry about your nipples. No, I'm not sorry. Your nipples are fantastic. No, I mean they've nothing to apologise for. They're fine and lovely. And they belong to you. And you're fine and lovely.'

The Indian idiot, Lat, was sitting behind Antonio Banderas, smiling and winking. He had no intention of moving.

'I came to apologise, Antonia,' Jamie continued. 'I apologise for mentioning your nipples in front of you. But you see I was pulling up that horrible Detective. He mentioned your nipples. And not in a nice way. He's not a fan. And I am.'

'You are a fan of my nipples?' Antonia's look changed from derision to incredulity.

'No! No! Well, yes. I'm a fan of all of you, including your nipples. But Detective Whatshisname is nasty and he wants to get his hands all over them. I was trying to protect you.'

'I can look after myself.'

'I know. But he's evil. And I had to say something. To let him know I wasn't going to stand for any of his Grampian Police hanky-panky. It was just unfortunate that when the word "nipple" came out, you came in.'

'You are so full of sheet.'

Verbal abuse, Jamie thought, was at least one step on from total indifference. Their relationship was progressing.

'I know,' he sighed. 'But I am sorry. Very very sorry to have caused you any hurt. And now that I've made a complete tit of myself, I'll go.

Antonio Banderas said nothing. The arms were still crossed. The hip was still stuck out. The look was steely – steel now made from ultra-hard, high molybdenum Steel.

Jamie put on his hard hat. 'You know,' he said, 'you're very nicely set up in here. It's very pleasant. Very high-tech. The rest of the rig's a bit... downmarket.'

'Get out,' she said. 'And close the door properly. I don't want to lose pressure.'

Lat grinned and winked. Jamie was growing to detest Lat.

Chapter 17 Poverty!

The only person in the tea shack was Bill the Mechanic. Peachy had warned Jamie about getting stuck in the tea shack with Bill the Mechanic.

Bill took a deep slurp of tea. 'I never introduced myself properly,' he began. 'I'm Bill McGibney. The Rig Mechanic. I fix things. Keep the rig running. I set my own standards. It's important to set your own standards. Setting the same standards as other people is,' Bill paused for dramatic effect, '... poverty.'

Jamie slurped his own rancid tea. There was an evangelical light in Bill's eye.

'Poverty lurks everywhere. And it's not always where you think it is. Alcohol is poverty. Where does it lead a man? To hangovers. Stabbings. Vomit. Depression. Cirrhosis. Accident and Emergency. Makes men attack each other. Attack their brothers. Attack their wives. Attack the working nurses that are trying to help them. Poverty.' Bill shook his head. 'Poverty.'

The rest of the rig had stopped listening to Bill years ago and Bill had stopped talking. Jamie could sense his gratitude at having a fresh audience.

'My father was the greatest man who ever lived. He said to me, "Son, God has given every person on this planet a special talent."'

'"What's your talent dad?" I said.'

'"Turning poverty into pleasure. God has put me on this planet to turn lead into gold."'

Jamie kept quiet. He'd decided to let Bill enjoy himself.

'He was the greatest man who ever lived. Poverty? We were rich beyond belief. My mother and father adored us. We were blissfully happy. Went for walks in the most glorious landscape in the world. There was always food on the table. And love around it. Now that's wealth.'

Jamie couldn't help but smile.

'Out here, you'd think everything would be about wealth, wouldn't you? Well it's not. This entire operation is a homage to poverty. Not paying men enough: poverty. Not having enough men: poverty. Not investing in spares and maintenance: real poverty. Things break. Lads get hurt. The rig goes down. The oil company or the drilling company lose money. Poverty. Poverty. Everywhere you look. In every rivet and every coat of cheap paint. Poverty!'

'This rotten tea is certainly poverty,' said Jamie.

'Thousands I've saved them. Thousands.'

This was a lie. Bill had saved them millions. When the rig broke down, the Senior Toolpusher and the Oil Company Rep had a handbag fight about who was going to pay for it while everyone stood about doing nothing. The toolpusher always lost and the rig went "Off Contract" and the drilling company started losing pots of money. Bill not only kept the Manticore running like a well-oiled oil rig, if something did break down, he worked like a demon to fix it quicker than anyone thought humanly possible.

'Flicking cigarette ash everywhere is poverty. You have guys come in here just after the stewards have cleaned it and it's spotless. Give them ten minutes and they've flicked their ash everywhere, dripped their teabags all over the counter tops and the place is a shit-hole. Poverty. But don't blame them.'

Jamie wasn't going to. He couldn't have got a word in if he'd tried.

'They're addicted to poverty. Takes a remarkable man to break free from poverty. Some of these guys are earning sixty grand a year and they're still poor. Gambling. Poverty! Drinking. Poverty! Smoking.' He drew on his roll-up. 'Poverty! E-bay. Poverty! Designer labels. Poverty! Petrol-guzzling four by fours with five hundred pound tyres. Poverty! It's the Vital Four Inches.'

He pointed to the space between his ears where his brain was.

'Change the Vital Four Inches and you change everything. Consider, the lowliest Subject of this kingdom now has access to better medical treatment than the Queen herself had fifty years ago. We have more wealth than we can shake a stick at. People are fitter. Living longer. But what do we see everywhere?'

'Poverty?'

'Drugs. Graffiti,' said Bill, not missing a beat. 'We've had to invent poverty just to stay comfortable. This country will never be rich until it thinks it is rich.'

In his scrupulous workshop, Bill could make you any part you wanted. Bill not only had the rig humming along sweetly, on his weeks at home he did odd jobs for cash. He fixed cars, maintained boats, even cleared guttering. In good weather he gardened too. He lived in a beautiful house in glorious gardens in an upmarket Glasgow suburb. His money-rich neighbours looked down on him - until they needed him.

'Never charge pensioners,' Bill went on. 'I practice my socialism. To each according to his needs. From each according to his ability.'

This was the extent of Bill's political education. He had taken these two phrases and run with them. He had made it his business to improve the quality of life for countless numbers of people. He was a man of exceptional ability. His wife was a demon ironer with a demon ironing business. His three grown-up children were successful and spookily well-adjusted. They were nothing more nor less than philanthropists.

'If we'd known the kids were going to do so well by folks, we'd have had more of them,' he said ruefully.

He even saw to it that the birds in his neighbourhood were well fed. Swallows on their way to Africa could count on Bill McGibney. He struck Jamie as the kind of guy who would drop dead in harness and have a lavish funeral.

The door opened and most of the night shift crew came in.

'Findon's asking questions,' said Mark Z testily.

'It's what he's here for,' said Ronnie the Roustie, improvising a cup of tea.

'I've enough to put up with out here without having to answer to that daftie,' said Peachy. 'They've asked us. We've told them everything.'

'We've told them fuck-all,' said Scottie.

'Fuck-all IS everything,' said Peachy. 'Webster's dead. Put him in a hole. Forget about him. End of story.'

'What sort of questions is he asking?' said Scottie.

Mark Z shrugged. 'He's asking all the wrong questions. It's nothing to do with Webster or the murder. All about who likes who. Who hates who. He's stirring things up. Opening cans of worms. He's..'

'... trying to get to the nitty-gritty.' Bill the Mechanic finished Mark Z's sentence.

'And what's the nitty-gritty?' said Phil the Driller, coming through the door and lighting a cigarette in one easy movement. Phil counted the faces which were inside and should have been outside – Mark Z, Scottie, Peachy, Ronnie the Roustie. Scottie got up and lit another cigarette as an act of defiance. He passed the light to Mark Z, who lit and passed to Peachy, who lit and passed to Ronnie. It was like Red Indians passing a pipe of peace. Or war; they were letting Phil know that they were going nowhere.

'The nitty-gritty started with that party,' said Bill the Mechanic.

'Just watch what you're saying in front of strangers,' said Phil.

All eyes turned to Jamie. He squirmed.

'Jamie's fine,' said Bill. 'I'll vouch for him.'

The tension broke.

'It was the creepiest party I've ever been to,' said Mark Z.

'Of course it was creepy,' said Ronnie, 'It took place in Fraserburgh.'

'It was deranged,' said Scottie.

'It was disgusting,' said Bill the Mechanic.

'It was deranged and disgusting,' said Mark Z.

'It was in Fraserburgh,' said Ronnie the Roustie.

'Only Webster could put on a party as weird as that.'

'Only Fraserburgh could host a party like that,' said Ronnie. 'Only Fraserburgh could produce a man as unhinged, unbalanced and unbelievably nasty as John Webster.'

Nothing good had ever happened to Ronnie the Roustie in Fraserburgh. He had met with little kindness in that place. Coming from Peterhead didn't help.

'What kind of party was it?' said Jamie.

'It was like a cross between The Addams Family and Debbie Does Dallas,' said Scottie. 'With me mixing cocktails. My arms were sore for weeks.'

'I bet those Russian lassies' arms were sore for weeks too,' said Mark Z, provoking a round of dirty laughter.

'It was Webster's attempt to bring us all down to his level,' said Bill.

'And it only worked in ninety-five percent of cases,' said Ronnie.

'Forty of us invited under pain of death to a "team-building" session. Absolutely no women allowed. Arrived to find Webster there with ten Russian hookers,' said Scottie.

'And four enormous Russian bouncers,' added Mark Z.

'The whole thing gave me the creeps,' said Bill, shuddering. 'You could tell he was planning something. A man like that never gives anything away for nothing.'

'How long were the girls over for? Did he make any money out of them?' asked Ronnie.

'He tried,' said Scottie. 'Didn't like it. Running a brothel wasn't the kind of business John Webster was suited to. Too many people having too much fun.'

'They won't put up with that in Fraserburgh,' said Ronnie. 'They're a righteous people - when they're not knocking lumps out of visitors.'

'Hey Scottie, how come you were mixing cocktails?' asked Mark Z.

'There was no way I was taking any drink at Webster's that I hadn't mixed myself. God knows where the night would have ended.'

'I couldn't get away quick enough,' said Bill.

'You missed the best bit,' said Ronnie. 'Webster had a room with a camera in it. For those that wanted to make their own porn film.'

Bill's head turned, naturally, to Peachy.

Peachy stood up to confront Bill. 'I watch porn, I don't make it!' Peachy's face was bright pink. His eyes were blinking furiously. 'Fuck all of you!' he shouted, and left.

The silence was a painful one.

'Don't worry Bill,' said Ronnie, 'we were all looking at Peachy.'

Bill shrugged. 'He's not a happy boy. Needs to realise his problems are over. Needs to relax.'

'Easier said than done,' said Scottie.

Ronnie was deep in thought. 'Did Peachy stay at Webster's that night?'

'No,' said Scottie. 'He stayed at my place. In Aberdeen. I kept an eye on him. There was no way I was leaving him to Webster's tender mercies.'

'I thought you were pretty pissed,' said Phil.

'That's what I wanted you to think,' said Scottie. 'I drank fruit juice all night.'

'Bill's got a point,' said Mark Z. 'It's no coincidence that Webster held that party just before the rig went into the yard at Rotterdam. He was up to something.'

Phil made an announcement. 'We'll be a couple more hours. There's a hydraulic hose burst.' He got up and left.

'Guess whose fault the burst hose was?' said Scottie. 'It was Phil. He's a fucking liability. He's going to hurt someone before this trip is over. Unless someone hurts him first.'

Chapter 18 Spudding the Well

'I could piss faster than that,' said Jamie gloomily. He was watching as a stream of drillwater was attempting to fill Active Pit 1 – Webster's pit. They had left it too late to begin mixing spud mud. Jamie had complained to everyone. No one had listened. Now they were in trouble. And they hadn't even started.

'We'll mix it thick and flush the last of that bastard's brains through the drill bit and onto the seabed. There'll be bits of John Webster's brain next to the wellhead,' said Scottie gleefully.

'I thought the cops had cleaned everything into tanks?'

'I'm bullshitting you Jamie. They were very thorough. I helped them drain the lines.'

'Are we going to be all right tonight?' Jamie was unable to conceal his nervousness.

'Of course we are. Relax. Webster's dead. Life is now a walk in the park. Phil the Driller will go nuts. He's an idiot. He's new in the job. He's not coping well, so he shouts. Anger is the default setting of every incompetent arsehole.'

'Was Webster incompetent?'

Scottie thought long and hard. He spat into the pit. 'He wasn't incompetent. But he wasn't an angry man. Anger was just one of his tools.'

'What was he, Scot?'

Scottie fixed his squinty eyes on Jamie and gave him a friendly smile. 'John Webster was evil,' he said. 'Do you believe in evil?'

'I'm not sure.'

'Webster was never going to get better. The misery would just have spread. Like AIDS. He'd have ended his days in an old folk's home making all the geriatrics unhappy. Many people are fundamentally decent. A few are like Webster. The secret in life is to be affable and cooperative. Then the world will greet you with open arms.'

'That's one helluva handle on the cementer's door,' said Dave the Night Pusher, bursting in. 'It's fucking brilliant. About fucking time too. Useless bastard welder needs a slap. Thank fuck for Bill the Mechanic. He's the only bugger around here that can do his job.'

'Is Bill the Mechanic a better welder than the welder?' said Jamie.

'You're a better welder than the welder,' said Dave. 'You mixed any spud mud yet?' He paced up and down, in manic mode.

'Jamie's just away to check the chlorides,' said Scottie.

'You're in shit' said Dave, glaring at them. 'We're about to start drilling.'

'I tried warning them,' Jamie wailed.

'That doesn't count as an excuse out here,' said Dave. 'If we're not ready to go in time, I'll tear you a new arsehole.'

'Hasn't there been enough bloodshed?' said Jamie.

'It's an oil rig,' said Scottie. 'There's always plenty of room for more.'

Dave walked away. He shouted back. 'Come and feel the new handle. Bill's done a brilliant job. It's painted and everything.'

'Dave's nuts,' said Scottie.

'Nice nuts, or nuts enough to kill the toolpusher?'

'Both.'

'He's definitely not affable and cooperative.'

'Life doesn't open out to him. Dave struggles.' Scottie reached down into the pit to take a sample of the water for Jamie. He used a specially designed sample catcher. It was a sample catcher peculiar to oil rigs. It was a sample catcher consistent with the oil industry's technological levels in the 21st century: it was an eight foot iron bar with a huge baked bean tin riveted onto it.

Chlorides were bad for spud mud. They prevented it from hydrating. The hydrating was something to do with flocculation. Flocculation was something to do with isomorphic substitution. Jamie had no idea what hydration, flocculation or isomorphic substitution were. If only he'd listened to his teacher. If only his teacher hadn't been a drunken, burned-out liar.

Jamie supposed that the mud lab was supposed to be his haven. The rig's interior designers had been somewhat complacent in conceptualising the space. The floor was made up of wooden pallets with twenty years' worth of debris wedged under. The bulkheads were off-white – white with twenty years of dirt on top. There were dried ejaculations of mud everywhere, even on the ceiling. Jamie figured these had come from mud checks gone wrong. The drawers were blue and broken. A tap on the end of an arthritic pipe was leaking into a foul metal sink. In keeping with the rest of the rig, there was rust everywhere. The testing equipment that Jamie required was huddled together on the limited worktops available. On the left was a viscometer, High-Pressure High-Temperature filter press, retort oven and Hamilton-Beach mixer. On the right were the chemicals, titration cups, beakers and pipettes. It was cramped. It stank. And the interior designers had gotten the mood lighting badly wrong.

Jamie studied Gray's recipe sheet.

Check Chlorides.

If the chlorides were less than 1,000 milligrammes per litre, everything would be okay. Everything rested on the test that Jamie was about to perform. He could feel the tension building inside him. He took 10 ml of the drillwater sample that Scottie had taken from the pit. He put it into a titration cup. He added a few drops of potassium chromate. It was supposed to turn yellow. It did turn yellow. Relieved, Jamie reached for the 0.282 nolar silver nitrate. His hand was trembling.

PING PONG went the Tannoy: 'Mud engineer, mud engineer. Call the drillfloor.'

'This is the mud engineer,' said Jamie in his best BBC voice.

'And this is the driller,' said Phil the Driller menacingly. 'How much mud have you mixed?'

'Loads,' lied Jamie.

'Bullshit,' said Phil the Driller. 'I'm only showing one pit full on my screen.'

'There's a problem with the sensors,' lied Jamie again. He was working on Hitler's principle that if you're going to tell a lie, it might as well be a whopper.

'We're going to start drilling in a minute. I'm sending someone down,' growled Phil the Driller, 'and if you're shitting me, there'll be another body in Active 1.'

Clearly Phil the Driller was a prime suspect for the murder of John Webster.

'Fill the pits! Fill the pits!' shrieked Jamie as he burst into the pit room. 'The driller's going to kill me!'

Scottie laughed. Peachy was beside him, smiling. They were filling another pit with drillwater anyway.

'You better hide,' said Scottie. 'Phil the Driller is an evil, vicious psychopath.'

Scottie laughed. Peachy was still grinning nervously.

'We're going to start drilling,' said Jamie. 'We've no spud mud, no kill mud, no nothing.'

'That'll teach 'em to leave an idiot in charge,' said Peachy.

'If anyone is going to look bad, it'll be Phil the Driller. He's supposed to coordinate everything,' said Scottie.

'He's sending someone down.'

'Good. They can help us mix. Trust me Jamie, we won't be drilling for a couple of hours.' Scottie smiled affably.

Jamie relaxed. "Affable and cooperative" might have sounded simplistic, but in Scottie's capable hands it undoubtedly worked.

Back in the lab, Jamie was confronted with the nolar molar conundrum. A molar was the atomic weight in grammes diluted in a litre of water. So what was a nolar? And why was it 0.282 nolar in the silver nitrate? It was something to do with chlorides weighing 35.5. Jamie multiplied 35.5 by 0.282 and got 10.011. This was hopeful. He reckoned that if he used less than 10 ml of the 0.282 nolar silver nitrate then the chlorides in the water would be less than 1,000 mg/l. Because you multiplied by 1,000 and divided by the size of your sample, which was 10. Or something like that.

As the ninth millilitre of 0.282 nolar silver nitrate went in, Jamie realised he was grinding his molars. Magically, the liquid suddenly turned bright red. Jamie grinned. It was like being in a Potions class at Hogwarts with Harry Potter. He looked at his pipette. He had used 9.9 ml. The chlorides were only just below 1,000. Would that be good enough?

'Hell yes,' said Scottie. We can add lime. That always works a treat. We'll get by. Phil the Driller's an idiot.'

'Oh is he?' said Phil the Driller. His eyes were wild (they were always wild) and his mustache was quivering. He squared up to Scottie. 'Remember. Webster's not here to protect you any more. You'll have to stand on your own. Like a man.'

'If you can manage, I can,' said Scottie.

'I'm gonna make your life a misery,' said Phil in a quiet, menacing voice.

Scottie stared back steadily. 'And I'm going to do everything to make you look stupid. Oh I forgot. You're doing that yourself already.'

'Your guardian angel's dead. What are you going to do now Scottie? No more promotions.'

'This is your first well as driller and you've no spud mud. How could you let that happen?'

Phil stiffened.

'Please,' said Peachy, 'there's no need to fight.'

Phil glared at Peachy.

'I tried to warn everyone,' said Jamie.

Everyone glared at Jamie. Dave the Night Pusher was right: it didn't wash as an excuse.

'We'll need kill mud before we can start,' said Phil.

'We'll have it,' said Scottie.

'Can you send us a roustie?' said Peachy.

'Away back to your porn,' said Phil. 'I hear you're the Porn King. Or are you the Queen?' Phil flicked Peachy's rag cravat.

Peachy took a step toward Phil. Scottie interposed himself between them. 'Ladies, ladies. That's enough.' He guided Phil out of the door. 'Send Ronnie down. We'll get two hoppers mixing on bentonite and then two on barite.'

Jamie was left with Peachy, who looked diminished. He was staring down at his boots. One leg of his coverall had ridden up. Jamie saw that Peachy was wearing red socks.

'I heard you the other night,' said Jamie.

'Heard me where?' said Peachy. He looked confused and vulnerable.

'I heard you crying. I came to help. You ran away.'

'I would never cry on an oil rig. That was someone else.'

'What's up, Peachy?'

'Nothing. It's been a shit trip. Even Webster dying hasn't helped. I need to get home.'

'I want you to know that I'm here. No strings. No conditions. Help in any form you want it. I won't tell anyone. I haven't told anybody about the crying. If you want to talk, come to the mud lab. It's quiet – even if it is a dump.'

Peachy smiled warmly. 'Thanks for the invitation to the dump. You're a gentleman. I'm fine, really. Webster was always able to get to me. There's nothing out here that's worth crying for. Tears turn to rust on an oil rig. Everything important happens on the Beach.'

Peachy shrugged, as if dismissing everything that he had just said. Then he looked directly at Jamie. 'I didn't kill him, you know, Webster. I swear. In the grand scheme of things, I was just a side issue.'

Jamie wondered whether Findon, or any other inept Detective would be hearing any of this. He also wondered what the Russian had to do with it all. There was so much he wanted to say to Peachy, so much he wanted to ask. This damaged and bewildered man seemed to be the key to everything. Yet Jamie could see that the brief moment of honesty and openness had passed. Peachy was staring at the ground. He would say nothing more.

'Don't take any shit from Phil. He's cracking up. He can't handle it,' said Jamie.

'I understand.'

They got on with the mixing. They threw cans of caustic soda and sacks of soda ash in from the tops of the pits. Jamie thought of how carefully he had measured his chemicals when training with Bert. There were no such niceties on the Manticore. Jamie's offshore career had got off to a desperate start.

Things quickly got worse. They'd put all the right stuff in all the right pits and none of it was looking good. Even Jamie could tell that the fluid was not what it should be. The three pits they'd mixed were all depressingly identical. They were full of a watery grey mixture with occasional lumps.

Jamie's first attempt at mixing mud was a complete and utter disaster. The entire rig, at half a million dollars a day, would soon be sitting idle because of his incompetence. A familiar knot tightened in his stomach.

'That won't hold barite up,' said Scottie, spitting into the dismal liquid. 'Are you sure the chlorides were okay?'

'I think there might be a wee problem with the chlorides,' said Jamie.

'What problem?'

'You know I said they were nine hundred and ninety parts per million?'

'Yes.'

'I think they're actually nine thousand nine hundred and ninety.'

'Tell me you're joking.'

'The silver nitrate I used was actually ten times stronger than I realised.'

'So you were wrong by a factor of ten?'

'Yes.'

Scottie threw his head back and laughed. 'Being out by a factor of ten is par for the course in the oil business. We'll make a rig man of you yet.' Scottie stroked his stubbly chin. 'No wonder it isn't yielding. It's picked up the seawater from the dead volume in the pits and from the lines. And bentonite doesn't yield in seawater. We can dump it and start again. Or we can throw chemicals at the problem.'

The phone rang. It was for Jamie. It was Phil the Driller. 'Where the fuck's my kill mud and my sweeps?' he shrieked. 'We're about ready to get going.' He hung up.

'Let's throw chemicals at the problem,' said Jamie.

Each large pit was supposed to get one 12.5 kg can of caustic soda and half a 25 kg sack of soda ash. Jamie and Scottie lobbed a further 3 cans of caustic and 2 full sacks of soda ash into each pit. They then added half a sack of lime just for the hell of it. They weren't following correct procedures. They weren't wearing the correct Personal Protective Equipment. They weren't referring to the Material Safety Data Sheets. When push came to shove Jamie's good intentions about safety went straight out the window.

Jamie knew what the problem was: no one had written a Risk Assessment for blind panic. He stuck a pH stick into the fluid. It was supposed to be 9.5. It was more like 13.

'Er, don't get any of the fluid on your skin,' said Jamie. 'It's, like, really really corrosive.'

'Oh look,' said Peachy. 'The mud's coming together.'

It was. It was looking nice and creamy. Then it got thicker. And thicker. And thicker. Then it got so thick that you could walk on it.

Jamie's stomach tied itself into some new knots. 'Holy shit.'

'That's spud mud,' said Peachy. 'That's exactly what we want.'

To prove his point he stuck a broom handle in it. It stood erect, just as John Webster had predicted.

Peachy and Scottie leapt into action. They added water to the thick fluid whilst transferring some of it into empty pits. Meanwhile, Ronnie the Roustie was heaving barite in as fast as he could at the hoppers. Before they knew it, they were looking at enough nice, thick mud to get them started.

'That worked a treat,' said Peachy incredulously. 'You're a genius Jamie, and you don't even know it.'

The phone rang. It was for Jamie. 'Where the fuck's my mud?' barked Phil the Driller.

'I know you're not going to believe this,' said Jamie, 'but we've got nine hundred barrels of kill weight mud and four hundred barrels of sweeps ready to go.'

'Holy fuck,' said Phil the Driller. He fell silent, crestfallen that he had no reason to shout.

Peachy, Scottie and Ronnie the Roustie were standing in front of Jamie. They were coated in chemicals. As he looked at them, Jamie realised that he was on a cushy number. All he had to do was issue instructions and perform a few tests. They did everything else. They performed all the heavy manual tasks for a surly, petulant driller. They were bathed in sweat.

'We've got a few problems up here,' Phil continued. 'It'll be a couple of hours before we start drilling. Are the boys there?'

'Are the boys here?' Jamie repeated.

Peachy, Scottie and Ronnie waved "No!" frantically.

'No one here just now Phil.'

'Where the fuck are they?'

Jamie faced an array of baffling mimes. Ronnie was waving a rag and pointing outside. Peachy was hopping on one foot and Scottie was pumping up an imaginary bicycle.

'Ronnie's lost the rag. Peachy's hopping mad and Scottie's got on his bike.'

'Are you fucking with me?' said Phil.

'No! I mean Ronnie's gone to the stores for some rags.

Peachy's checking out the barite hoppers and Scottie's working on the pumps.'

'If you see them, send them straight up.' Phil hung up.

'Fuck Phil,' said Ronnie. 'We're going to the tea shack.'

'Phil's a complete twat,' said Scottie. 'I told you he wouldn't be ready in time.'

'Phil IS a complete twat,' said Peachy. 'He borrows porn and never gives it back.'

Shortly before midnight the Manticore commenced drilling on Well 211/96-F. The ROV, the underwater vehicle, had dropped marker buoys on the seabed so that the rig couldn't lose the hole. Such things weren't unheard of and were deeply embarrassing to all concerned.

Rig: 'We have a slight problem out here.'

The Beach: 'What's that?'

Rig: 'You remember that 36 inch hole we just drilled?'

The Beach: 'Yes.'

Rig: 'Well we're buggered if we can find it.'

The Beach: 'You're fired.'

Once they were done drilling, the rig would pull the drill bit out of the water, break all the drilling assembly down and rig up to run conductor pipe. This pipe would be cemented into place with about 30 feet sticking up above the seabed. Then the wellhead would be placed on top and the marker buoys recovered. Not even the Manticore could lose a wellhead. Unless they dropped it. This wasn't unheard of either.

Scottie and Peachy had things cunningly arranged in the pit room. The rig pumps were lined up to suck from Reserve Pit 4. Reserve Pit 4 had twin seawater feeds which were left open. These filled the pit, which overflowed into the flowline and into Reserve Pit 5. The dump valve on Reserve Pit 5 was open so that any excess seawater returned to the sea. In this way, the rig pumps had a plentiful supply of seawater for drilling without Scottie and Peachy having to constantly monitor the situation. For every 45 feet of hole drilled, a fifty barrel sweep of spud mud would be pumped. This thick stuff would sweep any debris from the hole and prevent the pipe from getting stuck. At the end of the section, aka Total Depth, aka TD, a final, one hundred barrel sweep would be pumped to ensure the hole was totally clear. The hole would then be filled with kill mud. This thick and weighted mud was designed to keep the hole open until they returned with the conductor pipe. Its hydrostatic weight would also "kill" the well by preventing any harmful gases from coming up. Hence the moniker.

That was the theory.

Amazingly, the practice wasn't much different. The drilling went smoothly, apart from one brief interlude.

'Come on upstairs and we'll annoy Phil,' said Scottie.

They went into the doghouse, the aptly-named home of the driller. Phil was at the controls and the place was mobbed – Nigel the Night Company Man, Dave the Night Pusher, Elvis the Night Directional Driller and Stevie the new AD.

There was a horrible vibrating sound. The drillpipe was vibrating horribly. Phil's mustache was also vibrating horribly. His face was panic-stricken.

'Vibrating drillpipe is Golfing With The Wrong People,' said Dave petulantly.

'It's probably just a boulder,' said Scottie.

'I know!' shrieked Phil. 'What the fuck have you brought that idiot up here for?'

'To see how effortlessly you deal with pressure,' said Jamie.

Nigel the Night Company Man laughed. Dave scowled. Having the client laugh at his driller was also GWTWP.

'I thought I'd let Jamie see what vibrating drillpipe looked like,' said Scottie. 'Part of his learning curve.'

'Learning curve? More like a learning ditch,' said Phil. 'Well he's seen it now, so he can fuck off. And so can you.'

'Shouldn't you clear the drillfloor, Phil?' said Scottie. 'Mark Z and Ronnie the Roustie are on the drillfloor. The vibration could shake anything out the derrick. There's a high chance of a dropped object. It's not safe out there.'

Phil glared at Scottie. Dave whistled and gestured to Mark Z for him and Ronnie to clear off.

'Good point Scottie,' said Nigel. He lifted the telephone and made a tannoy. 'Due to the vibration could all personnel keep clear of the drillfloor until further notice. Roughnecks will be tannoyed for the next connection.' He hung up. 'Everyone apart from the driller and the directional driller better shove off.'

Phil stared at Scottie with undisguised hatred.

Back in the pit room, Scottie was grinning. 'Phil should have known to clear the drillfloor. I had to tell him his job. Total humiliation.'

'He'll want to pay you back for that. And me.'

'He tried to make you look stupid and you stood up to him. You've already learned the number one lesson out here: don't take shit from any man. He can't touch you. You don't work for him. And he knows you're more than a match for him. He can't touch me either, because he's an idiot and I'm not frightened of him. Next time he asks for a sweep, we'll give him seawater instead of spud mud and see if he notices.'

They did. He didn't.

'He should see it on his pump pressure and on the pit levels,' said Scottie. 'He's not fit for the job. He's dangerous.'

'Like the toolpusher?'

Scottie smiled. 'No one's that dangerous. The dearly departed toolpusher was always having to cover for Phil's calamities.'

'I thought you were his favourite.'

'Webster did that to annoy people. The person it annoyed most was me. He knew that. Who, in their right mind, would want to be Webster's favourite?' Scottie stared intently at Jamie.

'Fair point,' said Jamie. He noted Scottie's stare. This was a guy that you didn't want as an enemy. 'What about the sweep that we missed? Doesn't that make us more likely to get stuck?'

'No. We were drilling the boulder a long time. The seawater will have swept the hole clean. We're pumping fast. Your stuff's just for show.'

The 36 inch section was TD'd shortly after 5.30 am. This sent waves of suspicion running through the day shift crew. By the time night shift had swept the hole clean and killed the well, it was time to handover and let day shift do all the hard work of pulling out of the hole, breaking up the 36 inch Bottom Hole Assembly, making up the 30 inch conductor pipe handling gear and running that in − assuming they could find the hole they'd just drilled. Handovers between drillcrew members were performed with elation on the part of night shift and sullen resentment on the part of day shift.

There was little for Gray to do. Scottie and Peachy had remade spud mud as they went along. The kill mud for the next section could be made without Gray's participation. It was just as well, because Gray was cracking up.

Chapter 19 The £200K International Oil Executive

Jamie knew straight away that there was something wrong. After the handover, Gray came down to the mess to eat with him. They had never shared a meal together. It was breakfast for Gray: he had sausage, bacon, egg, beans, black pudding and a potato scone. It was dinner for Jamie: he had sausage, bacon, egg, beans, black pudding and a potato scone. There was no other hot food available for the night shift. It didn't exactly help them to maintain a balanced diet. They didn't seem bothered. There weren't many health food fanatics aboard. Besides, the night shift were buzzing. It had been a good night's drilling, they had finished the section and left all the dirty work for the boys on days. Even Phil the Driller was elated.

'I'm worried about the displacement,' said Gray.

Jamie didn't know what a displacement was.

'After we've finished with water-based mud, we'll have to displace the well to oil-based mud,' Gray explained. 'Swap them over. Dump all the WBM into the sea. But you've got to make sure you don't put any OBM in the sea.'

'Especially with police aboard,' said Jamie helpfully.

Gray's eyes widened in panic. 'Shit! I hadn't thought of that! Putting oil in the water is illegal. You can get fined or arrested. It's not like the good old days when you could heave anything over the side.'

Jamie, already in detective mode, made a brilliant deduction. 'It's those tree-hugging environmentalists,' he said.

'I know!' wailed Gray. 'We put so much as a litre of oil over the side and they'll frog-march us straight to the Ministry of Brown Trout. They'll send spotter planes over and everything. It's awful. An environmental incident is the worst thing we can do out here.'

'Apart from killing someone.'

'We've killed someone already!'

'I was talking about accidentally killing someone. Not smashing their head in and throwing them in a pit.'

'This is the worst trip of my life. I thought Webster's death would make me happy. I need to speak to Beryl.'

'Who's Beryl?'

'The wife.'

Gray's face assumed a haunted look, so Jamie changed tack. 'When is this displacement? We've no oil-based mud aboard. The last of that went back in tote tanks with bits of Webster's brain in it.'

'We'll displace after the 17 ½ inch section. We drill that with potassium chloride. And I haven't used that kind of mud in years. Oh God, someone help me. People have no idea what the pressures are like out here.'

'I'll talk to Walter and see if we can get you on the blower to Beryl.'

'That would be wonderful.' Gray's face was like that of a child's. 'You know, you do one hundred good trips out here and all people remember is the last, bad one. We all snap in the end. Offshore careers always finish badly. Look at Webster.'

'Webster's offshore career was finished badly for him by somebody else.'

'There's no happy endings on an oil rig,' said Gray.

*****

'What is it son?' said Walter.

'Why does everybody call me 'son'?' said Jamie. 'I'm thirty years old.'

'We don't mean anything by it.'

'It's patronising.'

'There's a lot worse happens on an oil rig.'

'Fair point.'

'Don't take it to heart. It's a term of endearment. We like you.'

Walter's face looked soft and almost vulnerable. Jamie could suddenly see more of the man and less of his job. Jamie also felt as if he'd just grown three feet taller.

'What can I do for you, son?' Walter smiled.

'It's Gray. He really needs to talk to his wife.'

'Not another one,' Walter groaned. 'I've had six in so far. Near greetin'. There are some things an OIM shouldn't have to listen to. The sooner the world knows we've bashed the Pusher's head in, the better. Why is the oil industry so obsessed with secrecy?'

'Tax evasion?'

'Why couldn't Gray ask me?'

'He's in a bad way, Walter.'

'The whole rig's in a bad way. I keep telling the police that we need to get some fresh faces out here. They won't listen. They've sent a top Senior International Oil Executive to come out to give us all a pep talk. Wait until you meet him and see what two hundred grand a year gets you. And they're threatening us with a life coach. Some twenty-five year-old with big tits and a PowerPoint presentation.'

Jamie got out of his chair. 'I'll send Gray up.'

'I'll be a lot happier once we've got conductor pipe cemented in the ground and the wellhead landed off,' said Walter. 'Are you involved in this cement job?'

'I'm taking weights.'

'Good,' said Walter. 'Not even you can mess that up.'

***

The TV lounge was packed. Everyone who could be spared was there. All seats were taken. Jamie had struggled to secure himself a piece of carpet. 'I don't even know why I'm here,' he said. 'I don't work for Manticore Drilling.'

'You heard the tannoy,' said Bill the Mechanic. 'Attendance compulsory for all personnel.'

'You're on our rig,' said Desperate Dan, 'so you can suffer with the rest of us. You are about to witness a performance by the most impressive executive in our organisation.'

'He's got a well-deserved, international reputation,' said Peachy.

'His rise up the ranks has been astonishing,' said Scottie.

'Sounds impressive,' said Jamie. 'What's he called?'

'Stuarty Higgins.'

Walter arrived with Findon in tow and an insignificant-looking man bringing up the rear. This was the two hundred grand Senior International Oil Executive.

Walter cleared his throat. 'We are gathered here today,' he began, 'because Stuart has been kind enough to come out to discuss safety issues relating to the incident.'

Stuarty shuffled forward. He was wearing what Jamie would come to see as standard outfit for occasional offshore types in their fifties – jeans, checked shirt, mustache and not much hair. He was wearing proper shoes. The crew were all in tattered trainers.

'Right boys,' said Stuarty, sliding his hands nervously into his pockets, 'this is one of the sorrier trips I've had to make offshore. To say that Houston is disappointed would be an understatement. I've had a lot of explaining to do and I'm not happy. I mean it's hard enough keeping this kind of hanky-panky out of the Aberdeen

Press and Journal. But there's been international interest. From Glasgow. And Edinburgh. From big papers. I've been rushed off my feet. And let me tell you boys that every minute I spend on the incident is a minute I'm not spending on looking after your safety.'

'Thank fuck,' whispered Peachy, loud enough for most of the room to hear. There were a few titters. Several people studied their tattered trainers. Walter's eyes roamed the room looking for suspects.

'A few more murders,' whispered Bill, 'and we'll have that arse out of our hair forever.'

'Now boys,' Stuarty continued, shuffling his feet, 'I wasn't a big fan of John Webster myself, but come on, fair is fair. What went on was right out of order. I mean, it was uncalled for.'

'Uncalled for?' whispered Scottie. 'Every bastard north of Perth was calling for it.'

Even Walter smiled at that one. But Stuarty's ears had been damaged by too much unprotected time with noisy shale shakers in the bad old days. He went on. 'Put yourself in my shoes,' he said, 'it's embarrassing having to explain away something like that. The Manticore is the talk of the fleet. And not in a good way.'

'I bet all the other rigs are jealous,' Jamie found himself saying. Several people nodded.

'And how do you think John Webster felt, eh? Smacked on the head and tossed into a mud pit like some old....' Stuarty struggled to find the right word.

'Tie wrap?' someone suggested. People were now laughing openly.

'It's not funny boys,' said Stuarty as emphatically as he could. 'And we found all kinds of junk in the bottom of the pits too. Mud pits are not dumping grounds for all your old shite.'

The room mulled over the implications of this unfortunate statement.

'Tie wraps and rags block the valves and the strainers to the mud pumps,' Scottie whispered to Jamie.

'Dead bodies don't help much either,' added Bill.

'To get back to the most serious issue,' Stuarty continued, 'let me tell you that Houston are worried. Very worried. I mean we can't have this. Smacking people about the head with steel bars and dumping them in mud pits is no way to treat rig management. Houston thinks there could be copycat episodes. And let's face it, there's a lot of unpopular toolpushers out there. So I hope youse are happy. This rig's copybook is well and truly blotted.' Stuarty paused to let the shame sink in.

'Fucking typical,' said Peachy, 'he talks to us as if we all did it.'

'No, we just wish we all did it,' said Ronnie the Roustie.

'And think about this,' said Stuarty, 'John Webster's two wee girls. They'll never see their father ever again. Daddy the toolpusher will never put on that yellow survival suit, he'll never climb up into that chopper and he'll never be coming home.'

'Hurray!' Someone let out a mock cheer.

'HURRAY!!!' The entire room let out a real cheer. Then the noise got louder. And louder. Jamie could feel the hairs begin to stand up on the back of his neck. He had never sensed an atmosphere like this in his life. He struggled to draw breath. It was as if the poisonous atmosphere in the room was sucking the very life out of the air. Jamie now began to feel his face reddening. His heart was pounding in his chest. He was frightened and elated at the same time. People started to clap their hands together. Then the chanting began.

'KILLER! KILLER! KILLER! KILLER!'

Jamie's was not the only red face in the room. Walter's face was red. Stuarty's was scarlet. Unconsciously, Stuarty backed away from the crew, into a corner. He blinked in astonishment. He was too frightened to make eye contact with anyone.

'KILLER! KILLER! KILLER! KILLER!' The chanting went on.

People were clapping. People were cheering. People were whistling. It was an awful cacophony. Jamie felt that John Webster would have approved of it. His presence here was palpable. Yes, John Webster would have loved it. If only someone else had died.

Findon stood with his mouth agape, exaggerating his stupidity. He too was staring into space.

'KILLER! KILLER! KILLER! KILLER!' Some people were stamping their feet.

Jamie pulled himself together and drew a deep breath. Otherwise, he would have fainted. He scanned the room. Just about every face had some colour in it. Some faces were contorted with hatred. Some were contorted with glee. Some were smiling indulgently. Some were aghast, but were chanting despite themselves. There were four people who weren't joining in with the mob at all. Jamie made a mental note of them.

'KILLER! KILLER! KILLER! KILLER!'

Things were reaching a crescendo.

'KILLER! KILLER KILLER! KILLEEER !!'

Everyone stopped. There was silence. The room was exhausted.

Jamie didn't know whether the killer was present, but he did know that these people were capable of murder – as a mob.

Stuarty had meandered back centre-stage. 'Where was I?' he mumbled.

Desperate Dan said, 'You were telling us how cuddly John Webster wouldn't be putting on his ickle survival suit, donning his Care Bear lifejacket and skipping onto a My Little Pony helicopter anytime soon. Bounding back up Walton Mountain to meet his ex-prostitute Russian wife and his two wee deranged daughters.'

'Three wee deranged daughters,' corrected Bill.

'Stuarty said two,' said Desperate Dan.

'Webster always said three,' said Bill.

'That's right. Three,' said Ronnie.

'Lads, lads,' said Stuarty, 'let's not argue. There's been enough unpleasantness already. I can assure you that John Webster only had two daughters. I've met them myself.'

'So why did he always talk about his three girls?' said Jamie.

'I don't know,' said Stuarty wearily. 'He only had two children. There's no point in trying to fathom John Webster's idea of a joke. Those two wee lassies are bereaved. Think about that.' Stuarty left another shameful pause.

'But what's disappointed me most, boys,' continued Stuarty in his gravest voice, 'is the complete and utter lack of cooperation with Grampian Police.'

All eyes alighted on Detective Findon. He seized his moment. 'Grampian Police are big enough to let bygones be bygones,' he said. 'After all, we're a forgiving bunch.'

This comment was met by a silence of stunned incredulity.

'I'm pretty confident that there's a murderer here in this room,' Detective Findon continued. Think on that boys. Look around. Somebody here has taken a human life. Look at the man next to you. It could be him. Ask yourself this: "Am I comfortable sitting next to a killer?" Well, are you? Do you feel lucky? Because the question we all have to ask is: "Who's next?" And you won't be chanting for the killer then, will you? Because you'll be dead. Think about that. And Webster won't be the only one who isn't putting on his survival suit and not getting on the chopper and not going home to his two or three wee daughters. You won't be either, because you'll have your head dented and you'll be face down in one of those mud pit things with that horrible brown liquid in your lungs. Someone here knows something. The killer definitely. Maybe somebody else. Maybe two people know something. If you're a person who knows something, think about what you can do to help your fellow rig pigs. Protecting the killer doesn't help him. We'll get him in the end. Someone will spill the beans. I've got psychological training you know. People crack in my presence. I'll wear you down. I'm just warning you. And I can promise the killer a fair trial. Maybe it was all a big accident. Somebody slipped with a hammer in their hand and then panicked. There could be extenuating circumstances. Maybe tempers got a bit frayed or it was a bit of hanky-panky that got carried away.'

'Hanky-panky?' whispered Peachy. 'With John Webster?'

'By all accounts, John Webster was not a popular man. There could be a reduced charge of manslaughter. Temporary insanity. There's a load of dingbat judges always ready to fall for that one. You could be back out here in a couple of years. And what's a couple of years inside? From what I've seen so far, conditions in prisons are far better than they are out here.'

The entire room gave Detective Findon a heartfelt round of applause.

Stuarty gritted his teeth. Walter nodded philosophically.

'But let me warn you.' Findon jabbed the air as he built to his climax. 'Obstructing the course of justice is a serious crime. It will be viewed seriously. Protecting a killer is not a minor crime. So come forward now and all will be forgiven. Don't make me have to break you. It won't be pleasant.'

Findon ended his speech with his grim frown.

'Are there any questions?' said Walter.

It was Desperate Dan who spoke for them all: 'When's the next pay rise?'

Chapter 20 Bring Out the Gimp, It's a Cement Job

Jamie went to bed to fantasise about sunlit Andalusian evenings with Antonio Banderas, naked together in a moonlit jacuzzi. Horses would whinny in the corral and crickets would chirp among the dusty vines. And there would be a few cactuses here and there. Jamie then slept soundly, in the knowledge that when he got up he would get to participate in a cement job. More amazingly, he'd finally get to meet an elusive character known as "the cementer".

He was half-man. He was half-mattress. He was a knuckle-dragging, Frankenstein-foreheaded freak. He was Kevin the Cementer and he was a much maligned character on the Manticore. It wasn't really his fault. Cementers got a bad rap offshore. It was the job.

The cementer's job involved long periods of inactivity followed by short bursts of intense effort which ended in disaster. The cement either set too quickly or it never set at all. If it never set, the rig was fucked. If it set too quick, the rig was really fucked.

And to rub salt in the wounds, the cement companies charged an absolute fortune for what could only be described as, er, cement.

The cementer was also endowed with the biggest pump on the rig. So he was called upon to do any pressure testing, generally the Blow Out Prevention stack which had to be certified at least every 21 days.

In between cement jobs and pressure testing, the cementer slept. There was no truth to the apocryphal story about the cementer who lay dead in his bunk for five days before anyone noticed. Kev, however, did his profession proud, kipping down for eighteen hours at a stretch and on one legendary occasion for a full thirty-six hours without even waking up to go to the bathroom. He spent the entire week afterward thinking that Wednesday was Tuesday and Friday Thursday and no one took the trouble to disabuse him of the notion until his crew-change day, when the medic came into his room to wake him up for the helicopter briefing. Kev had a whole hour to pack, complete his paperwork for the hitch and scribble some hasty handover notes for his "back-to-back", the colleague who replaced him for two weeks.

'Youse are bastards,' he had said.

'Serves you right,' they had replied.

Kev had kept himself in ignoramic bliss by religiously watching porn instead of the news. He had also managed to avoid all computers, particularly his own. Cementers and computers didn't mix.

This cement job was relatively simple. The 30 inch conductor pipe was to be secured into place in the 36 inch hole which they had just drilled. More than enough cement would be mixed and pumped to fill the 3 inch gap between the outside of the pipe and the hole. The inside of the conductor pipe would be left empty since all the other sections would be drilled through it and all the casing strings run through it. Casing was steel tubing into which the small pipes which carried the oil from the reservoir would eventually be placed. You started at the top drilling 36 inch hole and running 30 inch conductor pipe. The holes then got smaller as you got deeper and so did the strings of casing until you were drilling an 8 ½ inch hole into the reservoir. It wouldn't have worked the other way about, as you couldn't have got a 36 inch bit 10,000 feet down into the reservoir if you only had an 8 ½ inch hole at the top. There was method in the madness. When the 8 ½ inch hole reached the reservoir, 7 inch liner was run inside. Liner differed from casing in that casing came all the way to the seabed and was sealed at the wellhead whereas liner hung off the end of the last casing string, generally 9 5/8 inch casing. You had to drill in different sections and run different casings to isolate the different pressure zones in the rock formations. Otherwise, Jamie's fluid would have been too heavy at the top of the well, causing losses and too light at the bottom of the well, causing hydrocarbons to come up a bit early and then probably migrate out into rocks nearer the surface. All this, no doubt, had been discovered at great length and under huge duress by oilmen the world over.

It was no wonder that Jamie was confused.

Kev had been rigging up for the past two days, doing what he liked doing second best; swinging a sledgehammer and knocking things together. His favourite thing was swinging a sledgehammer and knocking things apart. Destruction was always more enjoyable. He had batch tanks and chemical tanks that all needed connecting to his unit. It was a big job and Freddie was no use.

Freddie came with the unit. The bizarre arrangement was that the oil company had awarded the cementing contract to Topset, Kev's employers, but on board the Manticore had installed a Sqweezjob cement unit. Sqweezjob had the responsibility of maintaining their unit. Sqweezjob had some wonderfully well-trained cementers. And Sqweezjob sent these cementers to work on their lucrative contracts. To the Manticore they sent Freddie. He muddled along. The unit muddled along. Somehow the jobs got done.

Freddie always seemed to be on the point of drawing his last breath. He had the worst wheeze in the North Sea. Nobody knew how he had got into the job in the first place. Freddie had been a social worker and had got fed up dealing with reprobates. He came into the oil business to deal with nicer people, do as little as possible and smoke himself to death. Freddie had been everyone's top choice for a death on the rig before Webster had, unnaturally, croaked it.

Just watching Freddie struggling into his coveralls was painful. His wee pickled Presbyterian face grew redder as the wheezing increased and his arm searched in vain for a sleeve. Jamie was already better at putting on his coveralls after four days. The secret was to hold them by the collar, let the legs fall to the ground and step inside. Freddie hadn't figured this out in fifteen years. His mind was elsewhere.

'We'll be ready to go in about six hours,' he gasped, as Jamie helped him find the final arm, 'so we'll let everybody eat early and then kick off just after midnight.'

Exhausted by his exertions, Freddie sat down and lit a cigarette. 'Technically speaking, I should only touch the unit, but I like to give Kev a hand,' he lied. Freddie hadn't touched the unit much in fifteen years either. He was good with a paintbrush, so the place at least looked well-maintained, but the mechanics were a disaster and he never had enough spares.

Looking at Freddie, Jamie surmised that he wasn't exactly a suspect in the murder of John Webster. The effort would have killed him along with his victim. Freddie's file had probably joined Jamie's in the "Completely Incapable" pile.

Kevin burst in like a lion, just out his cage, released into the wild, with some hunting to do. Or like a cementer, just out his bed, released into the tea shack with a cement job to do.

'What's happening? What's happening?' he said, jerking his head from side to side.

'Relax,' wheezed Freddie. 'We've hours yet. You get a good sleep?'

'Always. Always.' Kevin's eyes stared wildly. His hair sat up wildly. His head bobbed around wildly.

'Are you Kevin the Cementer?' said Jamie. 'I was beginning to doubt you even existed.'

Kevin crushed Jamie's hand, pumped it three times and stared deep into his eyes. It was the most disconcerting handshake Jamie had ever received. If Bill the Mechanic was barking mad and Dave the Night Pusher was downright nuts, Kevin the Cementer was barking nuts, downright mad and very likely to explode. Bed was probably the best place for him.

'Are you the latest mud mutt? And you're taking weights?'

'I'm raring to go,' said Jamie amiably.

'Looks like we're scraping the bottom of the barrel, Freddie. There's no roughnecks to take weights 'cos they're all up the floor, fixing Phil the drill's latest fuck-up.'

'Oh that's awful,' said Freddie, who liked to hear bad news. 'What's he done now?'

'Crowned the Top Drive.'

'Oh my, that is serious.' Freddie could scarcely contain his glee. It was important to have people around who were more incompetent than he was. It kept him in a job. Freddie's job had been safe for fifteen years.

Kevin the Cementer might have been barking insane, but he was able to read the bewildered look on Jamie's face. 'Crowning the Top Drive,' he explained, 'is when the driller lifts the Top Drive up the derrick and fails to stop, so it hits the Crown Block at the top.'

'Aren't there automatic brakes to stop that kind of thing?' said Jamie.

'There are. But Phil's a superstar. He managed to over-ride them. He's such a genius that even he doesn't know how he did it.'

'Questions will be asked on the Beach,' said Freddie.

'Questions are being asked on the Beach,' said Jamie. 'Somebody rubbed out the toolpusher, remember?'

'Imagine if he'd still been alive,' said Kevin. 'Phil would be over the side, swimming for it.'

'Webster would have shredded him,' said Freddie. 'Is it not still a cause for dismissal?'

'Demotion, more like,' said Kevin. 'You never know, the Webster incident might save him.'

'It might save him for a couple of trips,' said Freddie. 'But Phil won't be a driller on here in the New Year. Mark my words.'

Kevin the Cementer did mark Freddie's words. Freddie was an expert on cock-ups and catastrophes. He was a student of ineptitude. It was his life's work.

Scottie arrived with Peachy in tow. Peachy looked more worried than ever. Scottie had a smile on his face and a twinkle in his eye. 'Have we all heard about Phil the Driller's crowning glory? It was brilliant. Right in front of the client and the night pusher. Totally unable to blame anybody else. What a twat.'

'Didn't stop him shouting at us,' Peachy muttered.

'And we had our backs to it. Tragically, so did Phil. All we heard was the beautiful, sickening crash. The entire rigfloor shook. Then it was just Phil's mustache that shook. And it's still shaking now.'

'What about my cement job?' said Kevin.

'Top Drive seems okay. Walter's keen to get the cement down there and make the well safe. Then they can think about derrick inspections and the like. I'm just sorry that Webster wasn't here. That would have been fun to watch.'

Freddie, who had struggled out of his coveralls, went back inside the accommodation.

'Is it just me,' said Jamie, 'or did Freddie come in here, get changed into his coveralls, have a cigarette, get changed back out his coveralls and go inside without actually going outside?'

'Freddie works in mysterious ways,' said Kevin.

'You've just witnessed Freddie doing an entire shift,' said Peachy. 'We won't see him again tonight.'

'Thank fuck,' said Kevin.

Scottie lit up and sat down. 'So, what's the latest rumour?'

'A well-stacked woman's coming to present to us on health issues,' said Jamie.

'Holy moley,' said Scottie, 'you're well-informed.'

At 11 pm, the entire night shift crew went into the mess to make the most of the rotten food that was available at that time of night. In the good old days, the Manticore had a night shift chef and the midnight meals were lovely. Chocolate biscuits were plentiful in the tea shack too. Then oil hit $12 per barrel and the chef went, to be replaced by a night baker. He was charged with reheating whatever had been prepared in the day and baking the bread for the next day. The food on nights quickly became inedible. Oil at $12 per barrel had a lot to answer for. Chocolate biscuits had never been seen on the Manticore since.

And so, with everyone in the early stages of indigestion, the cement job began in the early hours of Monday morning. Jamie hovered beside the cement unit, poised to take weights.

Jamie had imagined that dealing with pressurized hydrocarbons on multi-million dollar oil wells obviously called for a highly-sophisticated, electronic, real time, state-of-the-art method for measuring the density of the drilling fluid or cement designed to contain these dangerous pressures. Jamie was wrong. The multi-billion dollar oil industry had decided to make do with a crock-of-shit device commonly known as a Pressurized Mud Balance.

Here is the deal:

Take your Mud Balance (badly machined cast iron plus rivets plus scaled beam plus poor welds plus counterweight plus lead chamber plus Allen screw plus wee lead bits plus spirit level bubble) and fill with drilling fluid or cement or whatever dubious fluid you wish to weigh.

Pop on lid and screw into place with securing ring.

Some of the fluid should squirt out of the nozzle.

Aim this fluid at suitable receptacle (jug / shaker ditch / an enemy)

Take plunger and draw fluid inside.

Place plunger over nozzle and pump down until nozzle rises.

The Mud Balance is now pressurized

Clean excess fluid from Mud Balance (It has probably squirted everywhere anyway because the nozzles never seal properly)

Place mud balance on fulcrum and slide counterweight until spirit level bubble centres.

The Mud Balance is now balanced.

To ascertain mud weight, read off the scale on the beam where the wee arrow points on the counterweight.

Please note that errors may occur due to air in the balance (you didn't squirt); miscalibration (you're an idiot); grit in the badly designed Allen screw; grit anywhere else for that matter; the wee bits of lead moving about; broken seals; a dodgy fulcrum; a dodgy bubble; a dodgy derrickman.

Every oil well drilled on the planet uses this useless piece of shit. The amazing thing is: it seems to work.

Jamie practised taking weights using a jug of water. He sprayed most of it over himself in the attempts to pressurise the balance. Reassuringly, his weights approximated to the weight of water, which was conveniently marked by a line on the scale. By an amazing coincidence, water weighed exactly 1 sg. Disconcertingly, it weighed a little over 8.3 pounds per gallon and a little over 430 pounds per thousand feet. Jamie, however, took comfort from the fact that the wee arrow was pointing right at the line. All was well.

'You'll need these.' Kevin thrust a dust mask and a pair of ear defenders into Jamie's arms. 'We're looking for 13.2 ppg. That's pounds per gallon.' Kevin spoke into a walkie-talkie. 'Ronnie the Roustie, this is Kevin the cement unit.'

'Go ahead' squawked Ronnie.

'Please confirm we are lined up to blow though cement from silo four.'

'Silo four lined up. Just give us a shout.'

'Roger that.'

Jamie was thrilled. There was something about walkie-talkies that made him feel incredibly manly. It was boys and their toys. And he was a vital cog in the machine.

Kevin mounted his unit, where he was joined by Nigel the Night Company Man. He started up his diesel engines and Jamie realised why he needed the ear defenders. Jamie stood at the bottom and waited for a jug of cement to be passed down to him. There was some blaring on the walkie-talkies. Then the cement mixing started. Then Jamie realised why he needed a dust mask. A fog of cement dust rose.

Presently, Kevin leaned down with a jug. Jamie took it. It was heavy. Jamie dropped it.

'Mor muck's make,' shouted Kevin from under his dust mask.

Jamie slid around in the spilled cement, retrieved the jug and handed it up to Kevin. Kevin smacked Jamie over the head with it. 'Met the fire mose and mose that down or it'll mucking met,' said Kevin.

There was a large red fire hose coiled up in the corner. Jamie grabbed the nozzle. And twisted it on. There was quite a bit of pressure in it. There was quite a kick. He shot a spray up at the unit, dousing Kevin and Nigel.

Kevin threw a plastic bottle at Jamie. 'The mucking floor!'

Jamie hosed the floor until the cement was just sandy water. The floor became totally slippery. Another jug was lowered and Jamie carefully took it over to the small table where the mud balance was set up. Everything went okay until Jamie tried to pressurise the balance by pumping it up with the plunger. The nozzle on the lid was supposed to stand up, like a little erection. Jamie tried five times. He couldn't get an erection. He looked up. Kevin and Nigel were standing with their arms folded impatiently. Jamie was useless. He couldn't get it up.

Jamie drew up another load of cement with the plunger. He put it on the stem and pressed down with his right hand for all he was worth. With his left hand gripping the barrel of the plunger, Jamie eased this hand back. Cement sprayed everywhere. Jamie's safety glasses got it. His face got it. His coveralls got it and the wall got it. Jamie reeled back, gagging. Some cement had even gone into his mouth. He tried to wipe his glasses, but smeared cement all over them, scratching them in the process. He looked down at the mud balance. Finally, he had managed an erection.

Jamie dunked the balance in a bucket of water and wiped it clean with a rag. He put it on the fulcrum and nudged the counterweight along to centre the bubble. There was a whiteboard with numbers written on it and two magnets. Jamie positioned the magnets, one on 12 and the other on .5 ; weight 12.5 ppg.

Kevin gave Jamie the thumbs up and went back to pulling levers and opening valves. Jamie pressed with the plunger to depressurise the balance. Having finally managed an erection, Jamie was unable to get rid of the bugger. He ended up swinging the balance like a hammer and striking the nozzle off the table. This worked. He cleaned the balance and gave the jug back to Kevin, slipping on the floor as he went. He barely had time to dip his safety glasses in the water before the next jug came; weight 12.5 ppg. Two more jugs; both weighed 12.5 ppg. The next jug was really heavy; weight 15.1 ppg.

Kevin went nuts. He threw another plastic bottle at Jamie and came at him down the ladder. 'Mot the muck do you call that?' he yelled. He looked at the balance. It was balanced. It was reading 15.1. 'Mucking useless munt!'

Kevin went back up on the unit. He and Nigel yelled at each other and waved their arms about. The phone rang. Kevin shouted abuse at Phil and slammed the receiver down. More yelling. More arm waving. They pumped the cement.

The fog became thicker. The cement unit was disappearing. Jamie could feel the extractor fan at his neck. There was just one problem: it wasn't sucking, it was blowing. Some useless munt had wired the fan up the wrong way. It was going in the wrong direction. But this was soon the least of their worries. The unit fell silent. The diesel engine had died.

Kevin tore his face mask off. 'Useless little bastard!'

Jamie wasn't sure what he'd done, but he thought of making a run for it. He was convinced that Kevin was going to attack him. The cementer slid down the ladders and was onto Jamie in a flash. He grabbed Jamie by the scruff of the neck and dragged him out to the sack-store.

'The useless little wheezing cunt!' Kevin yelled. 'I'll kill Freddie! He told me he'd filled the diesel tank!'

There were six jerry cans in the sack-store. Kevin and Jamie each lugged one back to the unit, Kevin cursing Freddie every step of the way. At the diesel tank, Kevin rammed his face into Jamie's. 'Tell anybody that I ran out of diesel and I'll murder you. I want all six cans in there!' Kevin went back up his ladder and threw a plastic funnel at Jamie.

Jamie had only got about half a can in when the engines started. Kevin got on with mixing. When it came to the sixth can, Jamie could barely lift it up to the funnel. He spilled diesel everywhere, most of it over himself. He was one spark away from total immolation. He got the fire hose and sprayed it all over the place, making sure that he got a complete soaking himself. Nigel gave him a thumbs up. Then the jugs started coming again: 10.9 ; 11.4 ; 12.6 ; 13.8 ; 13.7. More yelling, more waving arms, more calls from the driller. More abuse. More pumping.

Finally, the engines died and Nigel came down from the unit. 'That went rather well,' he said.

'But none of the cement that we pumped down the hole was the right weight,' said Jamie.

'It never is.'

'Shouldn't we tell someone?'

'Are you insane? We can't have people telling people things. The oil industry will grind to a halt.'

'So I tell everybody that we pumped all the cement at 13.2 ppg and didn't run out of diesel?'

'That's what they want to hear. So that's what we'll tell them.'

'And if the well collapses?'

'We'll blame the seabed,' said Nigel.

'But why not just mix the cement at the right weight and not run out of diesel?'

'Because we're useless. Jamie, think of the people who were useless and lied out here twenty years ago. Where are they now? Behind big desks in Aberdeen and Houston, running the show. They expect us to be useless and lie. Nobody wants to hear bad news. Bad news just upsets people. Nobody cares about the half million people killed in the earthquake, they just want to see a baby plucked out the rubble.'

Nigel put his arms on Jamie's shoulders and looked him in the eye. 'Jamie, Kevin's a useless cementer. I'm a useless night company man. Walter's a useless OIM. And you're a useless mud engineer. You're going to mix the wrong things, get the wrong weights, change the wrong properties. Everything you touch will turn to rat shit. Your career will lurch from one catastrophe to the next. But nobody cares. Just make sure that you pluck a baby out the rubble.'

'But isn't that why the world is totally corrupt and totally awful?'

'That is exactly why the world is totally awful and totally corrupt. But that is also exactly why the world works.'

Chapter 21 A Little Feminine Help

There was a lonely character in the smoking tea shack. Phil the Driller's hand was trembling as he lifted the cigarette to his mouth for a short, nervous puff. His mustache was trembling even more than his hand. His eyes were wide and vacant, while his mind tried to apprehend the doom which awaited him. Jamie left Phil to himself and went to the non-smoker where he too sat alone.

While Phil seemed to be losing his wits, Jamie felt that he was gaining his own. He was amazed at how the weaknesses in others made you feel stronger. He was more amazed that it had taken the trauma of coming to work on an oil rig to make him realise it. The old made you feel young. Fools made you feel wise. Cock-ups made Freddie feel competent. Cowards made you feel brave. Yes, even cowards performed a useful function on the planet. People should thank them, Jamie thought – although no-one had thanked him these last thirty years. From his new-found position of strength, Jamie realised that he was in a position to help somebody. But he would have to overcome some fear of his own first. He would have to go to the logging shack and talk to Antonio Banderas about a pressing matter.

Phil had looked like the loneliest man on the planet. All that was missing was the albatross around his neck. Nobody would go near him now. He was a Jonah. In the olden days they would have keel-hauled him, made him walk the plank, or tipped him the Black Spot. So, in a way, things had improved. Phil merely faced demotion. And humiliation. It was enough.

Jamie went to the logging shack. 'I've come to ask you a favour.'

'I thought you'd come to apologise,' said Antonio Banderas.

'What for?'

'For being a man.'

Jamie found himself able to laugh. He was, indeed, gaining his wits. They were alone. Lat, mercifully, was winking somewhere else.

'I'm worried about Gray,' said Jamie.

The Iberian brow furrowed. 'He's not worried about you.'

'He doesn't have to. I don't need others to worry for me. I worry enough for myself.'

'If I were you Jaime, I'd be worried too.' Antonio Banderas tried to keep a straight face, but couldn't resist a smile. That smile meant more to Jamie than he could ever have imagined.

'The thing is Antonia, Gray's in a bad way. The whole Webster thing has been too much for him. He's been bubbling on the phone to his wife. He's getting sedatives from the medic.'

'Half the rig is getting sedatives from the medic. He's had to order extra supplies. I thought they were supposed to be North Sea tigers. They're more like North Sea pussies.'

'Who told you this?'

Antonio Banderas put her head in her hands. 'The medic,' she groaned. 'And the entire rig. Everyone is spilling their guts to me. Because I am a woman. It's unbearable.'

Jamie thought about placing a consoling hand on her shoulder, but decided better of it. 'I'll make you a cup of tea,' he said. 'De-ionised.'

'Yes, of course, it's Britain. Tea will solve everything.'

When they sat with their de-ionised tea, it was very nearly romantic.

'I notice that you weren't clapping during the rig manager's pep-talk,' said Jamie.

'I don't applaud killers.'

'Me neither.'

'I noticed. You were too busy watching the room. Do you think you are going to find the killer?'

'The police will never find the killer.'

'The police don't want to find the killer. That's why they sent Findon. He's a fool.'

Jamie watched Antonia closely. She had spoken the three words so matter-of-factly, but she had written off a man's life.

'If you find the killer Jaime, do you think you will impress someone?' She was now looking closely at him.

'Mainly myself.'

She shrugged. 'I guess you need all the help you can get.'

'Will you help with Gray? Sit with him at breakfast? Listen to him? He needs some tender, loving care from a female.'

'All right. Of course I'll help. But he's not the person in biggest trouble.'

'Who do you think that is?' said Jamie.

They looked at one another for a moment.

'Peachy.' They said the word together.

'I was able to speak to him privately. I told him I'd be there for him. Unconditionally. He says he's fine, but I'm worried.'

'You're worried about Peachy, you're worried about Gray...' Antonia was smiling, but Jamie wasn't quite sure why.

'I'm a worrier. I can't help it. To be honest, it's been a relief to have other people to worry about. I've been worried about no one other than myself for too long. I've been isolated. It's not healthy. Anyway, enough about me. I'm not important. Gray needs help and Peachy needs help. So I'll help.'

Antonia leaned back and looked lovely. 'I don't mean to be rude,' she said, 'and I know that you have only begun, but you are in the wrong occupation.'

'Why's that?'

'You are not selfish enough to work in the oil business. Everything that happens on here is to do with money. We come. We make a hole. We get some money. We go away and forget about each other. Money flows through the hole. It makes rich people richer. There is no sentiment. Nothing is done for goodness. This is Webster's industry. He dedicated his life to it. He gave his life for it. You have no place here.'

'And here was me just beginning to get into the machinery and the challenges and everything. It might not be a kind industry, but surely there's a place for a kind man in it?'

'Every minute that you spend out here will be a minute wasted. You don't understand the brutal numbers. I do. Maybe they'll toss me into a mud pit. Maybe it's all I am good for.' Antonia was now scowling. She forced herself out of it and brightened a little. 'Perhaps it is time that I moved on. I will help Gray as you asked. I don't think that I can do anything for Peachy. He gives me the creeps. He always has. His pastime disgusts me. He knows this and will never trust me. I notice that he didn't applaud the killer either.'

'Nor did Bill the Mechanic,' said Jamie.

'Or Ronnie the Roustie.' Antonio Banderas smiled.

'What was his excuse?'

She shrugged. 'Why would he tell me?'

When Jamie went outside, he was beside himself with excitement. Was Antonio Banderas's passionate love affair with Ronnie the Roustie on the rocks? Was there now room in her life for a spotty mud man? There was no time to waste. There were things to be done. But what was to be done? If catching a killer wasn't going to impress her? Striding across the oily pipedeck, it came to him: the way to impress Antonio Banderas was to not impress Antonio Banderas. He would do nothing, except his job. Yes, he would be amazingly, outstandingly, heroically and unbelievably good with drilling fluids. She would be impressed by his effortless proficiency and turned on by the nonchalant way that he refused to impress her with it. He would show her that he could take or leave this industry, just as it could take or leave him. If he was going to move on as she had suggested, he would do it on his terms. Jamie had been too needy, too keen to please. She had almost told him as much herself. Women liked men who were indifferent to women. And Spanish women liked men whose balls clacked together when they walked into a room.

From now on, Jamie was going to be cool, cruel and competent.

Chapter 22 Gumbo

It was during the drilling of the 24 inch section that Jamie became totally comfortable in the job. It was more difficult than the 36 inch section. It was a longer section. They drilled deeper. There were more and more frequent sweeps to be pumped. They coped admirably and never had to resort to the guar gum, which would have stank and blocked the mixing lines and the strainers to the pumps. Jamie was even able to thicken the spud mud by judicious additions of lime. The cement job on the 18 inch casing was a model of its type. The weights were all approximately okay. The job was good. The derrick was undamaged. The Manticore was back on track. There was just the small matter of the murdered toolpusher. If they struck oil, no one would be bothered.

The speed of operations even allowed them to run the riser before the weather deteriorated. The riser was the pipe which connected the rig to the well, isolating it from the wider environment. From now on, Jamie's fluid would operate on a closed loop, with rock cuttings being removed by the shale shakers.

Gray had improved under Antonio Banderas's attentions. She talked him down from the ledge, listened to his gibberish and sent him on with a smile on his face. It didn't improve his handovers, though.

'Tonight, said Gray, 'you're going to drill the 17 ½ inch section. It'll be fast. You might even finish it yourself. They'll run to bottom, then you'll displace the well to the potassium chloride mud which arrived today and is in the pits. There's potassium chloride liquor down the leg and there's a couple of pits of double-strength glycol. The specifications for the mud are in the program. Do the tests. Add the chemicals. If the mud gets badly out of shape, dump at the sandtraps and dilute the system with good mud from the pits. Easy. I think I'll take Beryl on a cruise.'

Gray left. Then returned.

'Oh, there might be a bit of gumbo.'

'What's gumbo?' said Jamie.

'It's thick clay. You'll know it when you see it.' Gray left again.

They held a Toolbox Talk in the doghouse. Since Jamie was notionally in charge of displacing the well from seawater to potassium chloride water-based mud, they let him lead the meeting. It was undoubtedly his finest moment on the rig so far. He was really, really competent.

'We're going to displace the well to potassium chloride mud and drill the 17 ½ inch section,' he began. 'And to do this with no accidents or incidents. You all have a pumping plan. Scottie will basically pump from Active 1, the Webster Pit, and top this up from Reserve 1. I'll be at the shakers and when I see good mud, we'll stop dumping and close the system in. I'll tell the loggers and the driller and then we'll drill out the shoe and drill ahead, dumping cuttings at the shakers. Are we set up to do that?'

'Roger that,' said Mark Z.

'And we'll take potassium chloride liquor up from the leg as required. Are the permits in place to do that?'

'Aye aye,' said Scottie.

'Any questions?'

'Is there a leak off test?' said Phil.

Jamie had no idea what a leak-off test was. 'No,' he said emphatically. No one contradicted him. 'Any other questions?'

'Now that we're on a closed-loop, I'll need you to let me know if you are dumping,' said Antonio Banderas.

'I will. We'll dump at the sand-traps,' said Jamie.

'It's easier to dump at the shakers,' said Mark Z.

'We'll dump at the shakers,' said Jamie.

'Excellent,' said Nigel the Night Company Man.

'We're Golfing With The Right People,' said Dave the Night Toolpusher.

'Let's TD this baby before the shift ends,' said Jamie. He really felt like one of the boys now.

'Okay,' said Phil the Driller. 'Hold on to your hats.'

Jamie went to the shale shakers. For the first time, they were turned on. They were making an awful racket and shaking like buggery. The entire shaker house was shaking like buggery. Jamie was armed with the primary tool of his trade: a plastic jug. The cacophony of the shakers was joined by the faint murmur of the pumps. Seawater soon flowed back along the flowline. Jamie took a sample with his jug. Yes, it was definitely seawater. Mark Z telephoned the driller to confirm that they had seawater returns at the shakers. Five minutes later, the returns turned milky and heavy. Jamie took a sample in his jug. It was the mud. Jamie signalled Mark Z, who closed a couple of valves, diverting the flow over the shakers. The system was closed in. The well had been displaced. Easy.

The first returns of rock cuttings took another ten minutes to arrive at the shakers. It was exactly what Jamie had imagined. There were small hard pieces; some with scrape marks from the drill bit.

'Cement,' said Mark Z.

'I never knew the North Sea had formations of cement,' said Jamie.

'It's the cement from the last cement job.'

'Oh.'

Things changed for the worse very quickly thereafter.

The nice, neat little cement pieces turned into a slight sludge. The slight sludge turned into persistent sludge. The persistent sludge turned into a catastrophic nightmare of thick, heavy sludge. It poured over the front of the shakers, taking rivers of Jamie's precious mud with it.

Desperate Dan broke out a fire hose.

'Don't,' Jamie wailed, 'you'll ruin my properties!'

'Fuck your properties.'

Desperate Dan turned on the hose and blasted away at the screens. He showered Mark Z with mud and clay. Mark Z was behind, raising the gates because the mud was overflowing the tank behind the shakers. The mud was also overflowing the front of the shakers. Jamie mouth went dry. This was a live well and he hadn't a clue what he was doing.

'Your fucking mud's mince!' screamed Mark Z, grabbing a second fire hose.

The hosing did help matters at the shakers. All Jamie could think about was the unwanted dilution. This would lighten the weight of the fluid, noxious gases would rise up from the formation and the rig would blow.

Mark Z threw a homemade metal implement at Jamie.

'Rake!'

It looked a bit like a rake. Jamie could see no weeds, but he assumed he was to pull the sludge from the top of the screens. Clay lumps the size of cow pats were coming over the top screens. Jamie pulled sludge and mud from one shaker. Things improved briefly. He moved along all four. He was engaged in an ordeal of Forth Bridge proportions. By the time he had finished the last, fluid was flooding over the front of the first. Mark Z was hosing behind him. Desperate Dan was on the phone, talking to somebody competent.

Jamie and Mark Z's rake and hose routine was working quite well. It calmed Jamie's nerves – a little. At least he was doing something positive for the cause. God alone knew what was happening to the properties of the fluid that he was supposed to be monitoring.

Jamie heard his name being called vaguely in the midst of this surreal scene. He was covered in shit. Clay and mud were seeping through his coveralls and leaking down his boots. His face was spattered and he could hardly see through his safety glasses. Was potassium chloride good for the skin and the lungs?

Extra bodies arrived. Ronnie the Roustie took Jamie's rake away.

'You were tannoyed. Phone the loggers.'

Jamie used his most commanding and competent voice. 'Mud engineer here. I believe you tannoyed me.'

'Jaime,' said an irritated Spanish voice, 'we seem to be taking losses. Are you dumping mud?'

Jamie looked at the bedlam in front of him. Fluid was leaking over the front of every shaker. Straight out to sea.

'Yes,' said Jamie.

'You were supposed to tell me! Are you trying to make me look stupid?'

'No.'

'Why are you dumping?'

'We can't help it, it's kind of dumping itself.'

'Are you a moron?'

'It's flowing over the front of the shakers.'

'Tell the driller to slow the pumps.'

Jamie phoned Phil the Driller. 'Slow the pumps,' said Jamie.

'Fuck off,' said Phil the Driller.

Jamie phoned Antonio Banderas. 'Phil told me to fuck off.'

'Change the screens,' said Antonio Banderas.

'Change the screens,' said Jamie.

'Fuck off,' said the roughnecks.

'The roughnecks told me to fuck off,' said Jamie. 'What do you want me to do?'

'I want you to fuck off!' shrieked Antonio Banderas. 'How long are you going to be dumping for?'

'Don't quote me on this, but I think we're going to be dumping pretty continuously most of the night,' yelled Jamie.

A third fire hose was trained on the shakers. On full pressure.

'But we're adding a bit of water as well.'

'How fast are you adding?'

'It's kind of difficult to say, Antonia.'

'How am I supposed to monitor the well?'

'Guess?'

Antonio Banderas let out a Spanish scream and hung up. When Jamie hung up, the phone rang straight away. It was Scottie.

'The weight's up. The Vis is up. And I need volume.'

'I'm shouting as loud as I can!' replied Jamie.

'I need more volume of fluid in the Active pit!' screamed Scottie.

'What do you want me to do?'

'Add something!'

'Add what?'

'What have you got?'

'I've got an idiot on the other end of this phone! Do you want water, liquor, or reserve mud?'

After thirty years of blissful dithering, Jamie encountered his first moment of decisiveness.

'Water.'

When Jamie burst into the cabin, Gray was watching a soap opera. One of the characters was undergoing a minor emotional problem.

Jamie was undergoing a major emotional problem. 'You've got to come out. All hell's broken loose,' he panted. 'Mud's pouring over the front of the shakers. They're hosing seawater all over the place. The weight's up. The Vis is up. I don't know what I'm doing.'

'You could at least have knocked,' said Gray woundedly.

'You better come,' pleaded Jamie shrilly.

'I've got every intention of coming,' replied Gray emphatically. 'But not outside.'

Gray lay back and scratched himself. He was indifference itself.

'What's coming over the shakers?' he said.

'Massive lumps of gooey stuff. It's horrific!'

'That'll be the gumbo. What are you adding?'

'Three seawater hoses at the shakers and more water at the pits.'

'Sounds like gumbo, right enough. You might want to add a bit of liquor now and again.'

'Are you not coming out?' Jamie tried to sound as pathetic as he could.

'No. You're fine. Sounds to me like you're on top of things. Consider it a learning curve.'

Jamie could quite happily have murdered Gray where he lay. He retreated slowly, staring at Gray's fat, callous form.

Gray motioned Jamie to close the door. 'And if anyone gives you any shit, tell them: "It's the gumbo". You'll be fine.'

Armed with three words, Jamie sauntered reluctantly back out into the war zone. He'd forgotten to pick up his spare pair of coveralls in the room, so he struggled into his soaked pair and squelched his feet into his boots. He didn't even have the time to get outside before Scottie tannoyed him. Jamie had already come to dread the tannoy's "PING PONG" call. His heart instinctively sank every time he heard it. He hadn't heard anyone else tannoyed all night. Maybe they weren't drilling at all. Maybe they'd sneaked away to play cards and were taking it in turns to torture him.

'The weight's fine but the Vis is through the roof.'

'Add a bit of liquor.'

'Can't.'

'Why not?'

'Active pit's full.'

'How come?'

'I added water. Like you told me to.'

'I'll be down in a minute,' Jamie lied. He had no intention of going down. All he wanted to do was crawl into the quietest hole he could find. And hide. Jamie hoped that if he avoided everyone for a couple of hours, all his problems would go away.

He staggered back outside, struggling with the watertight door. If he'd been able to notice, it was a beautiful autumnal night. But beautiful autumnal nights don't exist in hell.

Some base animal instinct took him back up to the shakers - anywhere but the pit room, where he would be faced with more decisions.

'IT'S YOUR FUCKING MUD!' screamed an unidentifiable, hose-wielding, clay-covered crewmember.

'IT'S THE GUMBO!' screamed Jamie.

There was now a raker on every shaker. There would have been a hose on every shaker too – if they had had enough hoses. The nightmare was growing.

A light flashed above Jamie's head. A siren sounded. It was a telephone call. It was for Jamie.

'Mud engineer!' he wailed.

'What about this vis?' said Peachy. 'We haven't added Glycol. And there's cans of polymer. I'm sure they're supposed to go in. And what are we doing for volume?'

'I thought the pit was full?'

'Not any more. Phil's drilling like a maniac, trying to make up for crowning the Top Drive.'

A tannoy went out from Phil. 'Roughnecks to the drillfloor. Connection.'

Half the guys in the shaker house dropped their rakes and hoses and departed. Mud flooded over the front of the shakers.

'Don't go!' Jamie pleaded.

'Fuck off!'

'Add reserve mud,' Jamie said to Peachy.

'What pit?'

'Any pit! I'm gonna check the mud and I'll get back to you.'

Jamie had no sooner hung up than the phone rang.

'Are you dumping again you foolish, idiotic, moronic, imbecilic, clown of a son of a whore of a bitch?' said a familiar Spanish voice.

Whatever else, Jamie was impressed by the girl's range of vocabulary.

'Er, the boys walked out to go and make a connection. I tried to stop them, but they told me to...'

'Fuck off.'

'Yes. And then mud flooded over the front of the shakers. And it still is.'

'You wretched, pathetic sorry excuse for a human being. I will see you in hell.'

'Well stuff you too honey. And stuff the Spanish donkey you rode in on.' Jamie slammed the phone down.

The flooding over the shakers stopped. The pumps had been turned off.

Jamie wandered over to Ronnie the Roustie, who was standing in the quietest part of the shaker house. 'That Spanish girl's got a bit of spirit.'

'Tell me about it,' said Ronnie.

'How did you manage to win her over?'

'Charmed her. Teased her. Provoked her. Drove her mad with desire. It's been non-stop sex ever since.'

It had been a bad night, but this last sentence really made Jamie want to weep.

'I'd be in there knobbing her now, if it wasn't for that Indian twat.'

'At least you're having a better night than I am.'

'The entire rig's having a better night than you are. Gray's dropped you right in it. Leaving you to survive a gumbo section alone on your first trip? Old bastard.'

All the mud had drained away from the shale shakers. The screens, which were supposed to sieve out the solids, had massive holes in them.

'No wonder the mud's getting heavy and thick,' said Jamie. 'The clay's going right through the screens. I'm really fucked now.'

'The raking fucks them. Best bet is to put on coarse screens. They'll last longer. Fine mesh will take out more clay at the beginning, but they'll puncture and let more through in the long run.'

'It's the weight I'm worried about. I don't want to blow the rig up.'

Ronnie smiled. 'You won't blow the rig up on a gumbo section. You're more likely to get the drillstring stuck.'

'Please,' said Jamie. 'I don't want to know. There's only so much worrying one brain can do.'

'All you can do tonight Jamie is to keep dumping and throw fresh mud and chemicals in when it gets too heavy or too thick. The driller's on a mission to make hole. He's not going to slow down or cut his pump rate for any man. Go and check your mud, it'll calm you down.'

The mud check didn't calm Jamie down. Every single one of the properties of his fluid was out of spec. It was too heavy. It was too thick. It had too many solids. It came as no surprise that there was too much clay in it. The big surprise was that he was even able to perform the test to find out that there was too much clay in it. This was an horrendous procedure involving hydrogen peroxide, a lot of heat and methylene blue. When he finally spotted the "halo" that marked an end point in the test, he almost fainted. There was an unbelievable amount of clay in the mud.

The phone kept ringing during the check.

'We need volume.'

'Liquor.'

'The weight's up.'

'Water.'

'Are you dumping again, you double-crossing, evil crock of sheet?'

'They're changing screens on the shale shakers. The driller won't slow the pumps. Shout at him.'

Jamie's heart was in his squelchy boots. It was time to admit defeat, confess to the company man, get Gray out of his bed and reserve a seat on the next chopper home. Having abandoned all hope, Jamie knew that there was only one place for him to go: the tea shack. It was busy. It was covered in clay. Jamie was expecting recriminations. Instead, he was given a cup of tea and a cigarette.

'You look fucked,' said Mark Z.

'I am fucked,' said Jamie.

'Have you got a plan?'

'No.'

'You really are fucked.'

Jamie sucked gratefully on his cigarette. It felt utterly delicious. Giving in was great. It was in this state of blissful resignation that things began to happen in Jamie's head. From somewhere in the ether, a memory appeared. The memory led to a concept. The concept led to an idea. The idea led...

'What's up with you?' said Antonio Banderas, blowing smoke elegantly through her pouting lips. 'You're smiling.'

'I've got a plan.'

At this, Dave the Night Pusher and Nigel the Night Company Man arrived. They were the only two people not yet covered in clay. Even Antonio Banderas had been splattered. Every 100 feet, the loggers were supposed to take samples of the rock that was coming over the shakers. Here, they'd been taking samples of sludge.

'What's up with your mud?' said Dave.

'Dunno Dave, what's up with your derrick?'

'There's nothing wrong with my derrick,' said Dave sullenly. 'The weight and the pump pressure's going up and down like a whore's drawers.'

'Whores don't wear drawers,' said Mark Z. Take it from me.'

Dave gritted his teeth. Not only was Mark Z not respecting his Toolpushing authority, he was making Dave look like he wasn't a man of the world. Two Golfing With The Wrong Peoples in one. Dave's Golfing With The Wrong People list was now over four pages long. His Golfing With The Right People list could be written on the back of an envelope. It was a tough life.

All of this made Dave even more determined to make Jamie look stupid. 'Your mud's out of control, you haven't a clue and you're in the tea shack,' he said.

'Your toolpusher's dead, your driller's out of control, you haven't a clue and YOU'RE in the tea shack. Welcome to the club.'

Stung, Dave opened and closed his mouth, but no words came out. He looked like a goldfish.

Jamie decided that the only thing to be done in a situation like this was to revert to full bullshit mode. 'I've just checked the mud,

Dave. All the properties are under control. We've got plenty of chemicals to get us to the end of the section. That's why I'm in the tea shack. Which property in particular were you worried about?'

'Well, em, the weight..'

'We're drilling through gumbo, Dave. Of course the weight's up and down a bit. The clay is blinding the shaker screens. We can't use fine mesh screens. We're using hoses. What do you want us to do?'

'Oh, I..'

'We're drilling up a storm, aren't we Nigel?'

'Oh yes,' said Nigel.

'You're happy with the speed we're drilling?'

'Certainly.'

'So what do you want Dave? You want us to slow down?'

'Suppose everything's all right

'Well you leave me to run the mud and I'll leave you to.....' Jamie left the word hanging as an insult. What did Dave do? He pissed people off, got in the way and mutilated the midnight report. He not only Golfed With the Wrong People, he spent most of his time in the rough.

Back in the pit room, Jamie did some quick sums.

'How far have we got to drill?'

'Six hundred feet,' said Peachy.

Jamie divided the chemicals he had left by six.

'Okay,' he said, 'every hundred feet, we need to add this.'

'Fuck me,' said Peachy. 'You've got a plan.'

'Scottie said to throw chemicals at the problem, so I'm going to throw every chemical we've got at it.'

'Just remember that we'll need a few hundred barrels of mud to cement with.'

'What do you mean?'

'When we come to cement the 13 3/8 inch casing, we'll need a few hundred barrels of mud to pump behind the cement to displace it. When we run the casing in the hole, that should give us some mud back, but sometimes you get losses. I'm just warning you.'

'Thanks Peachy. What's that mark on your neck?'

Peachy's makeshift cravat had slipped, revealing a raw, red mark on his neck.

Peachy pulled the cravat self-consciously back over the wound. 'On the drillfloor. We were man-riding. I wasn't looking where I was going. Grazed it on the metal tugger line. My fault. Didn't want to report it. Webster would have gone mental. You know what he was like. There weren't any incidents when Webster was aboard. Guys on here will put tape on a cut rather than report it. You know what I mean?'

'I know,' said Jamie, but he didn't.

Peachy drifted off to the sack-store. Jamie watched Scottie weaving in and out of the forest of valve handles, expertly avoiding the pipes which came down from the ceiling and those that lay on the metal deck. One valve was cracked open a little more, another cracked shut a little more. A torch was twisted on. A pit level was checked. The torch twisted off again. A call was made to the loggers. The Active pit (the Webster pit) had a float, whose indicator could be easily read off a scale. At a glance, the derrickman could see if the pit level was going down or up over time, indicating that the well was either losing fluid or gaining it. Here, the pit level was going down steadily. But that volume was being used simply to fill the hole that they were drilling so quickly. Antonio Banderas was doing those sums. She had electronic monitors in every pit. Scottie and Peachy told her about every transfer of fluid, every addition of every sack. When the sums didn't add up, it spelled trouble, sometimes big trouble. That was why she had been so angry at Jamie.

Scottie came over. Sweat was funnelling down his cheeks and dripping off his chin. He took his hard hat off, wiped his brow and spat into a pit. 'Weight's more or less steady,' he said. 'What's happening?'

'I've got a plan,' said Jamie.

'That's us fucked,' said Scottie.

They got into a regular routine of dosing the fluid with liquor and reserve mud. They stopped adding water. The hoses at the shakers were putting enough in. To add polymer, they poked holes in the cans and let it dribble in via the flowline.

The scene in the shaker house was apocalyptic. Wraith-like figures were moving around in a thick mist. The shale shakers were roaring angrily, disgorging steam and sludge and liquid. Condensation was raining on the entire, toxic scene. Jamie donned a mask and ear defenders and entered the fray. The principal sound he could hear now was that of his own breathing. The shakers were reduced to a mere hum and the blasts of the hoses sounded like little more than playful squirts. It gave a surreal sense to what was already a surreal experience. Jamie's glasses quickly steamed and reduced his field of vision to a couple of feet. In this sensory deprived world, he felt as if he was sleepwalking over the hoses and the slime.

'YOUR MUD'S SHITE!' they shouted.

'IT'S THE GUMBO!' he shouted back.

Jamie got the guys to turn the hoses off. The raking continued. Fluid flooded over the front of the shakers. Jamie told Antonio Banderas that they were dumping. He even told Phil the Driller. After five minutes, Jamie told the boys to start hosing again.

A magical thing happened: no one argued. It was as if they thought that Jamie knew what he was doing.

After the dump, Jamie went back down to the pits. Scottie was mopping his face with a rag. The pit room was an oasis of calm compared to the shaker house. The mud pumps provided a reassuring rumble.

'I've some absolutely astounding news,' said Scottie gravely.

'What's that?' said Jamie, a knot of fear forming in his stomach.

'The weight is spot on, so is the viscosity and the pump pressure has dropped 300 psi. Phil has stopped complaining. Your mud even looks like proper mud.'

'That's unbelievable,' said Jamie.

'Fuck knows how it happened, but your plan seems to have worked.'

'Incredible, isn't it?'

'We're going to TD the section by the end of the shift. They'll be throwing their hats in the air on the Beach. It's a major result.'

'And all down to my mud.'

Scottie spat and laughed. 'You've learned fast. Never let an opportunity to take credit pass you by. You'll have to fight Phil, though. He'll want to claim this as the product of his glorious drilling skills. The arsehole.'

'He'll want to repair his dented pride.'

'He needs to repair his dented derrick. Anyway, we'll be needing a slug and a hi-vis pill for TD.'

Jamie sighed. Out here, there was always something else that you didn't know. 'What the hell are a slug and a hi-vis pill?'

'We'll need about 30 barrels of heavy mud to put in the top of the pipe for when we pull out of the hole. It forces all the mud out of the pipe, so that when we disconnect on the drillfloor the boys don't get soaked. 1 ½ to 2 pounds per gallon heavier mud is normally good enough. A hi-vis pill is pumped around the hole to clear all the shite out before we pull out the hole. Stop us getting stuck on the way out. 50 to 100 barrels of thick shit. We can add some viscosifier to what's left in Reserve 3. I've already put mud in the slug pit and Peachy is weighing it up with barite as we speak.'

'You think of everything.'

'No, it was Peachy. Didn't want to get caught out. Terrified of Phil. Being the coward that he is, Phil's lashing out at Peachy after crowning the top drive. Well, he'll have to walk over me to get to Peachy.'

'I'm glad you're looking after him. I'm worried about Peachy. What happened to his neck?'

Scottie stared angrily at Jamie. 'Never you mind what happened to Peachy. He's fine. You want to sort yourself out. You're clinging on here by your fingernails. And you didn't tell me when you were dumping. I looked a right twat when I phoned Antonio Banderas.

'Sorry.'

'And I'm fucking sorry you were ever born.'

As Jamie squirmed under Scottie's glare, he suddenly felt very isolated. A man's screams would be drowned out by the din of the pumps. There were plenty of heavy, blunt instruments lying around. A picture formed in Jamie's mind of a bludgeoned, drowned body, rotating slowly in one of the darkened pits below his feet.

Scottie brightened. 'Let me worry about Peachy. He'll be fine.'

Watching Scottie growing moody and then brightening put Jamie in mind of Antonia and, particularly, Gray. So many people out here seemed to tend toward gloominess and then had to remind themselves to cheer up. Or in Gray's case, they forgot to remind themselves to cheer up. It was something to do with the peculiar set of pressures that everyone was under and that Jamie was coming to understand. People were isolated from their loved ones and living with the constant fear of the next catastrophe, which was never far away and potentially going to be their fault. All this in an industry obsessively driven by money. The best that could happen was they could lose their jobs and their livelihoods. In the worst case, they would all be blown to smithereens. Antonia was wrong: there was more kindness needed, not less.

Jamie now also knew that Scottie was the prime suspect. Anyone else committing a murder in the pit room would be concerned that Scottie could return at any moment. Or perhaps Scottie's absence was eloquent proof of his silent complicity? Or the murderer wielded enough power on the rig to make sure that Scottie was elsewhere? That, then, would be Phil the Driller.

Jamie looked around the scene of John Webster's final moments. As bad places to die went, this was as bad a place as any. It was a cold, functional, steel tomb. Valve handles protruded to spear the unwary. The only item of comfort was a cheap office chair, slashed, taped and disgorging its foam. The only sign of gaiety was the red and yellow paint marking the two mixing lines. The only decoration was a topless calendar above the derrickman's desk.

By the end of the section, the situation at the shakers had been brought under control. The clay coming over the screens was firmer and managed by occasional blasts of one hose. All raking had ceased. There was a bit of a to-do when the high-vis pill came back. It brought a huge amount of "shite" (the official term) with it. There was flooding, hosing and raking, as bad as anything that had been. Suddenly, the flow of clay dropped to almost nothing and Nigel the Night Company Man appeared at Jamie's shoulder with Dave the Night Toolpusher.

'Well?' said Nigel.

'Well what?' said Jamie.

'Jamie, you're supposed to tell us when you're happy with the shakers.'

'I'm a bit disappointed with the shakers, to be honest. They didn't really handle the gumbo very well.'

'Jamie, you're supposed to tell us that you are happy with the amount of cuttings coming over the shakers. That the low amount of returns indicated that the well is clear and it is safe to pull out.'

'Isn't there somebody more senior?'

'It's your job.'

'And if I'm wrong?'

'Dave and I will back you up.'

This was utterly unconvincing. Jamie studied the occasional lumps of clay bouncing off the top screens and the steady stream of fines coming off the bottom ones. The only thing that he was sure of was that if he delayed things until Gray came out, he wouldn't be popular. 'Looks okay to me,' he said.

'So we can come out of the hole?'

Jamie was gobsmacked. This wasn't a wind-up. The oil industry really would place such an important decision in the hands of a complete incompetent. 'Yes, let's come out the hole.'

Nigel called Phil the Driller. 'Flow check for ten minutes. If the well's static, pump the slug. We're coming out.'

'Your mud's shite,' said a Stewardess, mopping clay off the lockers.

'It's the gumbo,' said Jamie wearily. Everyone on the rig was an expert. He went into the smoko, where Walter was holding court.

'I've decided to go back on the tabs until I retire,' he said, drawing lustily on a cancer stick. 'There's too few pleasures out here, what with dead 'Pushers and Detectives and all. Here's the hero! Fancy a tab Jamie?'

Jamie gratefully accepted a cigarette.

'I didn't know you smoked.'

'I've started for similar reasons to yourself. I also intend to keep smoking until I retire.'

This got a good laugh – from everybody apart from Phil.

'I tell you what,' Walter went on, 'if I have to listen to one more conversation between Gray and his beloved Beryl, I think I'll top myself. I've never heard a married couple talk such utter drivel to one another. They call each other all these stupid names: Boo-Boo; Pinkie; Honey-Bun; Babesey; Darling Larlin. Yesterday, she called him her little Ramekin. What the hell is a Ramekin? And if I hear another word about the holiday home in the Dordogne...'

Gray, at handover, was in a great mood. 'Don't keep me too long, I'm having breakfast with Antonio Banderas. What a lovely girl she is. You should consider sticking your oar in there.'

Jamie considered wrapping his hands around Gray's fat, complacent neck and squeezing. 'Thanks for all the help with the gumbo. You dropped me right in it. You wouldn't even come out and help. You gave me no warning. No advice. No decent handover notes. Nothing.'

'And look how magnificently you coped. You're the toast of the rig. The Beach is delighted. I'd say I'm getting things just about right regarding your training.'

'Training?!!!'

'Only next time, ease up a bit. You used enough chemicals to drill the section twice over.' Gray got up and patted his stomach. 'Nothing for me to do today. Better make sure you've got enough mud. They'll probably cement the 13 3/8 inch casing tonight. They don't mess around running casing through gumbo. The hole doesn't stay open long. I'm off. I've got a date with a Spanish lovely.'

Jamie could only shake his head as he watched Gray's enormous figure recede. He was joined by Scottie. 'Gray doing your head in?'

'You know,' said Jamie, 'it's amazing there aren't a lot more murders on oil rigs. I'll quite happily add to the tally.'

'I can't guarantee you a murder, but I can guarantee you a fight.'

'Between who?'

'Me and Phil.'

Chapter 23 Midnight's Children

The room no longer depressed Jamie. This offshore prison camp had quickly become his reality. He was beginning to doubt whether he would ever see his loved ones again, although he was realising that in order to call them "loved ones", he had better start actually loving them. He was avoiding Antonio Banderas after the gumbo dumping debacle and was happy to slip into the room to watch a bit of television before going to sleep.

The news seemed to relate to people who were living on a different planet. The Manticore's reality was utterly removed from that parallel universe. Somehow it didn't seem right that the BBC weren't announcing the successful TD of the 17 ½ inch section and the heroics of the night mud engineer in the face of horrific gumbo. The rig's progress hadn't made any of the economic reports, the ongoing investigation into the toolpusher's murder was missing from the crime bulletin and the upcoming fight between the driller and the derrickman was totally absent from the sports section. The news was all wrong.

Jamie didn't so much sleep as fall into total unconsciousness.

That evening, Jamie received another comprehensive handover from Gray. 'The rig's on a burn. I've never seen anything like it out here. Just shows what the odd murder of senior management can do for productivity. You'll be cementing the 13 3/8 inch casing tonight. You won't be taking weights because you'll be needed in the pits. Now that we're on a closed system, you've to monitor for losses. Get dips from all the pits before you start and once you finish. At the end of the cement job, you should have gained a volume equal to the amount of cement mixed and pumped. Easy.'

Gray had done absolutely nothing all day. Jamie only discovered this when he came to do the midnight report. When they had been drilling with seawater and sweeps, it had been easy. Now, every barrel of volume and every sack and can of chemicals had to be costed.

Clients generally like to be appraised of how much money they're spending. Oil companies, perversely attached to the stuff, want to hear about it every single day of the operation. So, in the field of drilling liquids, was invented the Daily Mud Report. Generated each day at midnight, this document served to torture night engineers the world over. This was Jamie's first proper taste of it. Gray had double-crossed him again.

There was one important thing to be said about the Daily Mud Report:

No one ever read it.

There was another important thing to be said about the Daily Mud Report:

They only read it if they wanted to blame something on the mud company.

Jamie was about to be inducted into fellowship of the Service Companies' Meaningless Report Generating Brotherhood.

They were all at it: Directional Drillers (we're lost); Measurement While Drilling (we know they're lost); Loggers (we told you they'd get lost); Geologists (don't blame us, the rocks haven't moved); Wellhead Specialists (WE weren't lost); Fishing Companies (the whole well is lost); Cementers (who cares who's lost, we'll cement it up anyway); Environmental Services (all may be lost but we saw a lovely dolphin today) and the Mud Engineers (why it's the fluid's fault that everything is lost).

All the bedraggled night company man really wanted was a single figure from every company that he could total up into one big number of how much they'd spent that day. But that was too easy. No, the buggers had to hide the figures in three pages each of justification:

How We Spent Your Money Today

Drilling Contractor – On a rig that doesn't work, serving food you cannot eat.

Directional Drillers – On tools and men that won't do what we want them to.

MWD – On things that are too complicated to explain, but easy to charge for.

Loggers – On things you never wanted to know, but we like to tell you.

Geologists – On multiple excuses as to why the rocks aren't where we said they were.

Environmental – On binoculars, fetching weatherproof coats and beard-trimmers.

Cementers – On hideously expensive cement and fluffy pillows.

Mud Engineers – On providing a 24 hour scapegoat service.

It was meaningless, but it was important. There were more spankings handed out because of paperwork than ever there were for incompetence on the actual job. The incompetence was expected. The paperwork had to be perfect. Jamie had come out expecting the wild frontier. He now saw that his primary function was to be little more than an office boy. His daily struggle with the Daily Mud Report would now become the lowlight of every day.

It was to change the meaning of midnight for Jamie forever.

Jamie had been stuck in front of the computer since eleven o'clock, filling in fictitious values for mud checks that he hadn't done at times and depths that he could only guess at. Someone had helpfully filled in the specifications for most of the values and Jamie obligingly stuck to these. It made him look good. At least the fictitious fluid in the report would be in good shape. The volumes were a disaster. Jamie added virtual water, virtual liquor and virtual chemicals. He transferred imaginary fluid between pits and down the hole. He hid a hundred barrels in the Trip Tank, but this did no good so he dumped it instead. Then he realised his real problem: he needed to know how much fluid was in every pit, how many chemicals were left, how much liquor was down the leg and how much hole they'd made. The guys in the control room were less than helpful, refusing to dip the leg tank before 1 am. It didn't matter. Jamie was still tearing his hair out at 2 am. He went down to the sack-store to try and make sense of his inventory.

When he got there, he was confronted by a disturbing sight: Mark Z was striking Peachy repeatedly about the head.

'Where is it? You know where it is. Tell me!' The blows were becoming heavier.

Peachy cowered. He looked utterly wretched. 'He just used me! He didn't tell me anything! Please!'

'Leave him,' said Jamie.

Mark Z paused.

'It's all right Jamie,' Peachy pleaded. 'It's my fault.'

'Yes,' said Mark Z. 'Fuck off.'

'I'm going nowhere,' said Jamie. 'You're leaving him alone.'

Mark Z pushed Peachy to one side and confronted Jamie. 'That clown almost had me killed.'

'It's true,' said Peachy. His voice was distressed – and distressing.

'You're not going to solve anything this way,' said Jamie. 'Peachy, go away. Me and Mark will sort this out.'

'Don't you dare move,' said Mark Z.

'Peachy,' Jamie's voice was steady, 'I said go.' He looked directly at Peachy. 'You'll be fine. Go.'

'Sorry Mark.' Peachy skulked off.

Mark Z squared up to Jamie. 'So the mud engineer thinks he's a man?'

'You think you're a man by beating somebody as pathetic as Peachy? Beat me if you're going to beat anyone.'

'I might just do that. Come on into the pit room, we'll see if we can find a pit for you to hang out in.'

Jamie took a step back, to try and create some breathing space for himself. 'What's going on?'

'It's drillfloor stuff. Where the men of the rig work.'

'What are you looking for, Webster's money?'

'It's nothing to do with you.' Mark Z closed the space between them.

Jamie felt very isolated once again. It was chilling.

'Somebody else is going to die out here,' Mark Z said. 'It might be you.'

He backed off slowly. 'Stay away from me, Mud Man. You don't understand what's going on out here. You're out your depth. You're a prick.'

Jamie took a couple of moments to compose himself. He was frightened now. Mark Z was right. There was going to be another death. He could sense it, as he could sense that he was being watched. Jamie looked up. He saw Findon and Antonia standing on the gantry. Findon was grinning like a Cheshire Cat - a mangy, flea-ridden Cheshire Cat.

***

Jamie finished his report and sent it. It was all wrong, but now it was all right because everything on the rig was all wrong. If he wasn't killed, he'd be dismissed for incompetence. The cement job began at 3 am. Scottie diligently took dips of all the pits.

Peachy took Jamie to one side. 'Don't tell Scottie what happened. Please.'

Jamie made no reply. He looked closely at Peachy. He seemed to have cheered.

'I've got some fantastic porn you can have,' Peachy added, eagerly.

'It's okay Peachy, I won't tell a soul,' said Jamie. 'And I don't need porn.'

'Everybody needs porn.' Peachy's eyes were alive with possibilities.

'Of course,' said Jamie doubtfully. 'I'll drop by when I need it.'

Peachy winked. 'All tastes catered for.'

Scottie came over. 'There's a problem,' he said.

'Day shift shafted us again?' said Jamie.

'Exactly. We're supposed to displace the cement with 372 barrels of mud. We've only got 430.'

'What's up with that?'

'What's up with that is that there's forty barrels of dead volume in the bottom of each pit that I can't get to. So if we don't see any returns from pumping cement, we're stuffed.'

'Surely we'll get something back?'

'We started taking losses on the last few joints of casing,' said Peachy.

'Sometimes you get nothing back,' said Scottie.

'We're stuffed,' said Jamie.

'What do you want us to do?'

'Put 150 barrels of seawater in Reserve 2 and we'll add four sacks of viscosifier. Then add enough barite to get it to the same weight as the mud. It won't have any properties, but it'll be going inside casing anyway. So long as it's the right weight.'

Scottie looked at Jamie in amazement. He was impressed.

Jamie rang Antonio Banderas. 'We're filling Reserve 2 and mixing barite. Gray's shafted me again. He hasn't left me enough mud.'

Antonio Banderas groaned. 'Please tell me that I don't have to have another meal with that man. I think I'll kill myself.'

'I might have known,' said Jamie. 'Instead of you raising him up, he's dragging you down.'

'I think he wants have sex with me,' said Antonio Banderas.

'Most of the rig wants to have sex with you.'

There was a pause on the other end of the line. Then Antonio Banderas laughed. 'That may be true,' she said, 'but I am not so flattered. You are all desperate.'

'You've got us figured out. We are desperate. But you are beautiful too, so don't be so hard on yourself. Let me take over the impossible task of cheering Gray up.'

Antonio Banderas let out an Hispanic shriek of delight. 'I love you, Jaime,' she breathed.

Jamie felt his legs wobble. She was joking, but she had at least said the words. It was a start. 'What was Detective Findon doing?' he said.

'He really really wants to have sex with me. He has switched onto nights. He said that the suspects are on the night shift. The day shift all have good ali, ali..'

'Alibis.'

'Yes. The killer is one of us.'

An hour later, Jamie found himself in amongst the barite hoppers with a mallet in his hand. He was aiming random blows at assorted pieces of pipe in an attempt to clear a blockage. Kevin the Cementer came by.

'You almost look like a cementer. Give it here.'

Kevin seized the mallet from Jamie and began beating the shit out of any pipe that was within his reach. He was hitting them ten times harder than Jamie had managed, making Jamie think that Kevin would have had no problem felling Webster with a single blow. Kevin was grinning manically.

'What's so funny?'

'My bonus,' said Kevin. 'The more cement jobs I do, the bigger my bonus. Three this trip. I'm making a fortune.'

'You must be the only happy person on the rig.'

'Amazing, isn't it?'

'Tell me something.' Jamie steered Kevin over to a corner of the silo room. 'That wee silo tucked in at the back.' Jamie pointed to a vessel in the corner whose valve was locked off with a bright red plastic cover. 'What's in it?'

'Not cement,' said Kevin. 'That's a new hopper from Rotterdam. I think it's filled it with ultra-finely ground calcium carbonate.'

'Chalk?'

'Yes.'

'To put in the mud if you lose fluid to the rock formation?'

'Exactly. It's good to have that stuff in bulk. Saves you opening loads of sacks. You can cure losses really quickly. Trouble is, if you transfer it over to the mixing hoppers, you have to use it all or tie up one of your hoppers. That's probably why Webster never got round to opening it. Typical Webster. Loads it, then refuses to let anybody use it.'

'But it's not on the control room's inventory.'

Kevin shrugged. 'Ask Webster. He was a law unto himself.'

In the sack-store, Scottie was filling the barite hopper. He gave Jamie the thumbs-up. The blockage had been cleared. Peachy stood, poised to continue mixing.

'Another half tonne ought to do.'

'Magic,' said Jamie. 'Do you know anything about the new silo with ultra-fine grind calcium carbonate that's under lock and key?'

'Fuck,' said Scottie, 'I'd forgotten about that.' He spat into the mixing hopper. 'Some Webster scam. That guy really was unbelievable. Never missed a trick. His profit on that hopper wouldn't be much more than one or two grand.'

'The control room has no record of it. It's not on my inventory. Can we use it?'

'The idea of robbing the Webster estate appeals to me, but I wouldn't. Not unless you're desperate.'

Peachy removed his dust mask. 'Don't touch it, Jamie,' he said. 'It's a Webster thing. No good will come of it.'

'It's just that Kevin the Cementer said it would be good for curing losses.'

'Kevin's a twat,' said Peachy. 'What does he know? It's a load of old crap. I helped Webster load it. It'll block the hoppers, block the valves in the pits, block the strainers to the pumps and then ruin the pumps.'

'So that'll be a "no" then,' said Scottie. 'Unless we're incredibly desperate.'

'No,' said Peachy. 'It's "no" and "never". You'll use it over my dead body.'

'I was only asking,' said Jamie. Peachy looked at Jamie fiercely.

'There will be nothing but trouble will come from it,' said Peachy, putting his dust mask back on. The weight indicator showed that hopper was full. Scottie closed the feed. Peachy opened the valve at the bottom of the hopper, barite cascaded and mixing resumed.

Jamie and Scottie stood back. 'He gets sensitive about blocked valves,' said Scottie.

'Mark Z was hitting him earlier. He's looking for something.'

'Let me worry about Mark Z,' said Scottie. 'I'll sort Phil out first.'

'Oh well,' said Jamie, 'at least we've got a bit of spare fluid. Do you think we'll need it?'

Scottie nodded.

He was right. Losses from the cement job were horrendous. They pumped cement down the well. They pumped mud from the pits behind it to put it in place. Nothing came back. Nothing. Total losses.

'It's a clusterfuck,' said Ronnie the Roustie in the tea shack afterwards.

'Not my fault,' said Kevin, his face spattered in cement.

'Nor mine,' said Phil the Driller, quickly covering his arse.

'There will be no cement to secure the bottom of the casing,' said Antonio Banderas.

'We'll never get a pressure test,' said Mark Z.

'We might need to have another cement job straight away,' said Nigel the Night Company Man.

'There's no mud to pump behind it,' said Jamie.

'We're Golfing With The Wrong People,' said Dave the Night Toolpusher.

Chapter 24 Men Die Earlier: It's All Their Fault

The next morning, there were recriminations for the cement job. Town shouted at the rig. The rig shouted back. Walter refereed.

'They tried to blame the mud,' said Gray at that evening's handover.

'I hope you told them we drilled the 17 ½ inch section in record time,' said Jamie.

'And I mentioned that nobody asked for anything to be put in the mud to stop the losses,' said Gray.

'Do you know anything about a small silo filled with chalk?' Jamie whispered. He and Gray were in a packed TV lounge. They were waiting for a presentation.

'I refuse to answer on the grounds that it might incriminate me,' Gray whispered in reply. 'Now that Webster's gone, I suppose we can use it.'

'I hear it works a treat.'

'Oh aye. A tonne of that into the Active and you can cure losses in no time.'

'Peachy isn't so keen. Said it would block his valves.'

'Peachy's arse. He's an old woman.' Gray lowered his voice even more. 'I'm thinking about getting the leg over with Antonio Banderas.'

'You can't.'

'Why not?'

'She hates you.'

'Who told you?'

'She did.'

'I can't take much more of this,' Gray wailed quietly. 'There's a boat coming with oil-based mud. We've had a rotten cement job and we've no water-based mud left. What am I supposed to do? Leave it on board and plan for failure? Or take it off and plan for success?'

'Plan for failure,' said Jamie. 'That's the way of the world out here. Even I know that. Plan for failure with Antonio Banderas while you're at it.'

'I love her.'

'Oh God.'

'I want to sweep her up. We could live together in a hacienda. In Andalucia. With satellite telly.'

'No Gray, it's not going to happen.'

'We could have lots of little Antonio Banderases.'

'What about Beryl?' said Jamie.

'Beryl can piss off,' said Gray. 'She's been no support. She knows nothing about oil-based mud displacements.'

A stunningly attractive blonde came into the room. With five thousand pound breasts.

'Just forget about Antonio Banderas,' said Jamie.

'I think I have,' said Gray.

'Good Morning,' purred the blonde, sticking her chest out. 'I'm Nikki and I'm here to talk about Men's Health, How to Improve It and Why You All Die Before Women.'

The packed room hung on her every word.

Nikki was the perfect health package. Her teeth gleamed and her azure eyes shone. Her naturally fair hair was tied into a naturally upbeat ponytail. Her athletic body spoke eloquently of her suppleness and stamina in the bedroom. Her radiant cheeks even blushed at the embarrassing bits. But Nikki's crowning achievements were her five thousand pound breasts. Men couldn't take their eyes off them.

It was the best money she had ever spent. They were the basis of her business, the making of her fortune. She was earning the kind of money that would make City brokers choke. She couldn't have made more as a lap dancer.

Nikki had been packing them in all over the North Sea for the last three years. Oil companies were falling over themselves to prove that they were caring employers. The three grand a trip they paid Nikki assuaged their guilt about the hundreds of millions they'd forgotten to spend on safety. Toolpushers, weary of cajoling, ordering and bullying men into dreary safety seminars given by drone-voiced, oily-haired, shagged-out ex-drillers with chronic halitosis and one eye on retirement, cheered her arrival. With Nikki and her amazing attributes, a full house was guaranteed.

The reason that men didn't live as long as women came as no surprise. It was all men's fault. They had only themselves to blame, Nikki said. But she made it sound so sweet. Men were eating lousy food, bottling up their emotions, not exercising, failing to consult health experts at the first signs of trouble and committing suicide like there was no tomorrow. And for many of them there was no tomorrow, or at least less tomorrows than for their female counterparts.

'Could anyone tell me what their prostate does?' she asked coyly, blushing a little.

'It makes sperm?' volunteered Desperate Dan.

'I think you'll find that your testicles make sperm,' said Nikki forgivingly.

'He hasn't found his testicles in ten years,' said Mark Z.

'I'll find your testicles with the toe of my boot,' said Dan.

Nikki poked her breasts out like a veteran and continued. 'Prostate?' she said. Nikki liked to nip slagging matches in the bud before they led to ill feeling. She had seen and heard every kind of abuse and innuendo offshore. Still, however, she continued to blush. Her red faces did her credit. If only oil executives had maintained that facility, the planet would have been cleaner, healthier and more just.

'The prostate manufactures the semenal fluid, the fluid that the sperm swim in to their destination,' she said, finally.

'The crusty pages of a porn mag,' said Mark Z.

'Now,' Nikki continued, unfazed, 'for good prostate health, it's important that the system is flushed out on a regular basis. Either you, or a partner can perform the flushing.' Nikki reddened a little.

There was a moment's silence as the implications of this sank in – for most people.

'Is there any device that you use for this flushing?' said Detective Findon.

This was a question of such glaring stupidity that it was beyond response. Besides, no one was in a hurry to wind Findon up. Most of the guys were staring at the floor.

'As I said,' said Nikki sweetly. 'Either you or your partner might want to perform the flushing.'

'Perform it with what?' said Findon. 'Is there something I can get at the chemist?'

Peachy couldn't contain his laughter. Findon glared at him.

Nikki took a deep breath. 'Your system needs to be flushed out regularly through the end of the penis in an ejaculatory fashion and either you or your partner might want to do this.'

She really was a trouper.

A light went on slowly in Findon's head. 'Are you trying to tell us that wanking is good for your health?' he said.

'Yes,' sighed Nikki.

The room erupted into a cheer. Nikki beamed her beautiful smile. And blushed.

After the presentation, Dave Martin returned to his room and surveyed his lists with a big smile on his face. From "Golfing With The Wrong People" he crossed out "Wanking". On "Golfing With The Right People" he wrote, in block capitals, "FLUSHING".

***

'Arguing over botched cement jobs is poverty!' declared Bill the Mechanic.

'Trying to blame the mud is poverty as well,' said Jamie, enjoying a last cigarette before bedtime. 'I hear that Gray got a roasting at the morning call.'

'Poor bugger. He did what he could. Held his own. Just. He's outside now, getting into a flap about unloading the oil-based mud.'

'Are we planning for success or failure?'

'Half and half. They're taking enough OBM on to displace, but leaving enough pits empty to build more WBM if they don't get a test on the 13 3/8 casing. Are you going to do a health check with Nikki?'

'Of course. Not getting your health checked when it's free is..'

'Poverty.' Bill finished Jamie's sentence. 'Don't take the piss, son.'

Jamie was going to ask Bill if he knew about the upcoming fight, but he decided that if anything was poverty, fighting certainly was. It would only set Bill off. 'I notice you weren't cheering the killer with everybody else,' Jamie said.

Bill took a long sip of his coffee. 'And what do you read into that?'

'That you're too civilised to applaud a killer. Or that you're connected to the murder and you didn't want to look guilty.'

'The rest of the rig didn't mind looking guilty.'

'Exactly.'

Bill smiled. 'Very good, Jamie. But I'm just a man who doesn't applaud killers. I found an accommodation with John Webster and worked happily alongside him. Nothing changed.' Bill drained his cup and left.

Jamie went up to the service office. Antonio Banderas was sitting alone, going through her e-mails.

'You can apologize any time you're ready,' he said.

'Apologize for what?' A flash of dusky anger crossed her face.

'For being a woman. And you can cut out the fruity insults. I'm doing my best.'

'You were making me look stupid.'

'It's my first trip. You never had a first trip?'

'I was in a bad mood.' She sunk into her seat. 'We all need to get off of here.'

'I thought you, of all people, would be more relaxed.'

'Why?'

'All the sex you're having with Ronnie the Roustie.'

She sat up, furious. 'Who said I was having sex with Ronnie the Roustie?'

'I saw you kissing him during the Webster farewell party. I assumed...'

Her eyes were slits. 'Don't assume.'

'What did you kiss him for?'

'I wanted to see what it was like to kiss a roustabout.'

Jamie smiled to himself. The relief he felt was incredible.

Antonia tossed her lovely hair back. She shrugged. 'I am a curious girl.'

'You're some girl, Antonia,' Jamie sighed. Then he remembered himself. 'But in future, if you dish out abuse to me, you'll get bucket-loads of abuse back.'

'Okay.' She shrugged again.

'And no one will get off here until Findon has made some progress.'

'He's next door,' she said. 'With Peachy.'

Jamie pressed his ear to the wall. He could hear Findon's muffled shouts. He moved quickly.

'.. and if you think you can laugh at me and get away with it..' Findon paused as Jamie burst in.

Peachy looked up, fearful and confused.

'That's enough, Detective,' said Jamie.

'What the hell are you doing? This is a murder investigation.'

'Okay, so you made a fool of yourself about the flushing tool and Peachy laughed at you. That's no reason to bully him.'

'Get out of this room now.'

'No. We need to talk.'

Findon noticed Jamie's intensity. He jerked his head at the door, dismissing Peachy. Peachy fled.

'This had better be good,' said Findon.

'I can help you find the killer,' said Jamie. 'Making Peachy crack isn't going to help. He's already under pressure from Phil and Mark Z. I'm worried about what he might do.'

'I'll be the judge of that,' said Findon.

'The stakes are way higher than you think. I think Peachy's already tried to kill himself.'

Chapter 25 Displacement

Jamie was glad to be able to get back to the room to have some solitude. He needed to think about the way ahead.

Findon was utterly useless. That much was clear. He had no plan beyond bedding Antonio Banderas and pushing Peachy until he snapped. The problem was: if Peachy snapped he would die. The question was: had Peachy snapped and killed?

Peachy was central to everything.

Something bad had happened in Fraserburgh. Jamie was certain of that. Scottie was covering something up. So was Bill the Mechanic. Mark Z loomed violently on the horizon, as did Phil the Mechanic. Ronnie the Roustie stood enigmatically on the wings. These then, were the suspects. The Russian was the catalyst. In the middle stood Peachy.

Jamie slipped into Peachy's room. Peachy was sitting in a chair, staring at the wall. Porn was playing on a television in the corner.

'They know that you ransacked Webster's room,' said Jamie. 'What were you looking for?'

Peachy got up and turned the television off. 'I thought you'd come in for porn, but you don't like it, do you?'

'Turns out, I prefer the real thing.'

'Antonio Banderas?'

'I'm not the first fool in love. I won't be the last.'

'It could be worse. You could be a fool in porn.'

Jamie sat on the bed. 'Don't be so hard on yourself, Peachy. I'm not judging you.'

'I was looking for anything. Memory sticks. Papers. Anything he had on the lads. He must be a very wealthy man. The room was ransacked before I got there.'

'It was the Russian.'

'I know. It was all the Russian.'

'He killed Webster?'

'He did.'

'How do you know?'

'I saw him go into the pit room.'

'The police won't buy that.'

'They'll have to. There's nothing else to be said.'

'Peachy, I'm worried about you. I want you to know that there's nothing to be frightened of. Findon can't touch you. Nor can Phil. Or Mark Z. The rest of us are all here for you.' Jamie paused and looked directly at Peachy. 'The mark on your neck didn't come from a tugger line. I know you tried to hang yourself.'

Peachy relaxed into the chair and smiled warmly. 'It's good of you to be concerned. I think your imagination is running away with you. My problems are all in the past. I've decided to start a new life. I haven't been myself out here all these years. The person you are on the rig and the person you are on the Beach are two different animals. You'll find that out. It's a big gap in my case. Time to stop the double life. Stop the porn. You know, my wife is beautiful.'

'I'm sure she is.'

'Good luck with our lovely Spanish logger. You've come a long way in a short time. The rigs are good for you.'

'What are you going to do?'

'Get back on the tools. I'm a cabinet maker. The mortgage is almost paid. Kids are on their way. Time to set up in business. I think people are ready for quality again.'

'Quality.' Jamie smiled. 'I like it.'

'I appreciate you stopping Findon - and coming to see me. I just needed a wee bit of breathing space. I'll see this trip out. I'll be fine.'

'We can get you off any time you like.'

'And miss all the excitement? We're going to strike oil. I've got one well left in me.'

Jamie was at the door when Peachy called him back.

'Jamie? I've never introduced myself. I'm also called James. My name is James Anstruther.'

Jamie shook his hand. 'Pleased to meet you, James.'

Back in his room, Jamie felt as if a massive weight had been lifted from his shoulders, both with Peachy and Antonio Banderas. He took a long drink of water – the battle against dehydration was constant. He brushed his teeth and undressed. He put the lights out and climbed up into bed. He lay there feeling warm and delicious. Ronnie the Roustie was a wee liar. Antonio Banderas was gorgeous, loveable and available. It was still a slim hope, but perhaps Jamie could be in the hacienda in Andalucia. And he couldn't care less whether there was satellite telly or not. He and Antonio Banderas would be heavily engaged in other activities. In between times, he'd be happy to eat tapas and drink Rioja. Eastenders held no magnet for him. Life was going to turn out good. Even Peachy was happy. Jamie fell into a wonderful, deep and deserved sleep.

He awoke with Gray's hands tightly fixed around his neck.

'Jamie! Get up! Now!'

Jamie did get up. His head shot up – straight into the ceiling. 'Oyah!' His self-inflicted bedroom injuries were mounting. He was slow to learn that he wasn't at home.

Gray had a hold of his t-shirt, and Gray was falling backwards. Jamie slid out of the top bunk. He and Gray landed in a pile on the floor below.

'Oooohh,' said Jamie.

'Oooohh,' said Gray.

Gray had turned all the lights on. Amidst the fuzz, the stars, the concussion and the confusion, Jamie saw a clock. It read 14:30.

'What are you doing?'

'Displacing!' Gray shrieked.

'It's the middle of the night! I was having a great sleep!'

Gray grabbed a hold of Jamie once again. They were still on the floor. 'You've got to do it! You've got to do it!'

'Do what?' Jamie felt like he was being accosted by an old, rejected lover.

'Displace!'

'Displace yourself!' Jamie wiped Gray off.

Gray's hair was wild. His eyes were wild. His breath was wild. 'I can't do it! It'll go wrong. I know it will. We'll spill oil. They'll come for me!'

'Who?'

'The DTI! The government! Anyone! We can't hide anything! It's awful! We'll have a Pon violation!'

'I don't even know what a Pon violation is,' Jamie gasped, getting up. This was the worst waking up of his entire life.

'I'm begging you, Jamie. Don't make me do it.' Gray was on his knees, his hands clasped together. 'I'll do anything. I'll go down on you!'

'I do not want you to go down on me!'

Jamie heard someone stirring in the room next door.

Gray's eyes flicked around as he searched in his mind for something tempting to offer Jamie. A triumphant look appeared. 'I'll give you proper handovers,' he said. 'I promise.'

'Cross your heart and hope to die?'

Gray nodded like an obedient child.

Jamie got dressed quickly. He went upstairs and found Walter. Jamie got Walter to explain to him what the usual procedure for displacing to oil-based mud was. Then he went straight up to the doghouse for the Toolbox Talk.

The doghouse was full of grown-ups, all looking very serious.

'Are you running this crock-of-shit operation?' said a steely-haired middle-aged American. He was Brad Jackson, Nigel's boss, the company man on days. He was the client's representative that everyone had to answer to.

'I'm in charge,' said Jamie.

'And you know what you're doing?' said Brad.

'Yes.'

'What's your name, boy?'

'Jamie Chivers.'

'Well you had better go and get your passport, because I don't believe a fucking word that comes out of your mouth.'

Jamie felt his mouth go dry. His knees took a little wobble. Brad had a steely look to go with the steely hair. The only thing that gave

Jamie a crumb of comfort was that some of the other grown-ups were smirking. Stuarty the Rig Manager, was looking both grown-up and useless. It was quite a feat.

'Well boy, let's hear your Toolbox Talk,' said Brad. 'Then we can decide whether we're gonna run your sorry ass off this rig with your pal.'

That was it: Gray had been fired. Strangely, this news relaxed Jamie. He cleared his throat. 'Okay we've cemented the 13 3/8 casing. We tagged cement and we successfully pressure tested the casing to 3,000 psi.'

'A fucking miracle,' said Brad.

Jamie continued. 'There's water-based mud in the hole and we have oil-based mud in the pits and the sand-traps, which are presently bypassed. We are going to displace the well to oil-based mud safely and with zero discharge of oil into the environment. Returns are presently lined up for dumping over the side at the shakers. We'll pump from the Webster pit, dumping until 100 barrels before we expect any OBM back.'

'Where will you be?' said Brad.

'I'll be at the shakers, checking in case the OBM channels and comes back early.'

'Amen, brother.'

'100 barrels before OBM, which is after 7,000 strokes of the pumps, we'll stop pumping and seal everything in. Once we're happy, we'll start pumping again, diverting returns to Reserve 2 which is our slops pit. Once I've identified good OBM, at the flowline, we'll close the system in on the Webster pit, Active 1 and bring the sandtraps online. Any questions?'

There were none.

'Is everybody happy?'

Nods all round.

'One final point,' said Jamie. 'Have all water-based liquids been dumped from the pits?'

'Yes,' said the Driller, a pock-faced, hard-boiled looking guy.

'Has the Trip Tank been emptied?'

No,' said the Driller.

The entire doghouse looked at Jamie with respect. They thought he knew what he was doing. Jamie said a silent prayer of thanks to the Gods of drilling – and to Walter.

They then proceeded to enact the plan to the letter. The water turned to oily water, then to watery oil and then to oil-based mud. It was a perfect displacement. By four o'clock Jamie was back inside. He found Gray in the service office.

'I'm going to bed,' said Jamie. 'I won't be up before eight. You can get on with drilling. Brad says you're being run off.'

Gray smiled serenely. The thing that he had feared for most of his life, when it came, was a blessed relief. Jamie watched the man transform. The weight lifted and the spirit blossomed. It was the most sublime moment of Gray's life: being fired.

When Jamie woke up, he realised that he was sleeping like a baby. Literally. He was taking in so many new sights, sounds and ideas that his little brain was being overwhelmed. It was sending him into deep unconsciousness each night in order to process the stuff.

One of the benefits of going into the smoko half an hour after crew change was that you were likely to have it to yourself. The night shift wouldn't have their first break for an hour and the day shift were inside, showering and eating. The downside of going in at this time was that if anyone did come in, it was likely to be someone like Dave the disastrous Night Toolpusher. So it proved.

'You heard about the fight tonight?' said Dave softly. Dave's piggy face was clouded by worry.

Jamie drew a delicious lungful of death from his cigarette. 'Has it been arranged for tonight? Fantastic! I'd prefer Scottie to win, but he's a bit thin. If it turns dirty, Phil could wipe the floor with him. Who's running the book? What are the odds?'

'Ronnie the Roustie's running the book. The odds... What am I saying? Never mind that! What do you think?'

'About what?'

'Is it Golfing With The Right People?'

'Who cares?'

'That's easy for you to say, you're not senior management.'

'Neither are you.'

Dave bit his lip. 'Okay, but if I let it go ahead, senior management might blame me and that really is Golfing With The Wrong People.'

'But you'll disappoint the entire drillcrew. That's a lot of Wrong People to be Golfing With. They'll never forgive you'

'They can't fire me.'

'But they can make your life a complete misery for the next six months.'

'I suppose,' said Dave sullenly. 'Whatever I do, I'm Golfing With The Wrong People. I'm stuffed.'

'Sometimes Dave, you've just got to play golf. You can't always pick who you play with.'

Dave's brow furrowed. This was introducing a whole new concept into his philosophy.

'Listen Dave. There's another head of steam building up. The fight will let the entire crew blow a gasket. Let the boys have their fun. Then you'll not only be Golfing With The Right People, you'll be the leader in the clubhouse.'

Dave's face brightened. Jamie was speaking his language.

'If you ban the fight,' Jamie employed his darkest voice, 'somebody really will flip. And it was management that got targeted before. And floating face down in oil-based mud with your head caved in is the worst kind of Golfing With The Wrong People.'

'Surely, it won't come to that?' Dave whimpered.

'You'll be the scapegoat.'

'Being the scapegoat is definitely Golfing With The Wrong People.'

'And if the fight is discovered, what's the worst they can do?'

'Make me a roustabout. I don't want to be a roustabout!'

'You can get another job. In Africa.'

'And end up on a video with some hooded psycho with a Samurai sword at my neck looking for ransom money? No thanks.'

'Relax Dave,' said Jamie. 'If they can brush John Webster under the carpet, there's plenty of room for a wee fight.'

Dave looked like a naughty little boy who had just been told that he wasn't going to be smacked after all. Yet again, Jamie felt strong.

'Is the Stuarty the incredibly important international oil executive still aboard?'

'He went home on a chopper an hour ago.'

'So what's stopping you?'

A malicious grin spread across Dave's puffy face. 'All right! Fight's on!'

Chapter 26 Fight Club

It was traditional. The two potential locations for a fight on an oil rig were on the drillfloor behind the draw-works (the big reel of cable that pulled everything in and out of the hole) or in the sack-store. It all depended on whether you wanted the driller to know about it or not. In this case, since the fight involved the driller, it was a moot point. They had it in the sack-store anyway.

They had manoeuvred Jamie's chemicals about to create a little amphitheatre and when they ran out of space, they simply threw the excess chemicals into the mud whether it needed them or not. The three pallets of chalk that went in cured some incipient seepage losses. This accidentally made Gray look good and stopped him from being run off. He was devastated.

Jamie was alerted to the fight's imminent start by the noise. He was in the mud lab performing his first oil-based mud check. He opened the emergency escape hatch and had a fine view of the spectators gathering below him. Most of the night shift were there and all of the day shift. Jamie left his aerial view and joined the throng at the heart of the action.

Ronnie the Roustie spoke with relish. 'This is just like the good old days,' he said.

Yes, the good old days. The fight marked a brief return to those glory, glory times of constant scrapping, sitting on the toilet smoking, scud movies every night in the cinema playing to packed houses, dumping anything you wanted over the side, frequent brutal accidents and men with big balls earning a fortune, running around with nine and a half fingers.

It was amazing they hadn't had to risk assess the mêlée.

Hazards: Pinch points; Puncture wounds; Sprains; Strains; Collisions with spectators and pallets; Slips, trips and falls; Bruised body, bruised ego, bruised retina; Ingestion of flying teeth...

'What are the odds?' said Jamie.

'Six to four on,' said Ronnie the Roustie.

'Who is six to four on?'

'Both of them.'

'But that means whoever wins, you win.'

Ronnie grinned. 'That's why I'm the bookie.'

'Who are you looking to bet on?' said Bill the Mechanic.

'My heart says Scottie, but my head says Phil.'

'I've got fifty quid says Scottie will win.'

'Done,' said Jamie. They shook on it. 'I'm surprised to see you here.'

'Sometimes poverty is where you don't allow guys to knock lumps out of each other. There's no harm in pain. Men are designed for it.'

Kevin the Cementer barged past, looking intent on maiming someone.

'I didn't know there was a support fight,' said Bill.

'There isn't,' said Peachy. 'He looks like that all the time.' Peachy laughed. He looked more relaxed than Jamie had ever seen him. Scottie was right: Peachy was worth fighting for.

The bit was in hard rock. Drilling was steady. Phil wouldn't be needed in the doghouse for at least two hours. Scottie's pit levels were steady. All systems were go.

The thing which startled Jamie most was the look in Scottie's eye. It was one of distilled and focused hatred. He wasn't affable and he certainly wasn't cooperative. Phil's face had FEAR written all over it - in block capitals. Every sweating square inch was an eloquent testament to the bully whose bluff had been called. Whether Scottie was frightened or not wasn't clear. It was impossible to see past the hatred.

Jamie began to doubt the wisdom of his fifty pound wager.

The major difference between the two men was in their art. Phil, for all his body-building, was at sea. He had perfected the art of vocal bluster. Scottie was a master in the dark arts of physical harm.

Phil's first two blows grazed Scottie's temples.

Scottie didn't waste any time counter punching Phil's over-developed torso. He punched him straight in the balls.

This brought Phil's hands down – as Scottie knew it would.

Scottie reflexively smashed his fist into Phil's face, spreading his nose all over it.

There would be no explaining the fight away now.

Phil charged with his head down, hoping to return the compliment with a head butt.

Scottie swerved and turned his opponent.

The only thing that Phil head butted was a pallet of lime.

This produced a puff of white powder.

Scottie punched Phil's left kidney.

Phil went down on one knee.

Scottie was on him and would have finished him off but he breathed in some lime. It stung his throat and lungs. He gagged.

Phil lashed out blindly with his right hand and caught Scottie on the cheek, drawing blood. Phil had donned a ring just for the fight.

Phil rose and shook the lime out of his hair at Scottie.

It was boxing, but not as they knew it. The fight had morphed into chemical warfare.

Scottie's eyes were stinging. He staggered back.

Phil rounded on him. He landed two more blows – a body shot and a head shot. It was his worst mistake. They did little more than revive Scottie. The lime in Phil's hair had combined with the sweat to form a strong alkaline liquid which now ran into his eyes. Phil spat on his fingers and rubbed his eyes to relieve them.

Scottie punched Phil's right fingers into his right eye.

Phil wafted out a left hand and somehow caught Scottie's right eye.

Scottie seemed nothing so much as offended by this effrontery. He drew his right arm back as far as it would go and delivered a hook to Phil's chin which had everything behind it - arm, shoulder, hips, and knees. The power came from all the way down in Scottie's boots.

Phil fell.

'Stop!'

It was Walter.

The spectators stood like the guilty schoolboys they felt themselves to be. Heads weren't exactly hung, but the body language was muted. Phil lay on the floor, his back wedged against a pallet. He was barely conscious, but conscious enough to feel for his jaw with his loose arm. Scottie cut the most incongruous figure of all. He was standing with his fists up, as if waiting for some invisible referee to resume the fight or declare a no-contest.

'I can't believe you're here,' said Walter to Dave.

'I didn't want to stop it,' Dave mumbled.

'There's no need to take this any further, Walter,' said Peachy.

'Look at him,' Walter snorted, looking at Phil. 'How are we going to cover that up?'

Neither Peachy, nor anyone else, had an answer to this.

'Give me a hand Dave.' Walter went to pick Phil up. 'We need to get him to the medic. Scottie - go to my office.'

Jamie was struck by the sadness of the entire scene. The fight, so keenly anticipated, had brought joy to no one. They had witnessed the demise of a man. Jamie went back to his lab. He closed the hatch as quietly as he could.

***

Walter and Brad had a pow-wow on the perennial topic of crisis management: damage limitation.

'Jesus fucking bastarding Christ,' said Walter.

'There's no brushing this one under the carpet Walter,' said Brad.

'The Senior Toolpusher is hammered to death. The derrickman gives the driller a kicking in the sack-store. What did I do to deserve this?' wailed Walter.

'It was easier than I thought,' said Scottie to anyone willing to listen in the smoking tea shack. He had a full house and was milking it for everything he was worth. 'I always knew I could take him. So much for all that fabulous body of his. And all that mouth. I've waited years to smack that wanker.' He sipped his bitter tea bitterly.

'I I I I wanted to lance the boil,' stammered Dave Martin to Brad and Walter's kangaroo court.

'Your job, your pension, your reputation. Everything,' said Walter, 'is hanging by a thread.'

'I h-hoped they could get it out their system and we could brush it under the carpet,' said Dave.

'The Senior Toolpusher's been murdered. There's no room under the fucking carpet you idiot!' yelled Walter.

'What I want to know Dave,' said Brad, 'is why you were so stupid as to let this thing go on at all. Do you think we're daft?'

'The entire crew wanted to see the fight. It was a pressure keg. I was thinking about safety.'

Mentioning safety was always Golfing With The Right People.

Walter buried his face in his hands. 'I've got a driller with smashed teeth and quadruple vision. Don't talk to me about safety, Dave.'

'Walter, you've got to fire this clown, get Phil to resign and put Scottie on a final written warning,' said Brad.

Dave realised that he was now most definitely Golfing With The Wrong People.

'Look on the bright side,' said Brad.

'There's a bright side?' said Walter.

'No Walter, now that I think about it, there's no bright side.'

Dave burst into tears.

Walter sighed and thought about the early retirement package he'd inevitably be offered.

Brad the Company Man sighed and thought about how Walter would never be offered early retirement. Manticore drilling couldn't afford to lose a toolpusher and a driller and an OIM. They were short enough of experienced senior staff as it was. No, Walter was going to have to work to the bitter end.

'I could feel his teeth smash, even through my knuckles,' said Scottie to a packed smoking shack. 'It was great. Trust Phil to fight dirty with the lime. Wasn't it funny when it ran into his own eyes?'

No one was laughing. Sympathy for Scottie had ebbed as his gloating had flowed. The crew had washed its hands of Scottie.

'What have you got to say for yourself?' asked Walter at the next leg of the inquest.

'I wasn't prepared to be bullied by Phil any longer,' said Scottie.

'You realise that you could be up on a charge of grievous bodily harm?' said Brad.

'I can't see Phil pressing charges. Can you?'

'Your behaviour's very out of character, Scottie,' said Walter.

'No Walter, this is the real me.'

Scottie smiled. Walter felt a chill in his spine.

'I'm going to put you on a final written warning,' said Walter.

'You can poke it up your arse. I tell you what, I'll see this hitch out. And then you can find yourselves another derrickman.' Scottie smiled affably and then left the room cooperatively.

Scottie looked in on Jamie in the service office and smiled kindly. Jamie was certain of one thing: there was no way that Scottie could have been the killer. He was incapable of the kind of restraint that the calculated killing of John Webster had required. If he'd attacked, Webster's head would have been mashed to a pulp and he'd have been soaked in Webster's blood. Scottie, when roused, had no concept of "enough". He was a killer all right. But he wasn't John Webster's killer.

Chapter 27 Aye Fond Kiss

There was more to be swept under the carpet. Ritchie the Medic decided to enjoy a cigarette in his room as he watched his favourite soap opera. He fell asleep and set himself on fire. The smoke detector went off. The fire team arrived. Ritchie was smouldering in front of them. It was all they could do to hide the evidence and try and save Ritchie's job for him.

Walter saw right through it and went mental. He had the scorched medic brought to his office for a closed-door bollocking.

'You spend your entire life lecturing others on safety and then you go and do this? How am I supposed to tell the Beach that our beloved medic, in charge of all things healthy, not only smokes like a chimney, he smokes in his own room – a sackable offense – and he can't even do that properly? He sets himself on fire watching Eastenders! No wonder you fell asleep, watching that crap.'

But Walter was unable to maintain the pretence of seriousness. He began to smile.

'Oh Lord,' he sighed. 'You think you've seen it all out here. But there's always some balloon with a new fuck-up to present at your door. Bludgeoned toolpushers. Smashed-in drillers. Self-immolating medics. What the fuck have I done to deserve you lot? No money's worth this. Your job's safe, Ritchie. I won't be telling anyone. I can't be arsed with the paperwork. We'll put the muster down to a faulty smoke detector.'

The real muster drill didn't go much better. It was a fiasco.

The scenario was to be a fire in the laundry. Fires in the laundry were common, mainly due to tumble-driers overheating. In preparation for the drill, the Stewardess turned off the tumble-driers. She forgot to cool them down first. One of them caught fire. The Stewardess put the fire out.

Then the fire team arrived.

'We're here to put out the fire,' they said.

'Fuck off,' she said, 'I've already put it out.'

'No, we're here to put out the fire,' they insisted.

'I'm telling you, it's already been put out,' she insisted back.

'Now don't start any fucking nonsense,' said the fire team. 'Let us go about our business.'

'Don't you lecture me,' said the Stewardess indignantly.

It took about five minutes to ascertain that one side was talking about an imaginary fire, while the other was talking about the real thing. It almost came to blows.

Everyone else mustered as normal.

Amid all the confusion of the murder, Jamie had lost all track of the days and the months and, for that matter, the year. It was only the chill in the evening air that reminded him that they were firmly in autumn.

'It's easy to lose track out here,' said Peachy. He was standing, looking bewildered, by the lifeboats, in a lifejacket.

They were all standing, looking bewildered, by the lifeboats, in a lifejacket.

'The only reason I know that it's Saturday night,' Peachy continued, 'is because of this boat drill.'

'It's always good to get a couple of boat drills under your belt,' said Bill the Mechanic. 'Means you're going home soon, although this hitch feels like it'll go on forever.'

'Amen,' said Ronnie the Roustie sadly.

They all looked old and tired, Jamie thought. The industry had taken its toll on them. Or perhaps it was just life. Or Webster. As the Muster Checker counted them off in the gloom, Jamie looked around. The rig provided a miserably grey and rusty backdrop. The crew milled around aimlessly like ghosts, dwarfed by the decaying superstructure behind them. The sky looked old and tired.

'This will be my last boat drill,' said Peachy. 'Hopefully.'

***

By 5 am on the Sunday morning, it became apparent that the 8 ½ inch section was going well. They were drilling up a storm. Phil had been patched up and sent to his bed. It turned out that they didn't need him after all. Dave had sulked all night in the client's office, knowing fine well that the operation could do without him. Scottie was back in the pits, cheerfully helping Jamie to maintain his fluid's properties. It wasn't difficult. A bit of base oil and a few sacks of viscosifier was all it took. The oil-based mud was very stable. If this rate of drilling continued, they'd be in the reservoir on Monday. The previous night's depression had been replaced by a curious optimism. Such was the weird pendulum of rig morale.

'Barring the odd murder, it's been quite a successful well,' said Bill the Mechanic, sipping an early coffee.

'If I get another cement job, it'll be my best trip ever,' said Kevin the Cementer, sipping a late coffee. Every coffee was a late coffee for Kevin. It was always time for bed.

'Maybe we should have more murders and fist fights,' said Jamie.

'With Dave and Phil gone, there won't be anybody left aboard that's worth murdering,' said Kevin.

'Except me!' said Bill. 'Killing Bill the Mechanic is poverty!'

'You old bastard,' said Kevin, smiling. 'You've just been winding us up.'

'At my age you take your entertainment where you can get it,' said Bill. 'Entertainment is wealth!'

The three men laughed. It felt to Jamie like the fight had served its purpose. The boil had been lanced and the poison drawn off. The age of bullying was over. The drillbit would soon be in the payzone. They'd all be going home soon. Life was good.

Peachy had given Scottie an enormous hug when he returned to the pit room. It was one of the most touching moments that Jamie had ever witnessed.

'There's nothing to worry about,' Scottie had said.

Peachy had smiled and nodded and the two of them had worked seamlessly together thereafter. It had been a joy for Jamie to watch. In a dreamlike state, he had wandered up to the logging shack. There, Antonio Banderas smiled at him, looking every bit as heartbreakingly gorgeous as ever.

'Antonia,' Jamie said, 'I can't keep this to myself any longer. I've fallen in love with you. I think about you all the time. Seeing you makes my day better. You're the most stunningly attractive woman I've ever met. I'd just love to be with you. In a hacienda. In Andalucia. With or without satellite television.'

Antonia looked at him, her brow creased. Jamie waited for the longest moment of his entire life until she spoke. 'Do you have to say this in front of Lat?' she said.

Lat was standing, unobserved, in the corner with his microscope. He wasn't winking. He was blinking. In astonishment. He grabbed his hard hat and gloves and left.

'Well?'

'You are not stable, I think,' she said.

'I haven't been stable since I saw you.'

'The new job. The strange rig. The people. Webster. It has deranged you.'

'I'm the most wonderfully deranged man on the planet.'

'I am not sure.'

'How can I prove it to you?'

She said nothing. She half-shrugged. She looked at Jamie coyly.

Of course. It was obvious what Jamie had to do to prove the power of his love. He approached her slowly, knelt down so that their eyes were level, removed his hat and then kissed her with as much tenderness as he could find. When he felt her lips responding to his, Jamie knew that his life had improved beyond anything that he could ever have dreamed.

When they separated, her lovely, wonderful eyes were shining fiercely with passion.

'Have you ever done it on a rig?' said Jamie.

'What kind of a question is that you feelthy peeg? Get out!'

Jamie's hands went up in an involuntary act of surrender. 'No, I..'

'Get out! You disgust me!'

'That wasn't what I meant, Antonia. Please...'

She seized his hard hat and cracked him over the head with it. 'OUT!'

Jamie's eyes were watering. He was retreating. She threw the hard hat at him, scoring a hit to his chest. Right in the heart.

'Out! Out! Get out! And I never want to see you again! Ever!'

Her finger was pointing somewhere towards Norway. Jamie went to the tea shack.

Chapter 28 Tears for Souvenirs

In the tea shack, Kevin the Cementer and Bill the Mechanic were discussing the finer points of drilling theory in the context of global economic patterns set against the background of Peak Oil.

'The Client is a fucking cheapskate bastard,' said Kevin emphatically. 'We should have drilled a 12 ¼ inch section. Not gone straight from a 17 ½ to an 8 ½.'

'They're cutting corners,' said Bill. 'Saving money. Pure poverty.'

'Talking about cutting corners,' said Kevin, 'the handle you put on my door is a bit on the big side. Couldn't you grind it down?'

'It's already ground down,' said Bill. 'I'm sorry. It was a rush job. Webster wanted it done pronto. You could say it was his last request.'

'What's up with you?' said Kevin, noticing Jamie's quizzical look.

'Nothing. It just reminds me,' said Jamie. 'I've something I need to check in the control room.'

'So we've a John Webster memorial handle as well as a John Webster memorial pit?' said Kevin. 'That's a scary thought to take to bed with you.' He got to his feet and went out.

'You don't look yourself, Jamie. Is there something wrong?' said Bill.

'I need some advice. You're a meticulous man?'

'It's the secret of success.'

'You do things by the book.'

'Always.'

Jamie thought for a moment, then he changed tack. 'Can you keep a secret?'

'I suppose this is about Antonio Banderas?'

'Of course it is. I did something really stupid. It ended with her yelling "Out. Out. Get out and I never want to see you again. Ever."'

'And what's your problem?'

'She never wants to see me again.'

'Boy, have you got a lot to learn about women.'

Jamie brightened. 'You mean there's hope?'

'When a woman says, "Out. Out. Get out and I never want to see you again. Ever." She doesn't mean "Out. Out. Get out and I never want to see you again. Ever." She means, "Out. Out. Get out and don't come back for at least a few hours but when you do come back, you'd better be crawling on your hands and knees, begging for forgiveness. Then I might consider forgiving you." And she always will forgive you. Women are like volcanoes, Jamie. They're okay to be around, most of the time, but when they blow, you have to get well clear. And this one is Spanish. Expect regular eruptions.'

'Do I have to beg?'

'It's essential.'

'I can't just apologize?'

'Grovel.'

On his way to the control room, Jamie's heart was soaring. He had always known there was hope. The kiss had said it all.

In the control room, Jamie looked through old copies of Permits to Work. He didn't find what he was looking for. It wasn't a surprise. He knew now that Bill was concealing a secret.

*****

At 2 am, exhausted after another wrestling match with the Daily Mud Report, Jamie went back to the tea shack. Phil was sitting alone - because he was being left alone. He was a Jonah for a second time. Phil was completely finished. His brief, disastrous career as a driller was over.

'They'll fire me,' he slurred prophetically. He was sipping tea, realizing that this was the day before the helicopter flight that would take him away from the Manticore forever. 'I'll miss the old place. This has been my home for six months of the year for the past fifteen years.'

In misery, Phil was exhibiting exactly the kind of behaviour that he despised in others. But he wasn't others, he was him. And he was hell-bent on self-pity and nostalgia.

Jamie was hell-bent on nostalgia for the old, brutal Phil who at least had the benefit of being ridiculous. It was impossible to feel pity for pitiful Phil.

'Fifteen years blown. All over that wanker. Wait 'til I see him on the Beach. I'll bludgeon the bastard to death.'

'Bludgeoning people to death is... not advisable,' said Jamie, noticing a deranged glint in Phil's eye. 'Did you bludgeon Webster?'

'I had nothing to do with Webster,' said Phil.

This was said in such an offhand way that Jamie believed it.

'Bludgeoning seems to be the in-thing to do,' Phil continued, philosophically.

'Who do you think did it?' said Jamie.

'Peachy,' said Phil. 'You've no idea how hard Webster rode Peachy. Something was bound to break. You can't bully a man like that out here.'

'Didn't stop you trying,' said Jamie.

'With who?'

'With everybody. Especially Peachy.'

'You an expert on human motivation all of a sudden? What do you know about running a drillcrew?'

'I couldn't be any worse than you were.'

'True,' said Phil. 'I must be the worst driller in the history of the North Sea.'

'Yes,' said Jamie emphatically. He was unable to tell Phil that there were plenty more rigs in the ocean, that oil was a hundred dollars a barrel and that everyone was looking for experienced hands. Phil's smashed face matched his smashed career. 'Your smashed face matches your smashed career,' said Jamie.

'I know,' said Phil. Tears were pricking his blackened eyes, snot was running from his broken nose and tea was leaking through his broken teeth.

'I'll be amazed if you ever work in the North Sea again,' Jamie added, really rubbing it in.

'I know.'

'In fact, I'll be amazed if you ever work anywhere again.'

'Oh God,' said Phil.

'I mean, you were mentally unhinged before. I can't imagine that all those blows to the head have done you much good.'

'I'm finished,' said Phil. 'Finished.'

The tears had now grown big enough to course down Phil's fat, unshaven cheeks. What with the bruises and the nose and everything, it wasn't a pretty sight.

'You're not a pretty sight,' said Jamie.

'You know what makes this all worse?' said Phil.

'What?' said Jamie.

'Knowing that you're going to have it off with Antonio Banderas.'

'Face it, Phil. You never had a chance with Antonio Banderas.'

'I know.' The tears were bigger and had turned into little rivers of self-pity.

Jamie checked over his shoulder to check that Antonia hadn't come in and overheard him again.

'I wouldn't have got into this mess if it wasn't for that sneaky little bastard Peachy,' Phil continued. 'Gets Scottie to fight all his battles for him. Filthy little pig. God knows what he got up to with those Russian girls at Webster's party. All night at it.'

Jamie turned and looked closely at Phil. 'I thought Peachy went home with Scottie?'

Phil shook his head. 'Webster insisted Peachy stay. Peachy was only too happy to bide on. I was in the minibus with Scottie. Scottie went home alone.'

***

At handover, Gray was miserable once more. The weight of the world was back on his shoulders. He'd been un-fired.

'Why don't you resign?' said Jamie.

'Beryl won't have it. I'd be happy with a few hours a week in a polo shirt at a DIY warehouse. She wants me to earn as much as I can before I stop. If I don't get myself fired, I'll be out here... until the end.' Gray's voice cracked.

'Look on the bright side, at least the mud is stable.'

Gray frowned. 'I wish I could say the same for me.'

There was one last thing that Jamie had to do before going to bed. He took a sheet of A4 paper, drew a large heart on it and wrote the word "Sorry" underneath. He slipped it under Antonia's door. She would likely crumple it into a ball and throw it in the bin, but it was a start. The crawling would come later.

Chapter 29 Losses

Early the next morning, which was 4:30 in the afternoon, Jamie went into the smoko for the first cigarette of the day. Scottie and

Phil were there, curiously at peace with one another now that neither had a future on the Manticore.

'What's happening?' said Jamie.

'Losses,' said Scottie.

'How bad?'

'Seepage losses have started again. We're losing oil-based mud at a rate of about five barrels per hour to the rock formation. They're throwing a couple of sacks of nutshells in each hour.'

'No, it's wheat husks they're using,' said Phil.

'It could be the chef's over-cooked vegetables as far as I'm concerned,' said Scottie. He and Phil chuckled.

'Let's take total losses and then a massive kick,' said Phil.

'And stick it right up Manticore,' said Scottie.

'End my drilling career with a massive explosion.'

'And a rig evacuation,' Scottie added.

Ronnie the Roustie came in. 'This trip just gets weirder and weirder,' he said, shaking his head. 'I gets back to my room last night and there's a sheet of paper on the floor. There's a heart drawn on it and "Sorry" written underneath.'

Jamie suppressed a smile.

'So,' Ronnie continued, 'I gets a warm feeling in my underpants. It can only be one person: Antonio Banderas. And it must mean that I'm back in with a shout. So I heads straight for her room. Goes in. Gives her, "How's about it Baby?" and she starts freaking out at me, calling me a "dirty pig" and doing all that Spanish ranting and raving. This goes on for about five minutes. I couldn't get a word in edgeways.'

Jamie dug his fingernails into his hand. He didn't dare laugh.

'She called me everything under the sun,' said Ronnie. 'Said that all men were the same and she was becoming a lesbian and she hoped I was proud of myself for helping turn her. She said she'd rather visit a sperm bank than have anything to do with a roustabout like me. I tried to tell her about the sheet of paper, but she was having none of it. She was waving her arms all over the place, stood there in satin pyjamas. Her soft hair's bouncing up and down. Her lovely brown skin is breaking out into small beads of perspiration. And her tits were jiggling. I was getting the horn all over again. I'd have jumped in there, but I don't think she was amenable.'

Ronnie licked his cigarette paper, rolled his fag and popped it into his mouth. He shook his head philosophically.

'I mean,' Ronnie concluded, 'what kind of a bastard draws a heart on a sheet, writes "Sorry" under it and puts it under your door?'

When the laughter eventually subsided, Phil wiped the tears from his cheeks. 'Lads,' he said, 'I've an announcement to make.'

The room grew quiet and serious. Phil cleared his throat.

'I'm sorry for being a dick.'

'You weren't a dick,' said Scottie. 'You were a complete and utter dick.'

'Then I'm sorry for that. It's sad that it's taken this to make me realise it. And I'm sorry that it's cost you your job, Scottie.'

'No harm done,' said Scottie, 'I was leaving anyway. You'll be back drilling before you know it. The industry's crying out for experienced hands.'

Phil extended his experienced hand. Scottie shook it.

'It was Peachy I was really worried about,' said Scottie.

'I know. I was a bastard to him. He's a nice fella. He didn't deserve it. I'll apologise to him.'

'I think Peachy's going to be okay,' said Scottie.

'Peachy has turned some kind of corner,' said Jamie, 'It's like he's made some kind of decision. He's transformed. He's happy and content. It's lovely to see.'

Jamie slipped away and went into the TV lounge to check the muster cards. They were sorted by room number. He identified Antonia's, went to her room, took a deep breath, knocked and opened the door slightly. The light was on. He went in. Antonia was at the far end of the room, in a combative pose.

'What is this? Another idiot?'

Jamie closed the door behind him. He dropped to his knees.

A stunned look crossed Antonia's face.

Jamie then bent down and crawled across the room on his hands and knees.

Antonia's look changed from stunned to stupefied.

'I'm so sorry about what I said. I'm begging for you to forgive me. I was wrong. You were right. I should have known. What an idiot I've been. I'm so sorry. How could I have been so insensitive at such a wonderful moment for us both? I've ruined everything.'

'Do you think this will make everything all right?'

'No. Of course not. But I hope you can find it in your heart to forgive me and let me try and make it up to you.'

Antonia turned away, flicking her hair dismissively. She looked at herself in the mirror. And then looked down at Jamie. 'You are beneath contempt,' she snarled.

'I am.'

'This is a good view. Looking down on you.'

'That's why I'm down here.'

'Shut up. That is where you belong. You should be on your belly, like a snake.'

Jamie thought about grovelling on his stomach, but he felt that his present begging position was demeaning enough.

'You know nothing about love. About how to unleash the true spirit and passion of a woman. You are like a Spanish man, a little baby who wants to take and take, who is passed from one mother to another, who is never a true man. I tried to think of a suitable punishment for you, but there is none. Then I realised; your punishment is that you are a man. You are doomed forever to have that ridiculous thing between your legs that does all your thinking for you.'

Jamie knelt, realising that Ronnie the Roustie was right. Antonia was magnificent in anger. He wondered if there was any man who could match up to her. He was also becoming strangely aroused. He redoubled his efforts to look contrite. His knees were beginning to hurt.

'Men and women? What is the point? It always ends in

disaster. Look at you. On your knees, begging. And we haven't even begun. What hope is there? How could I be such a fool?'

'I'm the only idiot here.' Jamie rose to his feet. 'I've fallen madly in love with you, Antonia. I think you'll probably break my heart. But I don't care. I couldn't bear to have my heart broken by anybody else.'

She looked at him. Her eyes were soft and tender. They appeared to Jamie to contain the mysteries of life itself.

'That is the biggest load of bullshit that I have heard in my entire life,' she said.

Jamie smiled ruefully. 'Would you give me your telephone number Antonia? Please?'

She shrugged. 'I'll think about it.'

Antonia held her head up, aloof, turning away from Jamie. He saw his chance. He moved close to her, held her gently and kissed her lightly on the cheek. It felt like a wonderful victory: she didn't hit him. Her eyelids lowered slowly and came back up. It had a tremendously erotic effect. As he left, Jamie was sure he could see the beginnings of a playful smile on her lips.

Jamie was in his room, innocently washing his hands when Gray burst in.

'Losses! Losses! We're taking losses! I pumped a pill. It didn't work. I pumped a bigger pill. It still didn't work. What are we going to do? All our fluid is slowly draining away.'

'At least it's not quickly draining away,' said Jamie.

Defeated, Gray sat on the bed and put his head in his hands. 'I knew I should have been run off.'

'How quickly are we losing?'

'Fifty barrels an hour.'

'How much mud have we got left?'

'Five hundred barrels.'

'Ten hours. Then what?'

'We top the well up with seawater. And wait for a kick.'

'How do you get a kick when you're taking losses?'

'It's awful. You lose your heavy fluid down one hole and explosive gases come at you from another.'

'Have you ordered more mud from the Beach?'

'I didn't want to admit defeat.'

'Doesn't losing mud mean more profits for our company?'

'I suppose so. But losing mud is what we're paid to avoid,' said Gray, studying the carpet.

'What about the hopper full of Webster's calcium carbonate?'

'We can't use that! We'll get into trouble!'

'Gray, we ARE in trouble.'

'Webster...'

'Webster's dead.'

'I don't care, I'm still frightened of the bastard.'

'Phone the pits and tell them to empty the barite hopper into one of the reserve pits. Then phone town and organise some emergency mud. There must be a boat or a rig with something. I'll go outside and organise the Webster hopper.'

'On your own head be it.'

'I'll take full responsibility. Now where can I get my hands on some bolt-cutters?'

'The Fire Fighters' Store, but it's not allowed.'

'Fuck that.' Jamie strode off. Gray was left trailing in his wake.

Jamie arrived in the sack-store, brandishing his bolt-cutters. He was met by Billy the Fish, the derrickman on days.

'Where's Gray?' said Billy.

'In the office, wetting himself. There's a hopper full of chalk we're going to add to stop these losses.'

'That Webster thing? Are you sure that's wise?'

'Webster's dead! How many times do I have to say it?'

'Have you told the company man and the driller about this?'

Jamie got straight onto the phone. 'Brad? We're going to add a hopper full of chalk to the Active pit to stop these losses.'

'Where did you find a hopper full of chalk?'

'Webster bequeathed it to us.'

'Is it fine or coarse?'

'Fuck knows.'

'How much is there?'

'Fuck knows.'

'How much are you going to add?'

'All of it.'

'Are you sure that's wise?'

'Have you got a better idea?'

There was a pause on the other end. 'Son, I like your style. Pile it in.'

'Drillfloor,' said the Driller.

'We're gonna be firing in a load of chalk from a secret hopper.'

'Isn't that something to do with Webster? Are you sure...?'

'Webster's dead! Please make sure the loggers and everybody else is informed.'

'It's your funeral.'

Whilst Billy lined up the mixing pumps on the Webster pit, Jamie took the bolt-cutters to the Webster hopper. The padlock yielded in seconds. Jamie opened the red plastic cover on the valve wheel.

Then something unexpected happened: a memory stick fell into his lap.

Jamie recoiled. The last person who touched this was most likely dead. It was another gift from beyond the grave from Webster. Jamie pocketed it. He opened the valve and traced the line. There was another locked valve to be opened further along. Billy the Fish joined him and they double-checked the line-up to the air system.

'This is weird,' said Billy. 'God knows what Webster was thinking of. I can do it, but the powder will have to be blown around the houses. All he needed to do was put a short line in there.'

Billy was right. After a bit of jiggery-pokery, they succeeded in filling the barite hopper in the sack-store.

Brad tannoyed Jamie. 'I've drawn up a work instruction for curing these losses. Could you come up and sign it?'

It was a long way up to the company man's office. Jamie burst in breathlessly, forgot to put on his overshoes and scribbled his name. 'See you in court,' he gasped.

There was no time to be lost. The loss rate had increased to over 100 barrels per hour. There were only three hundred barrels left in reserve. There was no mud to be had anywhere nearby. A delivery of new mud was at least a day away. They didn't have enough chemicals to make their own mud. Once the reserve was gone, they would be in trouble. They would have to rely on the last line of defence: the Blow-Out Preventor Stack. Things were getting dangerous. Gray had locked himself in the toilet.

'We've got 80 barrels of one hundred pounds per barrel LCM pill already made in the pill pit,' said Billy.

Jamie had no idea what any of this meant.

'How much of the chalk do you want us to add to it?'

'As much as it can take,' said Jamie.

It didn't take much time to add four tonnes.

'That's one helluva pill,' said Billy.

The pill was pumped into the drillpipe and allowed to soak into the formation.

'What do we do now?' said Jamie.

'What does the work instruction say?' said Billy.

'Fuck knows. I signed it. I never read it.'

They quickly built another pill, a mixture of sacks of nutshells and wheat husks and more chalk from the hopper. Then there was an agonising wait while the well was monitored. Billy sat on the burst chair and Jamie sat on an agitator motor, which was warm. They stared at the walls.

'If the rig blows, we won't know much about it,' said Jamie.

'We should be pretty safe here,' said Billy. 'Any gas or oil will look for the first source of ignition. If we're unlucky it'll be the mud pumps and the explosion will blow them through the bulkhead and kill us. Otherwise it's out that door, over the side and take our chances that the standby boat will get to us before we freeze to death. That's if the sea's not on fire.'

'What about lifejackets?'

Billy nodded at a green locker.

'Is that supposed to have lifejackets in it?'

Billy smiled. 'It's our own private stash.'

The telephone rang. Billy took some instructions. He lined the rig pumps up to the pill pit. They pumped away the second pill and stared at the walls.

'It's not looking good,' said Jamie.

'It is looking good,' said Billy. 'The losses must have slowed dramatically. Or they would have asked us for mud to fill the Trip Tank. And look.'

Billy pointed at the marker on the float on the Active / Webster Pit. It had risen by at least seventy barrels.

'We got almost full returns from pumping that last pill. We're actually looking very good.'

So it was. Static losses, which is to say losses when the pumps were off, were zero. They started the pumps slowly at 100 gallons per minute and staged up at fifty gallons per minute. At 500 gallons per minute they had established a loss rate of 4 barrels per hour. This was acceptable to drill ahead. This much was confirmed when Brad rang.

'I think we're through the loss zone,' said Brad. 'Can you dust in the rest of that chalk? It's working a treat.'

'No bother,' said Jamie. 'I think there was twenty tonnes at the start. I'm not sure how much is left, but I'm sure we can put it all in.'

'Who would have thought that John Webster would have bequeathed us something so useful?' said Brad.

'Some man,' said Jamie, fingering the memory stick in his pocket.

The chalk went in steadily enough. They established a rate at which it could be added to the mud without blocking the hopper on the mixing line. When the mixing hopper emptied, another four tonnes were transferred across, and another four. Jamie threw in odd sacks of various materials to finish off pallets. On the final transfer, they only got three tonnes across and Jamie found himself happily whacking Webster's hopper with a mallet to get the last of the chalk out. By the time the final dribbles went in, the losses had been completely cured.

Jamie plugged a few figures into his calculator. 'We've got enough mud to get us to bottom,' he said. 'If we don't take any more losses.'

'Sounds good to me,' said Billy.

Jamie did some more calculation. 'We can make up 100 barrels of premix. The oil to water ratio is a bit high, so we can make it 50:50. We can bleed that in to control weight and dust in barite if we need to. That'll give us a cushion of volume. But nothing for you to worry about. We'll leave the mixing to night shift.

Billy chuckled. There was nothing better than handing work over to the next shift. 'You'll do for me,' he said.

'You'll do for me too!' bellowed Brad as he strode into the sack-store. He gave Jamie a big ol' Texan slap on the back. 'Well done my man. You've saved the well. Saved us millions. Have a Coke and a Mars Bar on me.'

Jamie was elated. He wasn't just one of the team, he was now a valued member of the team. At no point in his previous life could he ever have said that. He sat on a pallet of nutshells, watching Billy sweep up. He pushed his hard hat to the back of his head. This was a big moment in his life. He hadn't cracked. He wasn't locked in a toilet. It would soon be shift handover. Jamie couldn't wait to share his success with Scottie and Peachy. But wait he did. He waited what felt like a long time for Scottie and Peachy to arrive.

But Scottie and Peachy never came.

In addition to the fluid losses, there had been one other loss. It was a grievous loss. Peachy's body had been found hanging from the shower faucet in his room. Nearby was a suicide note confessing to the murder of John Webster.

Chapter 30 Drilling Ahead

They drilled on.

'Bastards,' said Ronnie the Roustie.

'That shows where their heart lies,' said Bill, bitterly. 'This industry was, is, and always will be about money.'

'We're just appendages to an expensive hole in the ground,' said Mark Z.

'I thought Walter had more to him than that,' said Jamie.

Walter, Brad and Detective Findon were having a tête-à-tête-à-tête in Walter's office. 'I want all drilling to cease at once,' said Findon.

'Fuck that,' said Walter.

'We're almost at the payzone. The hole is unstable. It's important that we keep going,' said Brad.

'Fuck that too,' said Walter.

'So we're stopping? Good.' Findon smirked at Brad.

'No, we're drilling ahead,' said Walter.

'I forbid it,' said Findon.

'You forbid fuck-all on my rig. And you,' he jabbed Brad in the chest, 'can wipe that smile off your face. One of my boys is dead. I want you to stay in your office with the door closed. You're not to phone the drillfloor. The directional driller will call you when he needs guidance. I want you to understand that the crew is only working under duress. In my opinion, it's the least worst option. Do I make myself understood?'

'Yes sir,' said Brad.

'And now, I'm going to cut my boy down and have him laid out with dignity.'

'You can't touch him. It's a crime scene,' said Findon.

'It's a suicide scene,' said Walter.

'If you touch him, you're committing a criminal offence.'

Walter leaned back in his executive chair, 'You know, I've always wanted to find out if prisons were cushier than oil rigs. I won't have to do 21 consecutive 12 hour shifts without a day off. Free satellite television. And I won't have to worry about anybody's safety. Just my own.'

'The money's crap,' said Brad.

Walter stood up. 'That's not a problem, Brad. I've a bit put by. And now, if you'll excuse me gentlemen, I have to go and tend to my boy.'

Findon stood in Walter's way. He raised a finger and wagged it in Walter's face. 'I am telling you: drilling must stop and the corpse must remain untouched. I will hold you personally responsible for this.'

'No, you will hold me personally responsible for this.'

Walter unleashed his old right-handed haymaker. Findon never even saw the blow coming. It smashed into his jaw, whipping his head violently clockwise. He fell backwards, knocking over Walter's water cooler. Stunned and groggy, he lay on the carpet in a widening pool of liquid.

Walter surveyed his work with satisfaction. It confirmed his philosophy: things generally did turn out for the best once you'd fought for them. He wondered if he'd fought enough for Peachy.

Scottie was standing vigil at Peachy's door. Walter arrived with Ritchie the Medic. They had a knife and a stretcher. Scottie and Ritchie supported Peachy as Walter cut the rope. The body was borne gently onto the stretcher and carried to the sick bay.

'It's okay now, Peachy,' said Scottie. 'You're going home.'

Walter returned to his office to find a stain on the carpet where Findon had been. He took a few moments to compose himself. He had promised himself over thirty years ago that he would never shed a tear on an oil rig. He wasn't going to start now. But he was getting older. Emotions could no longer be marshalled as easily as they once had. Walter often found memories and feelings creeping up on him, calling him back to unwanted times, unwanted places and long-forgotten people. The dead were increasingly demanding his attention. And here was another, to be managed in the present and dealt with in the future. He took a deep breath and made what he hoped would be the last tannoy of his offshore career.

'This is Walter, your OIM. As you'll all be sadly aware, Peachy has taken his own life and confessed to the murder of John Webster. I'm asking you to remain at your work positions. We're in a good routine of drilling. To stop safely, we'd have to pull back to the 13 3/8 inch shoe, which would involve even more dangerous work in unbearable circumstances. Hopefully, we can limp through tonight and day shift can TD this bitch tomorrow morning and pull out the hole. Staying inside and dwelling on this isn't going to help any of us. Crew change is only a few days away. I ask you to maintain your incredible professionalism until then. There will be plenty of time for tears on the Beach. And I have a final, unimportant, announcement to make. This is it: my final hitch offshore. I've seen enough.'

Walter went up to the drill floor. With no Peachy or Scottie, Phil could help Mark Z in the pit room, with Walter acting as stand-in driller. He felt better. Drilling took him back to familiar territory. He'd been on the brake for ten years. It was apt that he should spend some of his last trip drilling. It was what the rig was designed to do. It was what he was designed to do as a man. Walter eased up on the brake, increasing the weight on the bit. His intuition was still sound. The secret was not to overdo it, but to pitch everything just right for the bit, the tools downhole, the fluid and the formation. The trick was to send the bit ever downwards, as fast as possible, towards the ancient black liquid that powered the planet.

Phil was also back to familiar territory. He'd been a derrickman for seven years. His eyes darted quickly around the pit room, checking that every valve was in its correct position. He reset the mark on the float in the Active pit. His feet carried him automatically over a dozen different trip hazards. Jamie was still smacking his shins into every one of them.

'How's the mud?' said Phil.

'The mud's fine,' said Jamie.

'You've learned quickly. That's the stock response from a thousand mud engineers the world over.' Phil allowed himself a brief, sympathetic smile. 'How is the mud, really?'

'Really, it is fine.' Jamie allowed himself a faint smile in response. 'When I heard about Peachy, I walked round the rig about four times, but I realised there was nowhere for me to go, so I got a jug of mud and did a full check to keep myself busy.'

'If only it was that easy,' said Phil morosely. 'Still, Walter's probably right to keep us going. Looks like he's had enough too.'

'Have you had enough?'

'I haven't had enough of the rigs, but I think the rigs have had enough of me. I really didn't mean to push Peachy over the edge.'

'I know.' Jamie tried to be as reassuring as he could. Phil looked as if he was likely to crack. It felt like the whole crew was on the verge of a breakdown.

'There's so much pressure out here. People don't understand. You're made driller and it's supposed to be great. And everybody at home is delighted for you. And it's more money. But you feel like you've got the weight of the whole rig on your shoulders. You've got Webster breathing down your neck. You've got Scottie undermining you, questioning everything you do. Then the roughnecks start questioning you. The next thing you know, you've got a mutiny on your hands. So you clamp down. Kick arse. Because you know you're only one step away from disaster. You're terrified that you'll miss something and somebody will get hurt. Or you'll break a piece of kit and lose your job. And nobody's helping you. Webster's a psychopath. And the night toolpusher Golfs With The Wrong People.'

'It's no wonder you freaked out,' said Jamie, trying to be calm while trying desperately to calm Phil down.

'And you're not sleeping, so then you add fatigue into the equation. Things are coming at you from all angles. Directional drillers. MWD. Loggers. Cementers. Casing hands. Wellhead boys. Mud engineers. Company men. And at every Toolbox Talk they say, "The driller will be the focal point for everything". And you just want to scream, "Make some other bastard the focal point for a change!" And you think about the money and the kids. And you grit your teeth. And then you lash out at the nearest victim you can find.' Phil's voice trailed off. 'And then Peachy kills himself.'

Phil swung his foot, kicking the heel firmly against a valve handle, forcing it even tighter shut.

'Peachy's death was nothing to do with you,' said Jamie. 'You've got Scottie to thank for that.'

Phil snorted humourlessly.

'The fight ended that problem, lanced the boil, call it what you want. Peachy knew that you weren't an issue.'

'I could have pushed him over the edge.'

'That was Peachy's problem. He realised he was way over the edge. And he could never find his way back.'

Phil seemed to accept this. Eventually, he nodded slowly to himself. An awkward silence grew. Jamie was stuck for something to say to a man he didn't particularly like, let alone know. What were men supposed to talk about? Football? Pornography? Cars? The pornographic behaviour of football stars in fast cars? Jamie finally understood the appeal of football. It ticked so many bloke boxes. In the end, Walter's logic of continuing to drill ahead was vindicated. The ice could be broken by talking about work.

'The mud's a bit thin,' said Jamie. 'We need to add a few sacks of viscosifier: FabOilVis.'

'What's the circulation time?'

'We're pumping at 500 gallons per minute. The entire circulating system is about 1500 barrels.'

'Does that include the Webster pit and the sandtraps?'

'Yes. So with 42 gallons in a barrel that's..'

'..about two hours,' said Phil. 'I'll shove a sack in every half hour. Then you check the mud in another couple of hours. You don't want to add that stuff too quickly. You make love to mud slowly, you don't try and shag it to death.'

Phil rubbed his bruised and swollen face. Now that the pressure was off, Jamie could see the human being that had been invisible before. It was amazing what death could achieve.

'I feel like I've completely misjudged you, Phil. You're ... nice.'

'I wouldn't go that far. I was a guy reacting badly to pressure. I'm not as brutal a person as you've seen. Whether I'm actually nice is another matter.' Phil paused. 'It's been quite a first trip for you. You've had to cope with a lot. Without much support from Gray. And yet you've helped him. And I know what you tried to do for Peachy. I appreciate what you've been trying to do for me here today. I just want you to look at me and answer one question: Do you really think that Peachy's suicide is nothing to do with me?'

'No. I'm certain that it wasn't. If it was, Scottie would have buried a bar in your head.'

'How come Scottie is so sure that I'm not to blame?' said Phil. 'What does he know that we don't?'

Chapter 31 All Our Sons

Jamie helped Phil get the four sacks of FabOilVis over to the mixing hopper. Phil wedged the first of the sacks in the hopper and whacked a hole in the bottom. The vibration from the mixing line emptied the sack efficiently over the next five minutes. Phil checked his pumps.

Ronnie the Roustie was manning the shale shakers. 'I've been promoted to roughneck,' he said ruefully. 'If we keep losing people like this, I'll be a driller by Christmas and OIM by Easter. They can promote me right back down to roustabout, or I'll be resigning too.'

'What's your problem?' said Jamie, 'You're obviously an intelligent guy. You could be the OIM.'

'I'm a contented underachiever. You make your accommodations with life and you live with them. Stuff responsibility.'

Things were obviously under control at the shakers, so Jamie went to the logging unit.

'The geology's changing, we're getting near the reservoir,' said Lat. 'No shows of oil yet.'

'How are we doing on the losses front?' said Jamie.

'No losses. Your special chalk worked wonders,' said Antonia.

'I'll tell you when we're dumping,' said Jamie.

'If you're dumping oil-based mud, I'll run you off myself.' Antonia smiled.

Jamie tried not to get too excited about one smile. He failed. He got really excited about the fact that Antonia had smiled at him.

Lat stood up. 'I'm off for a coffee and a smoko. I'll catch a sample on my way back.'

Jamie and Antonia surveyed one another warily.

'Well?' she said.

'Well Peachy's dead. Kind of puts my pathetic problems into perspective.'

'We have a saying in Spain: if you want to make God laugh, tell him your plans.'

'Never mind God,' said Jamie. 'My plans make you laugh.'

Antonia smiled. 'If Peachy's death has taught me anything it is to live more and to live better. He didn't live well. That is why, I think, he died.'

'I think you're right.'

'You did everything you could.'

Jamie took the few steps across the room, took Antonia's hands in his and kissed her very tenderly on the lips.

When the kiss was over Jamie opened his eyes. He felt wonderful. He had taken control. He felt like a man. Then he felt as if he was going to faint. Antonia grabbed his arm and helped him into a chair.

'Oh dear,' said Jamie, gratefully accepting a cup of water. Whether the water had ions in it or not didn't seem to matter any more. He tried to read the look in Antonia's face, but gave up. She was certainly concerned and she certainly found him funny, but apart from that, who knew? All he did know was that they had begun some kind of journey together. And that was a fabulous thing to know. And he knew that she knew that his heart was in the right place. And that was another fabulous thing to know. He gathered himself.

'Antonia, I have an unusual question for you. Please don't go mad at me until I explain why I asked it.'

'Go ahead. You couldn't do any worse than you've already done.'

'Are you related to John Webster?'

Continentals aren't very good at disguising emotions at the best of times. Antonia didn't even try. Her mouth hung open. 'Why would you ask that?'

'I think I know why Webster used to talk about his three daughters.'

'You think I am Webster's daughter?'

'No, but you must have been the only female in the room when he said it.'

'What do you want me to do, introduce you to my parents?'

'I'd love to meet your parents.'

'Maybe, if you're lucky.'

'If Webster only had two daughters and out here he talked about his three daughters, that makes me think that he was saying it to insult someone in the audience. Someone who was actually his son.'

'You think Peachy was Webster's son?'

'Someone in this crew is.'

'Do you believe that Peachy killed Webster?'

'No,' said Jamie. 'Peachy had snapped before Webster died. He was at peace at the end because he knew his life was over.'

'How sad.'

'I should have realised.'

'You did what you could for him Jaime. You stood up for him. You cared. Why do you think I am even talking to you now?'

Jamie had no reply to this. He hadn't imagined that he would impress Antonia in this way - which said a lot about her, and a lot about him.

'It was important that someone was trying to help Peachy,' Antonia continued. 'I couldn't. Peachy gave me the creeps. The pornography. It was his life.'

'I'm beginning to think that pornography is more about avoiding sex than anything else.'

'It is about avoiding intimacy,' she said.

'At the end, Peachy knew that.'

'How do you know?'

'Peachy told me himself.' Jamie paused for a moment in thought. 'James told me himself. His name was James.'

Antonia smiled warmly. Jamie could see her eyes searching his. He held out his hand. She took it. Intimacy. It was fabulous.

'I found Webster's memory stick when I opened his lock on the hopper.' Jamie handed it to Antonia. 'Do you mind if I use your computer? I'm frightened to open it in the service office. God alone knows what's on it.'

Antonia put it in her computer. It was password protected. She went online. She downloaded some software. It took a couple of minutes to work through. Then they were in.

She scanned through the contents. She opened a couple of files. 'Bank details. Interesting. Switzerland! My goodness. I didn't think that Webster was so sophisticated.'

'There!' said Jamie. 'Video files.'

Antonia clicked. There were a couple of dozen files to be perused.

'You might not want to watch any of these,' Jamie said.

'We might not want to watch this,' Antonia replied.

The window the home-made movies played on was mercifully small. After a couple of seconds of the first clip, Antonia fast forwarded. It made it a little more bearable. It was on the eighth or ninth film that Jamie felt his throat dry and a chill come over him. Antonia instinctively placed her hand on his forearm. This film unfolded in real time because Antonia was too stunned to remember to click. Her free hand had come off the mouse and was covering her mouth.

'Oh,' Antonia said.

The sound was barely a whisper, but it was more powerful than a scream.

Jamie turned his head from the screen. Antonia was motionless, paralysed almost. Gently, Jamie reached across her and clicked to close the movie's window.

The sound ended and the picture disappeared with finality. What was left was a list of file names on a monitor. Highlighted was FG56ytr.wmv . Jamie tried to make sense of the letters and numbers, but they were senseless. This anonymous-sounding file made chilling sense in John Webster's macabre universe. Jamie spoke. Antonia was unable to.

'Now we know why Peachy killed himself.'

Chapter 32 Drilling for Kicks

After a crap midnight meal and another struggle with the Daily Mud Report, Jamie spotted Walter in his office. He was about to go in, but saw that Walter was talking to a squawk box. Walter waved him in anyway.

'... they sent the same forensic team that were out here before. Not even three weeks ago.' Walter sighed. 'They're making rumbling noises about me spoiling the crime scene, but they can go take a flying fuck to themselves. I wasn't leaving James hanging there like that.'

'What were you thinking of Walter? You can't take the law into your own hands!' Stuarty the Rig Manager was squawking on the other end of the box.

'You're talking to a dangerous man, Stuarty. I don't care any more. About anything.'

'But there are procedures to be followed. It's what we pay you for.'

'Not any more. I'm taking early retirement.'

'Oh no you're not.'

'Oh yes I fucking well am. This is my last trip. I've cut one of my boys down from a rope today. If I couldn't help him, I'm not use to anybody out here.'

'I need you in place, Walter. I'm not going to make this easy for you.'

'I didn't expect a cocksucker like you to make anything easy.'

'I understand that you're under a great deal of stress, Walter.'

'I'm not suffering from stress, Stuarty. I'm suffering from an attack of clarity. I can see you for the unsupporting, arse-licking little worm that you are. You are a useless human being, Stuart. A waste of DNA. Unless there's something in it for you, you are not interested. Men like you add value to nothing. Nothing! And what have you got to show for it? An SUV and a nice kitchen. I bet you've got a nice kitchen, haven't you?'

'The wife's very happy with the kitchen. It's a German company most of the Aberdeen players use. Scottish design, though. The girl told me they'd just put a new one in for Willie Miller.'

'I hope your kitchen's worth it! Forty years of oilfield uselessness. Everything your grubby fingers touched turned to rat-shit. Took the credit for everyone else's good work. Tongue permanently up the arse of the nearest boss. You can't stop me quitting, Stuart. I'll give you a battle that'll turn your pubic hair white. If you've got any. You can't touch my pension. And you can't touch me. Stick your fucking OIM's job up your incompetent rig manager's arse!'

Walter jabbed the phone off with his index finger.

'Leaving?' said Jamie.

'If I'm not arrested first,' said Walter.

Jamie wondered what the world would be like if everyone was as liberated as Walter.

'I should have stayed a driller,' said Walter.

'Ronnie the Roustie was talking about being over-promoted. And he's a roughneck.'

'Ronnie the Roustie is a very clever man. He could easily do my job. Have you read any Bertrand Russell?'

'No.'

'He was a philosopher. Said the happiest man he ever met was his gardener.'

'I need to ask you a wee favour,' said Jamie. 'I want to check up on the night shift's original application forms.'

***

Back outside, there was trouble. When one pump packed in, they had to drill at a reduced rate. When the second pump went, they had to get Kevin the Cementer out of his bed (Where else could he have been?) to use his pump to keep mud moving around the bit. Dave the Night Toolpusher was allowed to man the brake. His job was to reciprocate the drillstring up and down. A stationery bit at a depth of over 10,000 feet with no fluid moving around it was a recipe for getting stuck. Bill the Mechanic was up, working frantically on the pumps. Scottie even came out and helped.

Jamie could only watch. His fluid was circulating so slowly that there was no point in treating it. Circulation time was now about twelve hours. There was nothing to do to the mud anyway. The FabOilVis had worked a treat and brought the fluid to the ideal thickness. Jamie helped Kevin with more canisters of diesel for his engine.

As the boys lowered a new pump module into place, Scottie came over to Jamie.

'Are you okay, Scottie?'

'I'm better than Peachy,' said Scottie, wringing his hands with a rag.

'I know why he killed himself.'

Scottie paused, sizing Jamie up.

'I found John Webster's memory stick.'

'I know something that you don't,' said Scottie.

'Who killed Webster?'

'All I know about who killed Webster is it wasn't me, and it wasn't Peachy.'

'So who was Peachy taking the rap for?'

'God knows. Peachy was finished as a human being. We both know why. My guess is that Peachy wanted closure for everybody. He wanted the evil to end. It was his best way of killing Webster once and for all.'

Jamie suddenly felt himself overcome by emotion. Peachy's confession to the murder of John Webster was his parting gift to the world he'd misunderstood so chronically.

Jamie wanted to go outside; take a walk; be alone. But there were people everywhere outside. There were people in the smoko, Gray was in the room. There was no peace to be found on an oil rig. He milled around the pit room, while Scottie checked his valves and wiped his hands obsessively.

'Tell me your secret,' said Jamie. 'You said that you knew something that I didn't.'

A rueful smile crossed Scottie's face. He led Jamie to a quiet corner and lowered his voice. 'Is it true that you used all of Webster's chalk to stop the losses?'

Jamie nodded.

'Oh Jamie, just a wee while ago I thought I would never laugh again, but now I don't think I can stop myself.'

Jamie felt his depression dissipate. A smile came to his own face.

'Did you really think that Webster would mess around trying to make a couple of grand's profit on a few tonnes of calcium carbonate?'

'Why not?'

Scottie laughed. He led Jamie to the mud lab, where they could be guaranteed total privacy. He shook Jamie's hand.

'I want to congratulate you, young man. On your first ever trip, you have created the most expensive drilling fluid in the entire history of oil exploration.'

Jamie's smile waned. He felt his throat tightening.

'That wasn't twenty tonnes of calcium carbonate. That was twenty tonnes of cocaine.'

Jamie's mouth dried.

'No wonder the pumps have packed in. They've had a fucking heart attack.'

Scottie grabbed one of Jamie's emergency eyewash bottles and doused his face with it.

'You have created a forty million pound mud system.'

'Holy shit,' croaked Jamie.

This, Jamie realised, was the understatement of his tiny thirty year life. The 1500 barrel active mud system had twenty tonnes of cocaine in it. Forty million pound's worth of white powder was presently circulating slowly through Kevin's pump, up to the drillfloor, down the drillpipe, out through the bit, back up the annulus, down the flowline, over the shale shakers and back into the pit that Webster had died in.

'Thank God Webster's dead,' said Jamie. 'He'd kill me.'

Jamie wondered if the cocaine had dissolved in the mud. Did cocaine dissolve? In oil? In water? The water phase of the mud was probably saturated with cocaine. The rest of the twenty tonnes was blocking the pores in the rocks and stopping the losses. Could they recover any of the coke? Boil the mud and make an oil-based mud crystal that everybody could smoke?

'There's probably about a hundred grand's worth still in the pipework,' Jamie said.

He remembered himself smacking the hopper with a mallet to make sure they got all of it out. What an idiot. Forty million quid's worth. That was more than lottery winners won. If only he'd known. A fraction of that could have set him up for life - if he'd been willing to deal in cocaine. Jamie knew himself well enough to know that he couldn't have anything to do with the drugs trade. They were all incredibly evil. They were all like, well, Webster. Jamie felt relief sweep over him. He hadn't blown anything.

Scottie was drying his face with blue paper towels. He was still chuckling. 'Do you want the good news or the bad news?'

Jamie's heart sank.

'You have a head start,' said Scottie

'Was that the good news or the bad news?'

'That was the good news.'

'Oh fuck. What's the bad news?'

'Some rather angry Russian gangsters are going to want to know what's happened to their cocaine.'

'But I didn't know!'

'Well you know now. Did you sign a work instruction?'

'Yes.'

'Might I suggest that you get hold of all the copies and destroy them? Not that it matters. One of the boys will spill the beans over a few pints. There's too many people know already.'

'What can I do?'

Scottie placed his hands on Jamie's shoulders. 'Pray that they kill each other before they come after you.'

***

There was a mist shrouded around the rig the next morning. Jamie had stayed up to bid Peachy farewell. Everybody had. The entire rig formed itself into a guard of honour between the sick bay and the helideck. They all had their hard hats in their hands. Heads were bowed.

The body was borne by Scottie and Mark Z, Bill the Mechanic and Walter, Ronnie the Roustie and Phil the ex-Driller. Phil was in his yellow survival suit and would be accompanying Peachy home. The helicopter stood ready, silent on the helideck. The entire rig was silent. The pumps had been stopped. The drillstring was stationery in the slips. They had no bell to toll. The fog horn sounded instead, three low blasts as the procession began. Walter had arranged for a piper to come out with the chopper. He stood, silhouetted by mist, and played a lament.

As the body was carried up the steps, everyone moved round to the pipedeck. The fire team had formed their own little guard of honour by the helicopter. Peachy was carefully and expertly placed aboard. Phil came to the side of the helideck. He raised his right hand, in salute and farewell, for both himself and for

Peachy. Those assembled on the pipedeck raised their hands in reply. Nothing needed to be said.

The piper played on as Phil climbed aboard, the other bearers retreated to a respectful distance and the fire crew manned their positions. The piper stopped playing and climbed aboard. The foghorn sounded another three times. The helicopter engines started slowly and the rotors began to turn. Soon the engines had built to a high whine and the rotors were a blur. The chopper sat for minutes as the pilots went through their checks and communications with the radio room. Then the engine whine grew in strength. The chopper rose twenty feet into the air, the nose dipped as if in a final bow of respect and then it climbed quickly, rising above the derrick. It banked and turned away. The sound diminished and died. Peachy was gone.

***

Jamie took two cups of decaf coffee into Antonia's room. They drank, sitting in silence, holding hands. They kissed, Jamie left and went to his bed. The limp lettuce sheets and dead pillow didn't bother him any more. He could have slept on a rope.

'Nearly there,' was Gray's handover to Jamie that evening.

Jamie went up to the doghouse to check in with Phil's replacement, who had come out on the chopper that Peachy had returned in. Both the driller and the assistant driller were from an agency. They had quickly formed themselves into a team, having little interest in the Manticore or its troubles.

'This is my first and last trip on this shithole,' said the Driller. 'You'll not get a service hand to come out here. Toolpusher dead. Roughneck dead. Who's next?'

Jamie stood with the pair in the doghouse. There was no more drillpipe in the derrick. If they wanted to drill further they would have to pick up some more from the pipedeck below.

Jamie noted the callousness beaten into the Driller's face. No one questioned his orders because everybody knew that he didn't give a shit. He had five years more drilling experience than Phil. That was the difference.

'You going to stand there all day and watch others work?' said the Driller. 'Why don't you fuck off and go mourn with the others?'

Jamie didn't need a second invitation. He crossed the deserted drillfloor and stood in the V-door. The sun was in its lower quarter and was fighting though a veil of cloud. The other rigs appeared curiously golden in its light. The Manticore was a surreal place at the best of times. Jamie wondered if he would ever experience normality again. The catwalk and the pipe deck were empty and derelict. Looking back across the drillfloor, Jamie saw the top half of the driller watching the pipe rotate. The assistant driller was recording futile data on a clipboard with a propelling pencil. They too were bathed in the golden light. The drillpipe rotated steadily and lowered itself slowly into the ground.

Despite the murdered toolpusher; the suicided roughneck; the randy roustie; the deranged and disgraced driller; the hapless leadership; the systemic skiving by some of the crew; the constant skiving by all of the service hands; the completely and utterly useless mud engineer; and unconscionable amounts of "flushing", the Manticore struck oil.

'We're in the payzone,' Lat announced to the tea shack.

'That'll keep the shareholders happy,' said Ronnie the Temporary Roughneck. 'That's what the planet's about these days: keeping shareholders happy.'

'I'm a shareholder,' said Kevin the Cementer. 'And I'm not happy.'

'Has anybody seen Scottie?' said Jamie.

'Not me,' said Kevin the Cementer.

'He was at the pre-tour meeting, so he's definitely... alive,' said Mark Z, giving voice to what everybody was thinking.

'That's what it's come to,' said Ronnie. 'Counting heads every day to make sure we're all still willing to live.'

Jamie slipped out. He went down to the pit room to make sure the derrickman wasn't trying to kill himself.

Scottie's inert form was slumped over the Active pit.

'Scottie!' Jamie yelled and ran to help.

Jamie still hadn't come to terms with the pit layout. He tripped on a valve handle and smashed his nose on an agitator motor. His nose was broken. There was blood everywhere. Scottie didn't notice. He had been bent over the pit with his tape measure, calculating the pit volume.

'We're gaining,' he said.

'I've broken my dose,' said Jamie, staggering to his feet, staunching the flow of blood.

Scottie phoned the drillfloor. 'We've gained five barrels,' he said.

'Bollocks,' said the Driller. 'The Spanish cow's phoned me already. You're both talking shite.'

'Stop the pumps, monitor the well on the Trip Tank and flowcheck,' said Scottie.

'Don't tell me my job,' said the Driller. He hung up.

Scottie threw Jamie a pristine white rag. He opened a cover on the flowline, looked at the level of the fluid in it and sniffed. There was an unmistakable whiff of petrol station.

He called the shaker house. 'Can you guys smell anything?'

'No,' said Ronnie, 'but we're getting shitloads of sand.'

Scottie dipped the pit again. 'Ten barrels,' he said.

'Waarghghfnnrr,' said Jamie.

Scottie got back on the blower. 'Will you shut the well in? We've taken a ten barrel kick. The flowline reeks of crude oil. And they're producing sand at the shakers.'

'There's nothing wrong,' said the Driller. He hung up again.

'If that arse doesn't shut the well in, he's going to blow the entire place to fuck,' said Scottie.

'It was the last thing that could have gone wrong,' said Jamie.

'Either that or there's going to be another murder,' said Scottie.

Scottie rang the logging shack. 'Are you showing a gain?

'Twenty barrels,' said Antonia. 'The Dreeler told me to..'

'He's a horse's arse,' said Scottie.

By this stage, the Active pit was getting dangerously full. Scottie skipped nimbly over the variety of obstacles, opened the suction valve from the Active pit to the red mixing line, opened the delivery valve from the red mixing line to Reserve 3 and switched on the red mixing pump. There was an echoey "boom" as the first of the fluid fell into the empty pit.

Scottie went back to the phone to call Brad. The line was engaged. Brad, too depressed to talk about Peachy, was talking to his wife about their upcoming Norwegian fjord cruise.

Scottie called Walter. It rang out. Walter was moping and smoking with everyone else in the smoking television lounge.

Scottie called the drillfloor again. It was engaged.

'Yeah yeah. Whatever,' the Driller was saying to a frantic Antonia. 'Honey, I can tell how a well is behaving just by the feel of the brake. I can tell you now: We are not taking a kick.'

'Scottie's transferring to another pit!' shrieked Antonia.

'He'll be filling it with seawater or something,' said the Driller. 'He'll be getting ready for the cleanup.' He hung up.

The Active Pit was still filling up. Scottie diverted the returning fluid directly into Reserve 3. Sweat was pouring from him.

'Get on the tannoy,' he shouted to Jamie. 'Tell Brad and Walter to get up to the floor and shut the well in!'

Jamie ignored the fire at the front of his face, dialled the number for the tannoy, waited for the bleep and spoke. 'Brad. Walter. Go to the drillfloor. The well bust be shut in. We're taking a kick. The Driller won't listen. This isn't a joke.'

He hung up. There was a pause which seemed like forever. Jamie had never been so happy to hear the "PING PONG" tannoy announcement. 'Brad...'

Brad felt his heart trying to rise up through his throat. He slammed the phone down on his wife. He kicked his shoes off. Forty years in the business had prepared him for this moment. He always left his boots inside his coveralls to ease getting dressed. His office had its own outside door with its own little changing area. He leapt into his boots, pulled on his coveralls, stabbed on his safety glasses and dunked on his hard hat. He opened the door. And started to run.

'Holy fuck!' said Walter.

He didn't bother with the niceties of PPE. He kicked open the fire door in the smoking television lounge and leapt outside. He was well into his stiff version of a sprint when he realised that he still had a cigarette in his mouth. He threw it over the side, but it blew back and landed in an oily puddle. Luckily, the oily puddle was more puddle than oil. The cigarette went out.

The two men collided at the corner at the foot of the stairs up to the drillfloor.

'Oyah,' went Walter.

'Aya,' went Brad.

'PING PONG,' went the tannoy.

'Somebody please shut the well in!' went Jamie.

Brad and Walter went up the stairs two at a time, like the young men they could hardly remember being. The drillfloor had never seemed as high up as it did now. Even here the smell of crude oil was overwhelming.

'Why didn't you go to the BOP controls in my office?' shouted Walter.

'Why didn't you?' said Brad.

'That idiot mud engineer said the drillfloor,' said Walter.

'We didn't have to listen,' said Brad.

'I'll kill the little fucker,' said Walter.

Reserve 3 was getting full too. Scottie diverted the returning fluid to Reserve 1.

'What now?' said Jamie.

'Pray,' said Scottie.

Walter and Brad burst into the doghouse.

'There's no panic,' said the Driller.

Walter and Brad leapt on the BOP controls.

Then Brad leapt on the Driller.

Down in the pit room, the level in the flowline lowered, then dropped to a trickle and then stopped.

After four hundred and fifty barrels of a kick, the well had been shut in. They were saved.

Chapter 33 Pulling Out the Hole

'It's not like Phil's,' said Ritchie the Medic. 'Your nose is properly broken. It's fabulous.'

'It's not fabulous at all,' said Jamie, who didn't like the way that Ritchie was groping his proboscis.

They were in the sick bay.

'You've cheered me right up,' Ritchie grinned. 'After Peachy. Poor guy. Still, this is turning out to be one of the best trips ever. All that brilliant stuff with Webster. Head caved in. Vacuuming the mud out his lungs. I even got to use the old shock pads. I had them turned up to ten.' Ritchie's face was a picture of pure glee. 'Then there was Findon's concussion. Smelling salts, freezing spray and painkillers. Phil's battle wounds. Ice and morphine. And now a cracking broken nose.'

'Glad to be of help,' said Jamie sarcastically. 'You know, we're only out here to make you happy.'

Ritchie mused, 'Now that I've tasted blood, so to speak, I'm pretty hungry for more action. Do you think the Army will take me?'

'You're too old.'

'I might chuck it in and, and … get into ambulances.' Ritchie's face lit up. 'Money isn't everything.'

'So I'm told,' said Jamie flatly. He wasn't interested in any problem other than the throbbing one on the front of his face.

'I could always do Botox injections for spare cash,' said Ritchie. 'You see, you can feel the break …. Right … here!' Ritchie yanked Jamie's nose.

'Aaaarrrgg!' Jamie yelled. 'You bastard! I knew you were going to do that!'

'What do you think?' said Ritchie.

'You've twisted it too far in the other direction,' said Antonia, who had been sitting quietly in the corner.

Jamie peered through watery eyes at the two faces considering his own.

'It's not bad for a first attempt,' said Ritchie.

'I kind of like it,' said Antonia. 'It has character. Before, it was... boring.'

'Antonia? I brought you here for support,' said Jamie.

'I am supporting you. We're fixing your face.'

'Shall I have another go?' said Ritchie.

Antonia considered Jamie, nibbling at the end of her finger.

'Can I have a look at a mirror please?' said Jamie. 'Do I get a say in this decision?'

'If your taste in clothes is anything to go by, your taste in noses will suck. Leave it to us,' said Antonia.

'I really like it,' said Ritchie, grinning like a maniac. 'I think I've done a brilliant job.'

'I think so too,' said Antonia, giggling. She ran her hand playfully through Jamie's hair.

Jamie could feel an erection building. How he longed to have her. Here they were. Bonding. Over his broken nose. He no longer cared about a mirror. As far as Jamie was concerned, if she was happy, his nose could be spread in five different directions. If that wasn't love, nothing was.

PING PONG went the tannoy. 'Mud engineer, go to the shakers.'

They had gone into well control procedures. Heavier fluid was pumped into the well via the kill line. Light fluid was bled off via the choke line. It then went through the Poor Boy Degasser, before being returned to an empty pit. It took four hours for the pressure on the well to be relieved.

It took a little, but not much longer for Peachy's death to relieve the pressure on everyone else.

Findon endeared himself to no one by stomping through the accommodation wearing a big smile and announcing to anyone who cared to listen (and anyone who didn't) that things had reached "a successful conclusion". In the tea shack, he'd even hinted to Kevin the Cementer that, as predicted in his speech, he'd "broken" Peachy. Kevin's response to this had been so terrifying in its intensity that Findon had stood up, turned, and fled. Kevin hadn't even got out of his seat. He'd merely growled. Findon hadn't mentioned it again. To anyone.

Findon was going home soon. They all were. A replacement crew had been organised and additional choppers were being laid on. The Manticore drilling crew had been deemed fit to be let loose on society once again.

'Poor society,' said Ronnie the Roustie.

The accidental adding of 40 million quid's worth of cocaine to the mud and potentially having Russian gangsters chasing after you fiasco had made Jamie even more determined to find out why Webster and Peachy had died. He had inadvertently become involved in the entire affair. His life could potentially depend on what he now had only a couple of days to find out.

Jamie went to the shakers to make sure that they were clear of cuttings and it was safe to pull out of the hole. Drilling had resumed, but only for a short while. TD, Total Depth, the end of the well, was called at 10,429 ft, once they had drilled far enough into the reservoir and then enough for a logging sump. Jamie had no idea what a logging sump was. Out here, there was always something else you didn't know.

They circulated until Jamie pronounced the shakers clean, pumped a slug and started to pull slowly out of the hole. Pulling too quick would have risked swabbing the well – the Bottom Hole Assembly was somewhat like the plunger in a syringe – and causing another kick. Once they got a couple of thousand feet above the reservoir, they would speed up and once they got inside the 13 3/8 inch casing, they would go like the clappers.

Jamie found Bill the Mechanic in the Smoking tea shack. It was 3 am. He was alone.

'Pumps okay now?'

'Fine.'

'So we can declare the enterprise a success?'

'Striking oil is not poverty.'

Bill smiled. 'It would normally make us happy. I doubt if this rig will ever be happy again.'

'I won't be back,' said Jamie.

'Not you as well? Had enough already?'

'It's not safe for me here. It's a long story. Tell me Bill, what was it you welded to the cement unit door?'

'It was the handle that John Webster gave me.'

'No it wasn't. You did the welding without a Hot Work Permit. A man as meticulous as you wouldn't do a thing like that. Unless you knew that Webster was already dead. And that all hell was about to break loose. You hid the murder weapon in the cleverest way you knew how.'

Bill's eyes widened in alarm.

'It's okay Bill, I'm not going to tell anyone, least of all Findon. What I'm saying is true, isn't it? You took the weapon that killed John Webster and turned it into a door handle.'

Bill nodded. 'I did. But you'll never prove it. There's no traces of Webster on there. I ground every surface thoroughly. Burned it. Quenched it.'

'Kind of apt, Webster's murder weapon becoming a permanent fixture on the rig.'

'He has a mud pit named after him. And the thing that killed him opens a door. That's what's apt. The man's death opens doors for a lot of people. We should thank the killer. He's saved a lot of lives. John Webster was a despicable man.'

'Who killed him?'

Bill fell silent for a moment. 'It was Peachy.'

'How did you become involved?'

'I was in the Moon Pool when I heard a shriek. That must have been when Peachy lost it. I came in as Webster fell from the first blow. I shouted and stopped Peachy from going into a frenzy. He had no idea how he was going to cover it up. He'd have launched the bar over the side. It would have been found by the ROV. And that would have been that. We put on slicker suits and got Webster into the pit. Then we hosed each other down and squeegeed everything into the pit. I made sure the slicker suits went into the wash and got on with the welding. That was the scary bit: no permit; no firewatcher. I knew the unit was pretty isolated, so it turned out okay. After the murder was discovered, no one was interested in a bit of welding. I don't think that the control room knew that it even happened.'

'You did well to calm Peachy down.'

'It was strange. Once he snapped out of it, he was fine. Calm. Logical. I thought he'd killed his demon.'

'He did think his demon had been killed,' said Jamie. 'But it hadn't.'

'Peachy had a bigger demon than Webster? What was it?' Bill was gobsmacked. His voice had risen slightly above the whisper in which they had been talking.

'It's not important any more. It died with Peachy. What's important is that it all ends here.'

***

Walter's body clock was as out of kilter as Bill's. Jamie found him in his office, attending to his own, final loose ends.

'What I would give for a glass of Bowmore 17 year-old malt whisky,' he said. 'That in itself is a sign for me to get out of this business. I never used to think about alcohol out here. Grab a pew. I'm sorry I can't offer you anything stronger than a can of coke.'

Jamie closed the door, cracked open the can and slouched into a chair.

'Feel free to put your feet on the table, Jamie. We'll let my successor worry about the scratches.'

Jamie put his feet up. Whisky sounded very appealing to him – for the first time in his life. He was ready for expensive tastes. 'Are you a whisky connoisseur Walter? Or a heavy drinker?'

Walter smiled. 'A connoisseur. My heavy drinking days are behind me. Or maybe they're ahead of me. I wouldn't be the first man to come off the rigs and drink himself to death.'

Jamie savoured his coke. 'With all the money he had in the bank, I wondered why John Webster kept coming out to the rigs. Was that it? To stop himself drinking himself to death? Was John Webster an alcoholic?'

Walter sipped from his own can of Coke. He removed his half-moon glasses and sat back. 'He was. Not many people knew it.'

Jamie savoured the syrupy sweetness of the cola, one of the few treats on the rigs. 'I suppose it makes sense,' he said. 'A two week bender at home. Then come out here. Dry out. Let the liver recover for two weeks. And because there's not even a sniff of alcohol out here, you get peace of mind.'

'"Peace of mind" is not a phrase that I'd associate with John Webster. He could think clearly out here, plot his schemes, devise new ways to make other people unhappy.'

'I can't believe John Webster's sole demon was alcohol.'

'John Webster had an entire squadron of demons.'

'I wonder where they came from? Bullied at school. Abused by his father. His mother. The usual suspects. I'd guess the drinking was a symptom of his problems rather than the cause. Drink would give him a respite from himself,' said Jamie.

'You're very perceptive, Jamie. I can understand why Antonio Banderas has picked you. She's no fool either. She can see that you're coming into your best years. You'll make a good couple. She's played you well. Kept you guessing. Sometimes you were wandering around here looking haunted. Your emotions are written all over your face. You'd make a rotten poker player.'

'I'm still not sure if we're a permanent item.'

'You are. Trust me. Seeing you two getting together has been nice, amidst all this carnage. It's been good to watch.'

'Did you find anything out, Walter?'

'I did.'

There was a knock at the door. Findon popped his head in. He was smiling.

'Off today. Mission accomplished. The chief is delighted. This would have been a messy one to have on the books. We would probably have needed a scapegoat. Out here, that's usually the mud engineer, isn't it?'

Findon cackled at his own joke. He jabbed a finger at Jamie.

'Told you I'd solve this, spotty boy. The result speaks for itself. Killer kills himself. We don't have to waste resources on a trial or a prison cell. If this doesn't get Antonio Banderas's knickers off, nothing will. And a final piece of advice. I'd stay away from Aberdeen if I were you. There will be nothing but trouble if I get my hands on you. Understand?'

Findon extended a hand toward Walter, who regarded it with disgust. 'If you cause Jamie, or any of my crew any trouble, we'll create a shit-storm that you and Grampian Police will never forget. Do you understand?'

Findon's hand withered and drooped to his side. He re-affixed his grin. 'Well, thanks for all the eh, cooperation, Walter. No hard feelings about the, you know, incident between us.'

Walter turned to Jamie. 'I never hit him hard enough.'

'I feel that you should be aware of something, Walter. There's a few troublemakers in your crew.'

'Just a few?'

'I've drawn up a dossier. I'll pop it by before I go. Complete psychological profiles.' Findon retreated to the door. 'I think you'll find it very revealing.'

And with a departing jab of the finger, Findon was gone.

'He came to an oil rig to discover that it was full of trouble-makers. It's just as well that criminals are stupid. Or we'd all be in trouble. It didn't take much to run rings round that clown.'

'The complete psychological profiles will be a laugh,' said Jamie. 'I wonder what he made of us?'

'Psychology? He's the only buffoon on the rig who doesn't know that Antonio Banderas hates him. Or that you and her are an item.'

'You'll be lucky if the dossier covers one side of A4.'

'You could write an entire book just about the night toolpusher.'

'Explaining your life philosophy to incompetent murder squad detectives and thinking you're impressing them is Golfing With The Wrong People.'

'There's enough material out here to occupy fifty psychiatrists for the next fifty years,' Walter sighed and sipped his alcohol-free drink.

'Peachy never killed Webster, did he?' said Jamie.

'Not a chance.'

'He didn't have it in him.'

'He couldn't even have witnessed it, or he'd have been bubbling to the police.'

'Do you know what Webster had done to Peachy that drove him to kill himself?'

'I can imagine. But don't tell me. It doesn't matter now. It doesn't even matter who killed Webster.'

'What happens on the rig stays on the rig?'

'Exactly. You know, when you finally decide it's time to go, the scales fall from your eyes and you begin to perceive things as they really are. We've successfully drilled the well we were asked to – under terrible strains. John Webster's evil juggernaut has been stopped, but not before it drove poor Peachy to his death. That's all there is to be said. We each mourn Peachy in our own way and we move on to the next well. Or in my case, an arboretum.'

'A what?'

'I've decided to plant trees on my land. Recreate the ancient woodland. Leave something positive behind. I might even plant a few veg. Build a chicken coop. Call it a smallholding. Walter goes green. Who'd have believed it?'

Jamie smiled. 'As you said Walter, when the scales fall from your eyes, a world of possibilities opens itself out to you.'

'I envy you your youth. And I envy you Antonio Banderas.'

'You've still got enough time to do some damage,' said Jamie.

'For sure,' said Walter. 'I know it sounds like a strange thing, but you've been lucky to see what you've seen out here.'

'It's been overwhelming.'

'Even the broken nose suits you.'

'Tell me Walter, the question that I asked you yesterday. Did you find anything out?'

'I did. But tell me why you need to know.'

Jamie smiled. He thought long and hard. 'Because I care,' he said. 'I care about what happened to Peachy. I was a man who cared about not very much. And now I'm a man who cares passionately about everything.'

'Findon was wrong. You're not spotty any more. The one disaster for you is that he's made you persona non grata in Aberdeen. The delights of that silver city are to be forever denied you. Whatever shall you do?'

'I suppose I'll just have to settle for second best. New York. Paris. Milan. Those shit-holes.'

Walter removed a thin file from his drawer. 'I got my spies in town to do your bidding. You were right. There was one person who, in his application form, had John Webster as his referee.'

'His son.'

Chapter 34 Cleanup

It was time to say goodbye to Gray. He was on that day's chopper with Findon. Jamie had been delighted to discover that he was due to leave on the Wednesday with Antonia.

'This time tomorrow, I'll be in France,' beamed Gray. He was wearing a natty shirt. 'You'll be stuck on here, wirelining!' Gray laughed, a gay, carefree laugh. His face had come to life again. There was even a spring in his step.

Gray was leading a double life: full of misery on the rig; full of joie de vivre at home. Jamie wondered if he really knew any of the people out here. It was like Peachy had said; on an oil rig, the gap between a person's work persona and their real persona could be enormous. Perhaps that was the reason why the industry attracted so many oddballs.

'What about the cleanup?' said Jamie.

'Forget about the cleanup. We won't see it. That's somebody else's problem.'

'Who's coming out for you?'

'Pig Pen!' Gray chuckled. 'The dirtiest man in the entire UK Continental Shelf. Wait until you smell the room once he moves in. I shouldn't laugh, He sleeps in the same bed as me.' Gray positively roared with laughter. 'He's called Connor Short. He's fine. You'll love him. Let's have breakfast. I'll buy.'

Antonia joined them for breakfast and Gray regaled the table with witty anecdotes, waving his arms about like a madman. Antonia shook her head in disbelief. It was quite a transformation.

Gray cleared his stuff out of the room. He took his bags to the radio room to be weighed and retrieved his survival suit from the grab bag. 'Jamie, it's been great. Goodbye.' Jamie felt a little stung. That was it. After all they had been through together. But that was life on the rigs. Gray was gone, never to be seen again.

Brushing his teeth, Jamie caught sight of himself in the mirror. The spots had indeed gone. Three weeks of clean living had ended a lifetime problem. He was a changed man. He had come a long way in a short time. Jamie sat down and thought about his own departure. He had two sleeps to go. Then he would pack his bags, don his survival suit and leave the rig for good. He had Russians to avoid. Tonight, he would confront the killer.

As he lay down to sleep, there was a light tapping at the door. He turned on his bedside light and drew the curtain back. Antonia came in. She was smiling and looking incredibly sexy.

'Your question, Jaime,' she whispered. 'Have I ever done it on a rig? My answer: not until now.'

Antonia eased herself out of her clothes sexily, staring all the time at Jamie, caressing her breasts to tease him. She climbed up to his bed. Jamie extinguished the light and they wrestled delightfully among the limp lettuce of the nylon sheets, making sparks as they made love.

***

Jamie had arranged to meet the killer at the murder scene. Gray's replacement, Connor, or Pig Pen, didn't inspire confidence. He was dishevelled and his breath stank. But he at least could be bothered to do a proper handover. He explained all about the process of wirelining and cementing the liner. He calculated which pits could presently be cleaned for the cleanup. He even drew diagrams. Wirelining was where they lowered tools into the reservoir on the end of a wire and then drew them back and forth, taking measurements which gave an idea about how much oil was down there. This had just started and would be going on all night. The pit cleaning couldn't begin until the next day when some dedicated cleaners would be coming out. Connor had even completed the midnight mud report.

In short, there was nothing for Jamie to do except confront John Webster's killer.

Jamie sat himself on top of the agitator motor on Active 1, the Webster Pit. The pit room was utterly silent. It was like a giant steel coffin.

'Hello Jamie. What can I do for you?' said the killer, coming in from the pump room.

Jamie took a look at the smiling character before him. He wasn't haunted by the killing at all. Perhaps it had even been good for him. Perhaps it was in the genes. 'Hello Scottie,' Jamie said. 'I thought we should have a wee quiet chat before you leave tomorrow.'

'About the cocaine?'

'About everything.'

Scottie let out a little sigh. 'Why not?' he pulled up the old, burst derrickman's chair and put his feet up. 'My last night offshore. Might as well make it a memorable one.'

Jamie suddenly felt vulnerable and alone. He wished he had told Antonia about this meeting. He took a deep breath. 'You're John Webster's son, aren't you?'

Scottie's affable smile vanished. 'I was John Webster's son, that's true. But the minute I leave this shit-hole of a rig behind, I won't be. I'm sure you understand why.' Scottie gave a smile filled with threat.

'I understand. I'd do the same thing.'

'You'd never do the same thing as me,' Scottie laughed. 'How did you find out?'

'It was the argument about how many daughters Webster had. Two daughters? Three daughters? Why would Webster do something like that? I knew that he must have been winding someone up. Someone who was in the room when he was saying it. It certainly wasn't Antonia.'

'I heard you got the leg over last night. Congratulations.'

'Thank-you,' said Jamie, trying not to blush. 'I suppose it was too much to hope for some privacy out here.'

'We take our entertainment where we can find it. Antonio Banderas was spotted leaving your room this morning at approximately 10:45 looking "refreshed". Findon had to be restrained from coming down and punching your lights out. It took two rousties to frog-march him onto the chopper. He was screaming the odds about seeing you in hell.'

'I think he means Aberdeen.'

'I heard he's barred you from Aberdeen. That must have been a blow.'

'Aberdeen has too many Russians for my taste.'

'I've destroyed all traces of your work instruction. When you resign your job, you'll need to get your company to remove all traces of your address from their files.'

'I was thinking of moving to Spain.'

'And live in a hacienda? In Andalucia? With satellite telly?'

'Have you been talking to Gray?'

'I've been listening to Gray. Everybody has. He'll be happily wrapped in Beryl's arms. Poor Beryl. If you're seriously moving to Spain, you'd better get Antonia to erase all details of her address too. I can do the business for you both on the heliport system.'

'I would have thought that it was very difficult to get access?'

'I was Webster's son. Remember?'

'How could I forget? You killed him. You're very much your father's son.'

Scottie's eyes narrowed, giving Jamie a sharp pang of fear. 'I did it to try and save Peachy's life. Peachy was beyond saving.'

'I saw the porn film with Peachy. Drugged. And the four men taking turns with him. Your father...'

'Will you stop calling him my father!' Scottie leaped out of his chair. He stopped, gathered himself and sat down. 'Webster couldn't load the cocaine on his own in Rotterdam. He needed someone he could depend on one hundred percent, because he knew he couldn't rely on me. He wanted to be sure that Peachy was his creature.'

'So he came up with a solution that was utterly sick. Blackmail the rig porn king by making him the star of his own porn flick?'

'That's the kind of logic Webster used. You understand him well.'

'Poor Peachy,' said Jamie. He never stood a chance. Webster destroyed Peachy's ... sense of himself. Peachy was killed by pornography.'

'I can almost hear Webster's laughter right now. He would have loved that.'

'What was the scheme with the cocaine?'

'Webster made contact with the cartel when he was in Russia. He loved them. Loved their attitude. Their particular brand of cruelty was right up his street. He saw all kinds of new avenues of evil opening up. Trafficking hookers. Blackmail. Extortion. Drugs. The plan was to move cocaine around the world, hidden in bulk cargoes. Webster had the hopper and the lines installed in the yard. He and Peachy loaded it up from a truck one night. The truck had unloaded from a boat from South America. The plan was for the Manticore to transfer it to a supply ship, which could unload at various ports in Europe.'

'But there was a fuck-up.'

Scottie smiled. 'Webster had bullied the guys in the Rotterdam shipyard. Made their lives a misery. Demanded all sorts of unreasonable shit. Rode them as only he could ride. They obviously decided to take some revenge and deliberately welded a blockage into the outlet pipe.'

'Karma,' said Jamie.

'The problem only manifest itself the night that they tried to offload. Webster went mental. Peachy told me about it. He thought that Webster was going to kill him that night. So the boat had to sail. Empty.'

'The next thing there's this phoney Russian assistant driller on board to noise up Webster,' said Jamie.

'That chilled him to the bone. That they could organise something like that behind his back. He went ape-shit and lashed out at the weakest victim he could find.'

'Peachy.'

'Peachy was only just keeping it together as it was. I found him in here swinging from a rope. He was seconds from death. He told me what had been done to him. He told me about the cocaine. He told me everything.'

'That's when you made your decision to kill Webster.'

Scottie nodded. 'I promised Peachy that I would save him. I thought that killing Webster would save Peachy.'

'Peachy, to all intent and purpose, was already dead.'

Scottie's eyes lowered. 'I tried. I really tried.'

'We all tried.'

'I didn't even care if I was caught.'

'You were lucky that it was Bill who discovered you.'

Scottie nodded. 'What are you going to do to me?'

'Do?' Jamie was perplexed. 'I'm not going to do anything. I'm not here looking for justice.' Jamie thought for a moment. 'Actually I am here looking for justice: justice for Peachy. I couldn't turn you in and live with myself.'

Scottie wiped his face with a mucky rag. 'I can't thank you enough, mate. It's weird, it feels such a relief to be caught. Maybe I'm not my father's son after all.'

'What did you feel after you'd killed him?'

'Elated. Horrified. Like I'd entered another world. Now I feel like I'm coming back to the real world. When I get to the Beach, I will be in the real world. I'll never be back out here.'

'Why did you come at all?'

'I never knew my Dad. He got my Mum pregnant and did a runner. She was smart enough not to try and find him. Then I was in my twenties and out of work. You're from a stable family, aren't you?'

'Yes.'

'It's written all over your face. Children are curious about their parents, even the horrible ones. Mum tried to warn me, but I didn't understand. I never dreamed it would end like this.'

'What did Webster want from you?'

Scottie shrugged. 'A son. A successor.'

'And then he started to refer to you as one of this three daughters in meetings, when you knew he only had two.'

'So he was calling me a big girl? That was the least of his crimes. I'm the lucky one.'

'What are you going to do with Webster's money?'

'I'm not going to touch it. His ex has already got a fortune. Webster provided for his daughters. And they'll get an enormous payout from the oil company. I don't have to worry about them. What's so funny?'

Jamie was thinking about the bank details on the stick. 'Nothing,' he said. 'For some people this is a happy ending.'

Scottie got up. 'The Russians will be looking for a scapegoat. They won't accept Webster's death on its own. Since you've done me a favour, I'll do you one. I'll take the blame. I tell the boys what's happened and I'll tell them to tell everyone that I added the cocaine to avenge Peachy's death. The Russians will never find me. Make sure they don't find you.'

Scottie shook Jamie's hand firmly and left.

***

The next morning, the drillcrew were in their going home clothes. They looked incredibly smart, if not exactly tasteful. They were already putting the dirt and the sweat of the rig behind them. Jamie thought that they looked like a bunch of brides in their going away outfits. Scottie was transformed. His clothes were expensive.

He looked like a young City broker.

Scottie caught Jamie's eye. He nodded. Jamie nodded back. It was the last they saw of each other.

Ronnie the Roustie and Bill the Mechanic caught Jamie's eye. They nodded. He nodded. He never saw them again either.

The initial results from the wireline logging were good. The well was successful. They cemented the 7 inch liner into place on Jamie's last night. There were no losses and Jamie stood at the shakers as the excess cement was circulated out. Some oil-based mud flooded over the front and filled a couple of skips. Later, they pumped the skips out over the shakers and the mud went back to the pits. The only other thing that Jamie had to do was to supervise some pit cleaning. Pig Pen had the cleanup in hand.

The reservoir had been secured. The shareholders were happy.

Brad signed Jamie's service ticket. Brad's going home clothes were much nicer than Jamie's. 'You've done a great job,' he said, pumping Jamie's hand. 'You're a fine man. Will we see you back?'

'No.'

'Half the crew has quit. The service hands won't come back. There's gonna be a lot of green hands out here. And that means accidents. There's more blood to be spilled on this rig.'

And so the ripples of Webster's evil spread still further.

They all left together: Jamie, Antonia, Brad, Walter, Kevin the Cementer and Dave the Night Pusher. The rest of the chopper was filled by catering crew and stewards.

Jamie doubted whether the Jamie who had left would even recognise the Jamie who was returning.

As the chopper rose, Jamie watched Walter. He took a last good look at his rig. It sat in the water looking rusty and small. It was difficult to believe that it was capable of so much or could play host to such momentous events. The chopper turned south-west toward Aberdeen. Walter never looked back.

Coming in to land, trees, grass and cows had never looked so thrilling. They were back in the land of the living. The heliport was filled with poor suckers just about to go in the opposite direction.

There were no Russians at the heliport. Jamie and Antonia found themselves behind Walter in the taxi queue. Everybody else had disappeared.

'Where are you two lovebirds off to?'

'Spain via Ayrshire.'

When the taxi pulled up, Walter asked, 'How much to Ayrshire?'

'Two hundred and fifty quid.'

'It's a deal. Get in, I'll give you lunch near Perth.'

Walter's home was a beautiful five bedroom cottage set in ten acres of its own grounds.

'The wages of sin,' he said.

Jamie and Antonia were treated to a tour of the estate, with Walter providing a running commentary on the trees that he was going to plant. Barbara, his wife, laid on a fabulous spread. Their world looked idyllic. She had her man home for good.

'It's either suicide or divorce,' she said, smiling.

They came out to see Jamie and Antonia off. One couple, just retired and settling down to the last part of their lives waved to a young couple about to embark on their own, doubtful adventure.

A week later Jamie found himself outside a Taverna. In Catalonia. With satellite telly. But he and Antonia weren't interested in television. They were recovering from the latest bout of fantastic sex, sitting outside, looking at the mountains and each other.

'Antonia,' he said, 'I've something I've been meaning to tell you. It's about me, some Russians and forty million pounds' worth of cocaine that I mistook for chalk. You know that I love you more than life itself. Do you promise not to shout?'

***

Over a thousand miles away, in deepest Aberdeenshire, Dave the ex-Night Pusher was recovering from his week-long bender. The time had come to fire up the laptop, update the CV and start looking for a job.

The minute he hit the first key, he knew that he was in trouble. He'd had the laptop in his office on the rig. Someone had sabotaged it. And Dave had no idea how to fix the problem. Each time a key was pressed, the computer let out a loud Homer Simpson "D'oh!"

Dave typed away with two beefy fingers. 'D'oh! D'oh! D'oh! D'oh! D'oh! D'oh! D'oh!'

Dave knew. It was Jamie. He had seen him scurrying out of the office that last morning. It had happened to him once more. He was well and truly Golfing With The Wrong People.

The End